The servant brought her cloak and Xavier took it from him.

He stepped towards Phillipa and placed it around her shoulders, so close she felt the warmth of his body. The touch of his hands on her shoulders caused a frisson of sensation down her back.

She disliked being so affected by Xavier Campion. It made her think of how she'd felt dancing with him. The thrill of coming close to him, of touching him.

The servant opened the door and the cool evening air revived her.

Phillipa crossed over the threshold with Xavier right behind her. 'I do not need an escort.'

He fell in step with her. 'Nevertheless, I need to do this.'

She scoffed. 'Do not be absurd. You can have the company of any woman you like. One of the gentlemen told me so.'

His step slowed for a moment. 'Phillipa, if any danger should befall you on this walk home I would never forgive myself for not preventing it.'

He sounded so serious.

'So dramatic, Xavier. I am not your responsibility.'

His voice turned low. 'At this moment you are.'

Welcome to
Diane Gaston's

THE MASQUERADE CLUB

Identities concealed, desires revealed…

This is your invitation to Regency society's most exclusive gaming establishment.

Leave your inhibitions at the door, don your disguise and indulge your desires!

Club proprietor Rhys, the most renowned gambler in London, finally meets his match in

A REPUTATION FOR NOTORIETY

Already available

And now Rhys's friend Xavier, the most devilish rogue in town, prefers to gamble with ladies' hearts in

A MARRIAGE OF NOTORIETY

the opera the night before. 'He is an Adonis!' one
had proclaimed and the name stuck.

Phillipa had not attended the opera that night, but
heard before all of them that he'd come to town. She,
too, glanced to the doorway.

Clad in the formal red coat of the East Essex in-
fantry, Xavier Campion looked as magnificent as a
man could look in regimentals.

He scanned the room, his brilliant blue eyes searching until reaching Phillipa. His lips widened into a
smile and he inclined his head before pivoting to
greet Lord and Lady Devine.

'He smiled at us!' cried one of Phillipa's friends.

No. He'd smiled at her.

Phillipa's cheeks flushed.

Did he remember her? They'd been childhood
friends in Brighton during the summers, especially
the summer when she fell and suffered her injury.

Phillipa's hand flew to her cheek, to where the
jagged scar marred her face. Not even the clever
feather her mother insisted be attached to her headpiece could hide the disfigurement.

Of course he remembered her. How many scar-
faced girls could be known to handsome Xavier
Campion?

She swung away, while the others giggled and
whispered to each other. She heard their voices, but

Prologue

London, Spring 1814

'Mr Xavier Campion,' Lady Devine's butler intoned in a baritone voice.

'Adonis is here!' gasped one of the young ladies standing near Phillipa Westleigh. The others shared furtive smiles.

Phillipa knew precisely who her friends would see when their gazes slipped towards the doorway. A young man tall and perfectly formed, with broad shoulders, a narrow waist, and muscled limbs. His hair would be as dark as the ebony keys on a pianoforte and longer than fashionable, but an excellent frame for his lean face, strong brow, sensitive mouth.

The young ladies had been tittering about him the whole evening. Would he come to the ball? Could they contrive an introduction? He'd been the main topic of conversation since they'd discovered him at

AUTHOR NOTE

The timeless theme of the fairytale *Beauty and the Beast* often reappears in romance novels, as well as in Disney movies, *Phantom of the Opera, King Kong* and more. Do we ever tire of this story? I've written it before, in my Mills & Boon® Historical *Undone!* eBook THE UNLACING OF MISS LEIGH (my *Phantom of the Opera* story), and now in A MARRIAGE OF NOTORIETY. I dare say I will write it again.

Part of the appeal of the *Beauty and the Beast* theme is its message—genuine beauty is what one has on the inside, not the way one appears on the outside. How many of us look in the mirror and forget this as we examine every flaw? How often do we gaze at models in magazines or celebrities on the red carpet and feel like garden gnomes in comparison? And how much do all of us want to be loved for who we are, not the way we appear?

I enjoyed exploring this issue once more, and giving my hero and heroine their own chance to discover that beauty isn't just skin-deep.

Dedication

For my new daughter-in-law Beth,
beautiful on the inside and the outside,
and a wonderful addition to our family.

As a psychiatric social worker, **Diane Gaston** spent years helping others create real-life happy endings. Now Diane crafts fictional ones, writing the kind of historical romance she's always loved to read. The youngest of three daughters of a US Army Colonel, Diane moved frequently during her childhood, even living for a year in Japan. It continues to amaze her that her own son and daughter grew up in one house in Northern Virginia. Diane still lives in that house, with her husband and three very ordinary housecats. Visit Diane's website at http://dianegaston.com

Previous novels by the same author:

THE MYSTERIOUS MISS M
THE WAGERING WIDOW
A REPUTABLE RAKE
INNOCENCE AND IMPROPRIETY
A TWELFTH NIGHT TALE
  (in *A Regency Christmas* anthology)
THE VANISHING VISCOUNTESS
SCANDALISING THE TON
JUSTINE AND THE NOBLE VISCOUNT†
  (in *Regency Summer Scandals*)
GALLANT OFFICER, FORBIDDEN LADY*
CHIVALROUS CAPTAIN, REBEL MISTRESS*
VALIANT SOLDIER, BEAUTIFUL ENEMY*
A NOT SO RESPECTABLE GENTLEMAN?†
BORN TO SCANDAL
A REPUTATION FOR NOTORIETY**

†linked by character
Three Soldiers mini-series
**The Masquerade Club*

and in Mills & Boon® Historical *Undone!* eBooks:

THE UNLACING OF MISS LEIGH
THE LIBERATION OF MISS FINCH

First published in Great Britain 2014
by Mills & Boon, an imprint of Harlequin (UK) Limited,
Large Print edition 2014
Harlequin (UK) Limited, Eton House, 18-24 Paradise Road,
Richmond, Surrey TW9 1SR

© 2014 Diane Perkins

ISBN: 978 0 263 23968 3

Printed and bound in Great Britain
by CPI Antony Rowe, Chippenham, Wiltshire

A MARRIAGE
OF NOTORIETY

Diane Gaston

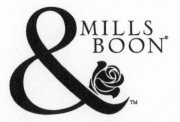

the grandeur inside. Sometimes when they were at play, she'd stop and stare, awestruck at his beauty. Many a night she'd fall asleep dreaming that some day, when she was grown, Xavier would ride in like a prince on horseback and whisk her away to a romantic castle.

Well, she was grown now and the reality was that no man wanted a young lady with a scar on her face. She was eighteen years old and it was past time to put away such childhood fancies.

'Phillipa?' His voice again.

She turned.

Xavier extended his hand to her. 'May I have the honour of this dance?'

She nodded, unable to speak, unable to believe her ears.

Her friends moaned in disappointment.

Xavier clasped her hand and led her to the dance floor as the orchestra began the first strains of a tune Phillipa easily identified, as she'd identified every tune played at the balls she'd attended.

'The Nonesuch'.

How fitting. Xavier was a nonesuch, a man without equal. There were none such as he.

The dance began.

Somehow, as if part of the music, her legs and feet

performed the figures. In fact, her step felt as light as air; her heart, joy-filled.

He smiled at her. He *looked* at her. Straight in her face. In her eyes.

'How have you spent your time since last we played on the beach?' he asked when the dance brought them together.

They parted and she had to wait until the dance joined them again to answer. 'I went away to school,' she told him.

School had been a mostly pleasant experience. So many of the girls had been kind and friendly, and a few had become dear friends. Others, however, had delighted in cruelty. The wounding words they'd spoken still felt etched in her memory.

He grinned. 'And you grew up.'

'That I could not prevent.' Blast! Could she not contrive something intelligent to say?

He laughed. 'I noticed.'

The dance parted them again, but his gaze did not leave her. The music connected them—the gaiety of the flute, the singing of the violin, the deep passion of the bass. She would not forget a note of it. In fact, she would wager she could play the tune on the pianoforte without a page of music in front of her.

The music was happiness, the happiness of having her childhood friend back.

She fondly recalled the boy he'd been and gladdened at the man he'd become. When his hand touched hers the music seemed to swell and that long-ago girlish fantasy sounded a strong refrain.

But eventually the musicians played the final note and Phillipa blinked as if waking from a lovely dream.

He escorted her back to where she had first been standing.

'May I get you a glass of wine?' he asked.

It was time for him to part from her, but she was thirsty from the dance. 'I would like some, but only if it is not too much trouble for you.'

His blue eyes sparkled as if amused. 'Your wish is my pleasure.'

Her insides skittered wildly as she watched him walk away. He returned quickly and handed her a glass. 'Thank you,' she murmured.

Showing no inclination to leave her side, he asked polite questions about the health of her parents and about the activities of her brothers, Ned and Hugh. He told her of encountering Hugh in Spain and she told him Hugh was also back from the war.

While they conversed, a part of her stood aside as if observing—and judging. Her responses displayed none of the wit and charm at which her friends so easily excelled, but he did not seem to mind.

* * *

She had no idea how long they chatted. It might have been ten minutes or it might have been half an hour, but it ended when his mother approached them.

'How do you do, Phillipa?' Lady Piermont asked.

'I am well, ma'am.' Phillipa exchanged pleasantries with her, but Lady Piermont seemed impatient.

She turned to her son. 'I have need of you, Xavier. There is someone who wishes a word with you.'

He tossed Phillipa an apologetic look. 'I fear I must leave you.'

He bowed.

She curtsied.

And he was gone.

No sooner had he walked away than her friend Felicia rushed up to her. 'Oh, Phillipa! How thrilling! He danced with you.'

Phillipa could only smile. The pleasure of being with him lingered like a song played over and over in her head. She feared speaking would hasten its loss.

'I want to hear about every minute of it!' Felicia cried.

But Felicia's betrothed came to collect her for the next set and she left without a glance back at her friend.

Another of Phillipa's former schoolmates approached her, one of the young ladies to whom she had introduced Xavier. 'It was kind of Mr Campion to dance with you, was it not?'

'It was indeed,' agreed Phillipa, still in perfect charity with the world, even though this girl had never precisely been a friend.

Her schoolmate leaned closer. 'Your mother and Lady Piermont arranged it. Was that not clever of them? Now perhaps other gentlemen will dance with you, as well.'

'My mother?' Phillipa gripped the stem of the glass.

'That is what I heard.' The girl smirked. 'The two ladies were discussing it while you danced with him.'

Phillipa felt the crash of cymbals and the air was knocked out of her just like the day in Brighton when she fell.

Prevailing on family connections to manage a dance invitation was precisely the sort of thing her mother would do.

Dance with her, Xavier dear, she could almost hear her mother say. *If you dance with her, the others will wish to dance with her, too.*

'Mr Campion is an old friend,' she managed to reply to the schoolmate.

'I wish I had that kind of friend.' The girl curtsied and walked away.

Phillipa held her ground and forced herself to casually finish sipping her glass of wine. When she'd drained the glass of its contents she strolled to a table against the wall and placed the empty glass on it.

Then she went in search of her mother and found her momentarily alone.

It was difficult to maintain composure. 'Mama, I have a headache. I am going home.'

'Phillipa! No.' Her mother looked aghast. 'Not when the ball is going so well for you.'

Because of her mother's contrivance.

'I cannot stay.' Phillipa swallowed, trying desperately not to cry.

'Do not do this to yourself,' her mother scolded, through clenched teeth. 'Stay. This is a good opportunity for you.'

'I am leaving.' Phillipa turned away and threaded her way quickly through the crush of people.

Her mother caught up with her in the hall and seized her arm. 'Phillipa! You cannot go unescorted and your father and I are not about to leave when the evening is just beginning.'

'Our town house is three doors away. I dare say I may walk it alone.' Phillipa freed herself from her mother's grasp. She collected her wrap from the footman attending the hall and was soon out in the cool evening air where no one could see.

Tears burst from her eyes.

How humiliating! To be made into Xavier Campion's charity case. He'd danced with her purely out of pity. She was foolish in the extreme for thinking it could be anything else.

Phillipa set her trembling chin in resolve. She'd have no more of balls. No more of hopes to attract a suitor. She'd had enough. The truth of her situation was clear even if her mother refused to see it.

No gentleman would court a scar-faced lady.

Certainly not an Adonis.

Certainly not Xavier Campion.

Chapter One

London, August 1819

'Enough!' Phillipa slapped her hand flat on the mahogany side table.

The last time she'd felt such strength of resolve had been that night five years ago when she fled Lady Devine's ball and removed herself out from the marriage mart for good.

To think she'd again wound up dancing with Xavier Campion just weeks ago at her mother's ball. He'd once again taken pity on her.

No doubt her mother arranged those two dances as well as the first. More reason to be furious with her.

But never mind that. The matter at hand was her mother's refusal to answer Phillipa's questions, flouncing out the drawing room in a huff instead.

Phillipa had demanded her mother tell her where her brothers and father had gone. The three of them had been away for a week now. Her mother had forbidden the servants to speak of it with her and refused to say anything of it herself.

Ned and Hugh had a rather loud quarrel with their father, Phillipa knew. It occurred late at night and had been loud enough to wake her.

'It is nothing for you to worry over,' her mother insisted. She said no more.

If it were indeed nothing to worry over, then why not simply tell her?

Granted, in the past several days Phillipa had been closeted with her pianoforte, consumed by her latest composition, a sonatina. Pouring her passions into music had been Phillipa's godsend. Music gave her a challenge. It gave her life meaning.

Like getting the phrasing exactly right in the sonatina. She'd been so preoccupied she'd not given her brothers or her father a thought. Sometimes she would work so diligently on her music that she would not see them for days at a time. It had finally become clear, though, that they were not at home. That in itself was not so unusual, but her mother's refusal to explain where they had gone was very odd. Where were they? Why had her father left London when Parliament was still in session? Why had her brothers gone with him?

Her mother would only say, 'They are away on business.'

Business, indeed. A strange business.

This whole Season had been strange. First her mother and brother Ned insisted she come to town when she'd much have preferred to remain in the country. Then the surprise of her mother's ball—

And seeing Xavier again.

The purpose of that ball had been a further surprise. It was held for a person Phillipa had never known existed.

Perhaps *that person* would explain it all to her. His appearance, the ball, her brothers' and father's disappearance—all must be connected somehow.

She'd ask John Rhysdale.

No. She would *demand* Rhysdale tell her what was going on in her family and how he—her half-brother, her father's illegitimate son—fit into it.

Rhysdale's relationship to her had also been kept secret from her. Her brothers had known of him, apparently, but no one told her about him or why her mother gave the ball for him or why her parents introduced him to society as her father's son.

A member of the Westleigh family.

Her mother had given her the task of writing the invitations to the ball, so she knew precisely where Rhysdale resided. Phillipa rushed out of the drawing room, collected her hat and gloves, and was out the door in seconds, walking with a determined step towards St James's Street.

She'd met Rhysdale the night of the ball. He was very near to Ned's age, she'd guess. In his thirties. He looked like her brothers, too, dark-haired and dark-eyed. Like her, as well, she supposed, minus the jagged scar on her face.

To Rhysdale's credit, he'd only given her scar a fleeting glance and afterward looked her in the eye. He'd been gentlemanly and kind. There had been nothing to object in him, except for the circumstances of his birth.

And his choice of friends.

Why did Xavier Campion have to be his friend? Xavier, the one man Phillipa wished to avoid above all others.

Phillipa forced thoughts of Xavier Campion out of her mind and concentrated on being angry at her mother instead. How dared her mother refuse to confide in her?

Phillipa had a surfeit of her mother's over-protection. She could endure a ball with no dance partners. She could handle whatever mysterious matters led to her family's aberrant behaviour. Just because an ugly scar marred her face did not mean she was a child.

She was not weak. She refused to be weak.

Phillipa took notice of passers-by staring at her and pulled down a piece of netting on her hat. Her mother insisted she tack netting on to all her hats so she could obscure half her face and not receive stares.

She turned off St James's Street on to the street where Rhysdale lived. When she found the house, she only hesitated a moment before sounding the knocker.

Several moments passed. She reached for the knocker again, but the door opened. A large man with expressionless eyes perused her quickly. His brows rose.

'Lady Phillipa to see Mr Rhysdale,' she said.

The man stepped aside and she entered the hall. He lifted a finger, which she took to mean she should wait, and he disappeared up the staircase.

The doors to rooms off the hall were closed, and the hall itself was so nearly devoid of all decoration that it appeared impersonal. Perhaps a single gentleman preferred no decoration. How would she know?

'Phillipa.' A man's voice came from the top of the stairs.

She looked up.

But it was not Rhysdale who descended the stairs. It was Xavier.

He quickly approached her. 'What are you doing here, Phillipa? Is something amiss?'

She forced herself not to step back. 'I—I came to speak with Rhysdale.'

'He is not here.' He glanced around. 'You are alone?'

Of course she was alone. Who would accompany her? Not her mother. Certainly her mother would never make a social call to her husband's illegitimate son. 'I will wait for him, then. It is a matter of some importance.'

He gestured to the stairs. 'Come. Let us sit in the drawing room.'

They walked up one flight of stairs and Phillipa glanced into a room she presumed would be the drawing room. She glimpsed several tables and chairs.

'What is this?' she exclaimed.

Xavier looked dismayed. 'I will explain.' He gestured for her to continue up another flight of stairs.

He led her into a comfortably furnished parlour and extended his arm towards a sofa upholstered in deep-red fabric. 'Do be seated. I will arrange for tea.'

Before she could protest, he left the room again. Her heart beat at such rapid rate that her hands trembled as she pulled off her gloves.

This was ridiculous. She refused to be made uncomfortable by him. He meant nothing to her. He'd merely been a boy who'd once been her playmate.

Defiantly she swept the netting over the brim of her hat. Let him see her face.

He stepped back in the room. 'We'll have tea in a moment.' Choosing a chair near her, he leaned close. 'I do not know when—or if—Rhys will come back.'

'Do not tell me he has disappeared as well!' What was going on?

He touched her hand in a reassuring gesture. 'He has not disappeared. I assure you.'

She pulled her hand away. 'Where is he?' she demanded.

He leaned back. 'He spends most days with Lady Gale.'

'Lady Gale?' What did Lady Gale have to do with anything?

Lady Gale was the stepmother of Adele Gale, the silly young woman to whom her brother Ned was betrothed. Both Adele and Lady Gale had been guests at her mother's ball, so Rhysdale might have met them there, but was there more to that connection?

Xavier frowned. 'You do not know about Rhysdale and Lady Gale?'

Phillipa waved a frustrated hand. 'I do not know anything! That is why I am here. My brothers and my father have disappeared and my mother will not tell me where they have gone or why. I came to ask

Rhysdale where they were, but it seems I've been excluded from even more *family* matters.'

There was a knock on the door and a manservant entered, carrying the tea tray. As he placed the tray on a side table, he gave Phillipa a curious look.

Because of her scar, no doubt.

Xavier nodded to him. 'Thank you, MacEvoy.'

The servant bowed and walked out, but not before tossing her another glance.

Xavier reached for the teapot. 'How do you take your tea, Phillipa? Still with lots of sugar?'

He remembered that? She'd had a sweet tooth as a little girl. That had been a long time ago, however.

She stood. 'I do not wish to drink tea. I came here for answers. I am quite overset, Xavier. I do not know why everything is kept secret from me. Do I look as if I cannot handle adversity?' She jabbed at her scar. 'I am well practised in adversity. My mother—my whole family, it seems—apparently thinks not.' She faced him. 'Something important has happened in my family—something more than Rhysdale's appearance—and I am to be told nothing? I cannot bear it!' She pressed her hands against her temples for a moment, collecting herself. She pointed towards the door. 'What is this place, Xavier? Why does my half-brother have a room full of tables where the drawing room should be and a drawing room on a floor for bedchambers?'

Xavier stared back at Phillipa, considering how much to tell her.

He preferred this version of Phillipa to the one he'd so recently encountered at her mother's ball. That Phillipa barely looked at him, barely conversed with him, even though he'd danced twice with her. She'd acted as if he were a loathsome stranger.

Her present upset disturbed him, however. Ever since they'd been children, he'd hated seeing her distressed. It reminded him of that summer in Brighton when the pretty little girl woke from a fall to discover the long cut on her face.

He admired Phillipa for not covering her scar now, for showing no shame of it or how she appeared to others. Besides, her colour was high, appealingly so, and her agitation piqued his empathy. He understood her distress. He would greatly dislike being left out of family matters of such consequence.

But surely she'd been told of Rhys's arrangement with her brothers?

'Do you not know about this place?' He swept his arm the breadth of the room.

Her eyes flashed. 'Do you not comprehend? I know nothing.'

'This is a gambling establishment.' All of society knew of it. Why not Phillipa? 'Nominally it is a gambling *club* so as to adhere to legalities. Have you not heard of the Masquerade Club?'

'No.' Her voice still held outrage.

He explained. 'This is the Masquerade Club. Rhys is the proprietor. Patrons may attend in masks and thus conceal their identities—as long as they pay their gambling debts, that is. If they need to write vowels, they must reveal themselves.' He made a dismissive gesture. 'In any event, it is meant to be a place where both gentlemen and ladies may enjoy cards or other games. Ladies' reputations are protected, you see.'

She looked around again, her expression incredulous. 'This is a gambling house?'

'Not this floor. These are Rhys's private rooms, but he is not here very often these days.'

She pressed fingers to her forehead. 'Because he is with Lady Gale.'

He nodded. Rhys's connection to Lady Gale ought to have been roundly discussed at the Westleigh residence.

He could tell her this much. 'Sit, Phillipa. Have some tea. I will explain.'

He reached for the teapot again but she stopped him with a light touch to his hand. 'I will pour.' She lifted a cup and raised her brows in question.

'A little milk. A little sugar,' he replied.

She fixed his cup and handed it to him. 'Explain, Xavier. Please.'

'About Lady Gale and Rhys,' he began. 'Earlier this Season Lady Gale came masked to the Masquerade Club.'

She lifted her cup. 'She is a gambler? I would not have guessed.'

He lifted a shoulder. 'Out of necessity. She needed money. She attended often enough for Rhys to become acquainted with her. In learning of her financial need, he began paying her to come gamble.'

'Paying her?' Her hand stopped before the teacup reached her lips.

He gave a half-smile. 'He fancied her. He did not know her name, though. Nor did she know his connection to your family.'

She looked at him expectantly. 'And?'

'They became lovers.' He took a breath. 'And she is with child. They are to be married as soon as the licence can be arranged.' He paused. 'And other matters settled.'

'Other matters.' Her brows knitted. 'Ned's courtship of Lady Gale's stepdaughter, do you mean?'

He nodded. 'And more.'

Rhys's gambling house and his affair with Lady Gale had hardly caused her a blink of the eye. Surely she was made of stern enough stuff to hear the whole of it.

She gave him a direct look. 'What more?'

'Do you know of Ned and Hugh's arrangement with Rhys?' he asked.

She shook her head. 'I am depending upon you to tell me all of it, Xavier. All of it.'

How could he resist her request?

Ever since her injury. What age had he been? Twelve? She'd been about seven and he'd never forgotten that summer.

How it pained him to see that little girl so wounded, so unhappy.

If only he could have prevented it.

He'd felt it his duty to cheer her up. He'd learned that summer that one should act, if one could. Not hold back.

So he'd made her his responsibility and worked to cheer her up.

It was not his place to tell her about her family's affairs, but....

He set his jaw. 'This past April Ned and Hugh came to Rhys and asked him to open a gaming house. They had scraped together the funds for it, but they needed Rhys to run it.'

'They asked Rhysdale to run a gaming house for them?' She sounded incredulous.

He took a sip of tea. 'Out of desperation. Your family was in dire financial straits. Did you know of that?'

She shook her head.

He might as well tell her all. 'Your father's gambling...and carousing...brought your family to the brink of ruin. You, your mother, everyone who depended upon the Westleigh estates for their livelihood would have suffered terribly if nothing had been done.'

Her eyes widened. 'I had no idea.'

'So Ned and Hugh hit upon the idea of a gaming house. Rhys agreed to run it, although your father gave him no reason to feel any sense of loyalty to the family. Besides taking half the profits, though, Rhys asked that your father publicly acknowledge him as his natural son.'

'Hence my mother's ball.' She caught on quickly.

'Indeed.' The ball was part of Rhys's payment. 'The scheme worked perfectly. The element of masquerade has made this place successful beyond anyone's hopes. Your family is rescued.'

She looked askance. 'If all has gone so well, where are my father and brothers?'

'They went to the Continent. To Brussels.' Ought he tell her this part? He peered at her. 'Phillipa, are you close to your father?'

She laughed. 'I dare say not.' She glanced away, her face shadowed. 'Should he chance encounter me, he looks through me. Or away.'

His heart constricted.

'Your father made trouble for Rhys, I'm afraid. He detested Rhys being the family's salvation.' She did not need to know all the details. 'Suffice to say your father challenged Rhys to a duel—'

'A duel!' She looked aghast.

'It did not take place,' he assured her. 'Your brothers stood by Rhys and together they forced your father to relinquish all control of the family's money and property to Ned.' Either that or publicly shame the man. 'They offered your father a generous allowance, but only if he moved to the Continent. Your brothers travelled with him to make certain he reaches his destination and keeps his word. He is to remain there. He will not come back.'

'He is gone?' She turned pale, making her red scar more vivid. 'I had no notion of any of this.'

He feared she would faint and he rose from his

chair to sit beside her on the sofa, wrapping an arm around her. 'I know this is a shock.'

He remembered how he'd held her as a little girl, when she cried about being ugly. He'd never thought her ugly. Certainly not now, although to see her face, half-beautiful, half-damaged, still made something inside him twist painfully.

She recovered quickly and moved from his grasp. 'How could I have been so unaware? How could I have not had some inkling?'

'It is not your fault, Phillipa. I am certain they meant to protect you,' he said.

'I do not need their protection!' she snapped. She looked at him as if he were the object of her anger. 'I do not need pity.'

He admired her effort to remain strong.

'I must leave.' She snatched up her gloves and stood.

He rose as well. 'I will walk you home.'

Her eyes shot daggers. 'I am fully capable of walking a few streets by myself.'

He did not know how to assist her. 'I meant only—'

She released a breath and spoke in an apologetic tone. 'Forgive me, Xavier. It is unfair of me to rail at you when you have done me the honour of exposing my family to me.' She pulled on her gloves. 'But truly there is no need to walk me home. I am no green girl in need of a chaperon.'

'If that is your wish.' He opened the door for her and walked with her down the stairs.

She stopped on the first-floor landing and pointed to a doorway with a half-closed door. 'Is this the game room?'

'It is.' He opened the door the whole way. 'You can see the card tables and the tables for faro, hazard and *rouge et noir.*'

She peeked in, but did not comment.

As they continued down the stairs, she asked, 'Why are you here in a gaming house, Xavier?'

He shrugged. 'I assist Rhys. As a friend.'

He was useful to Rhys. Because of his looks, men dismissed him and women were distracted. Consequently, he saw more than either sex imagined and, for that, Rhys paid him a share of his profits.

'Do you have the gambling habit, then?' she asked.

Like her father? 'Not a habit,' he responded, although once it had been important to prove himself at the card table. 'These days I play less and watch more.'

They reached the hall and Xavier walked her to the door. When he turned the latch and opened it for her, she pulled down the netting on her hat, covering her face.

The action made him sad for her.

He opened his mouth to repeat the offer to escort her.

She lifted a hand. 'I prefer to be alone, Xavier. Please respect that.'

He nodded.

'Good day,' she said in a formal voice and stepped away.

Xavier ducked inside and grabbed his hat. He waited until he surmised she would have reached the corner of the street, then stepped outside and followed her, keeping her in sight, just in case she should require assistance of any kind. He followed her all the way to her street and watched until she safely entered her house.

It was a familiar habit, looking out for her, one he'd practised over and over that long-ago summer in Brighton, when his duty towards her first began.

Chapter Two

Phillipa walked briskly back to her family's town house, emotions in disharmony. Her mind whirled. Rhysdale's gaming house. Her father's shameful behaviour.

Xavier.

She had not expected to see Xavier and her face burned with embarrassment that it had been he who exposed her family's troubles to her.

Her family's shame. Did there ever exist such a father as hers? What must Xavier think of him? Of them?

Of her?

She hurried through the streets.

How could she have been so insensible? Her family had been at the brink of ruin and she'd not had an inkling. She should have guessed something was awry. She should have realised how out of character it was for her father to hold a ball for anyone, least of all a natural son.

Seeing Xavier there distracted her.

No. It was unfair to place the blame on Xavier. Or even on her family.

She was to blame. She'd deliberately isolated herself, immersing herself in her music so as not to think about being in London, not to think of that first Season, that first dance with Xavier, nor of dancing with him again at the ball.

Instead she'd poured everything into her new composition. With the music, she'd tried to recreate her youthful feelings of joy and the despairing emotions of reality. She'd transitioned the tune to something bittersweet—how it had felt to dance with him once again.

Her mind had been filled with him and she'd not spared a thought for her family. In fact, she'd resented whenever her mother insisted she receive morning calls, including those of Lady Gale and her stepdaughter. It surprised her that she'd paid enough attention to learn that Ned intended to marry the artless Adele Gale. The girl reminded Phillipa of her school friends and that first Season when they'd been innocent and starry-eyed.

And hopeful.

Phillipa had paid no attention at all to her father,

but, then, he paid no attention to her. She long ago learned not to care about what her father thought or did or said, but how dared he be so selfish as to gamble away the family money? She would not miss him. It was a relief to no longer endure his unpleasantness.

Phillipa entered the house and climbed the stairs to her music room. She pulled off her hat and gloves and sat at the pianoforte. Her fingers pressed the ivory keys, searching for expression of the feelings resonating inside of her. She created a discordant sound, a chaos, unpleasant to her ears. She rose again and walked to the window, staring out at the small garden behind the town house. A yellow tabby cat walked the length of the wall, sure-footed, unafraid, surveying the domain below.

Her inharmonious musical notes re-echoed in her ears. Unlike the cat, she was not sure-footed. She was afraid.

For years she'd been fooling herself, saying she was embracing life by her study of music. Playing the pianoforte, composing melodies, gave her some purpose and activity. Although she yearned to perform her music or see it published for others to perform, what hope could she have to accomplish that? No lady wanted a disfigured *pianiste* in her musicale. And no music publisher would consider an earl's daughter to be a serious composer.

There was an even more brutal truth to jar her. She was hiding behind her music. So thoroughly that she had missed the drama at play on her family's stage. All kinds of life occurred outside the walls of her music room and she'd been ignoring it all. She needed to rejoin life.

Phillipa spun away from the window. She rushed from the room, startling one of the maids passing through the hallway. What was the girl's name? When had Phillipa begun to be blind to the very people around her?

'Pardon, miss.' The girl struggled to curtsy, even though her hands were laden with bed linens.

'No pardon is necessary,' Phillipa responded. 'I surprised you.' She started to walk past, but turned. 'Forgive me, I do not know your name.'

The girl looked even more startled. 'It is Ivey, miss. Sally Ivey.'

'Ivey,' Phillipa repeated. 'I will remember it.'

The maid curtsied again and hurried on her way.

Phillipa reached the stairs, climbing them quickly, passing the floor to the maids' rooms and continuing to the attic where one small window provided a little light. She opened one of the trunks and rummaged through it, not finding for what she searched. In the third trunk, though, triumph reigned. She pulled it out. A lady's mask, one her mother had made for her to attend a masquerade at Vauxhall Gardens during her first Season. It had been specifically designed to cover her scar.

She'd never worn it.

Until now.

Because she'd decided her first step to embrace life and conquer fear was to do what Lady Gale had done. She would wait until night. She would step out into the darkness and make her way to St James's Street.

Phillipa would attend the Masquerade Club. If Lady Gale thought it acceptable to attend, so could she. She would don the mask and enter a gaming house. She would play cards and hazard and faro and see what sort of investment Ned and Hugh had made in Rhysdale.

He would be there, of course, but that was of no consequence. If she encountered Xavier, he would not know her.

No one would know her.

That night Phillipa stepped up to the door to Rhysdale's town house. No sounds of revelry reached the street and nothing could be seen of the gamblers inside, but, even so, she immediately sensed a different mood to the place than earlier in the day.

She sounded the knocker and the same taciturn

manservant who'd attended the hall that morning answered the door.

'Good evening, sir.' She entered the hall and slipped off her hooded cape. This time she did not need netting to hide her face; her mask performed that task.

The manservant showed no indication of recognising her and she breathed a sign of relief. The mask must be working.

She handed him her cape. 'What do I do next? I am new to this place, you see.'

He nodded and actually spoke. 'Wait here a moment. I will take you to the cashier.'

The knocker sounded the moment he stepped away, but he returned quickly and opened the door to two gentlemen who greeted him exuberantly. 'Good evening to you, Cummings! Trust you are well.'

Cummings took their hats and gloves and inclined his head towards Phillipa. 'Follow them, ma'am.'

The gentlemen glanced her way and their brows rose with interest. How novel. Without her mask most men quickly looked away.

'Is this your first time here, ma'am?' one asked in a polite tone.

'It is.' She made herself smile.

The other gentleman offered an arm. 'Then it will be our pleasure to show you to the cashier.'

This was how she would be treated if not disfigured. With pleasure, not pity.

How new, as well, to accept the arm of a stranger when she'd been reared to acknowledge gentlemen only after a formal introduction took place. Would he think her fast for doing so? Or did it not matter? The gentleman would never know her.

She'd already defied the conventions of a well-bred lady by walking alone on the streets at night. She'd gathered her cloak and hood around her and made her way briskly, ignoring anyone she passed. Gas lamps lit most of the way and there had been plenty of other pedestrians out and about to make the trek feel safe.

Taking the arm of a stranger for a few seconds seemed tame after that.

He and the other gentleman escorted her to one of the rooms that had been hidden behind closed doors earlier that day. It was at the back of the house and, judging from the bookshelves that lined one of the walls, must have once been the library. Besides a few lonely books on the shelves, the room was as sparsely decorated as the hall. A large desk dominated the room. Behind the desk sat the man who had served her tea.

'MacEvoy,' one of her escorts said. 'We have a new lady for you. This is her first time here.'

MacEvoy looked her straight in the face. 'Good

evening, ma'am. Shall I explain how the Masquerade Club operates?'

'I would be grateful.' She searched for signs that this man recognised her. There were none.

He told her the cost of membership and explained that she would purchase counters from him to use in play in the game room. She could purchase as many counters as she liked, but, if she lost more than she possessed, she must reveal her identity.

This was how patrons were protected, he explained. They would know who owed them money, and those who needed their identity protected dared not wager more than they possessed.

Phillipa had little interest in the wagering, but hoped she purchased enough counters to appear as if she did.

'We will take you to the gaming room, ma'am,' one of her escorts said.

'That would be kind of you.' She knew the way, but did not want the gentlemen to realise it.

When they entered the room, it seemed transformed, a riot of colour and sound. The rhythm of rolling dice, the hum of voices, the trill of shuffling cards melded into a strange symphony. Could such noise be recreated in music? What might be required? Horns? Drums? Castanets?

'Ma'am, do you wish to join us in cards?' One of her gentlemen escorts broke her reverie.

She shook her head. 'You have assisted me enough, sir. I thank you both. Please be about your own entertainment.'

They bowed and she turned away from them and scanned the room as she made her way to the hazard table. To her great relief, she did not see Xavier. A pretty young woman acted as croupier at the hazard table, which surprised Phillipa. She'd not imagined women employed to do such a job. She knew the rules of hazard, but thought it insipid to wager money on the roll of dice. Phillipa watched the play, interested more in the people than the gambling. Several of the croupiers were women. The women players were mostly masked, like she, but some were not. She wondered about them. Who were they and why did they not worry about their reputations? Perhaps she was in the company of actresses. Opera dancers. Women who would not hide from life.

There certainly seemed to be great numbers of counters being passed around in the room. Those who won exclaimed in delight; the losers groaned and despaired. Happy sounds juxtaposed with despairing ones. She'd never heard the like.

She glimpsed Rhysdale. He circulated through the room, watching, stopping to speak to this or that person. He came close to her and her heart raced. He looked directly at her, nodding a greeting before passing on. She smiled. He had not recognised her.

She walked over to the faro table. If hazard was an insipid game, faro was ridiculous. One wagered whether a particular card would be chosen from the deck. If you placed money on the banker's card you lost, if on the winning card you won double.

Still, she ought to gamble. To merely gape at everything would appear a bit suspicious.

She stifled a giggle. Out in society, people treated her as if she did not exist. Here she feared them noticing her.

She played at faro and became caught up in the spirit of the game. She cried with joy when she won and groaned at her losses, just like the other patrons. She was merely one of the crowd. Even her deep-green gown blended with the tableau as if she were a part of the décor of reds, greens and glinting golds. Her anonymity became like a cloak around her, protecting her so well she forgot that, besides Rhysdale, there might be someone at the club who could recognise her.

Xavier defused some escalating tempers, interrupted some reckless wagers and otherwise performed the same tasks as always at the Masquerade

Club. His mind, however, continued to wander back to that morning.

Ought he have sent Phillipa to Rhys? Should it have been Rhys's choice of whether to tell her about her father, about the gaming house?

No. Rhys might have some of the same blood flowing through his veins as Phillipa, but she was a stranger to him. Xavier had known her for ever, even before her injury. He'd been close to her once. Her injury bound them together.

Or at least it bound him to her.

He'd been wrong to neglect her since the war ended. He should have sought her out before this. Made certain she was in good health and in good spirits. Perhaps that was why she was so cold to him at the ball.

Perhaps he would call upon her soon. See how she was faring after what he'd told her this afternoon.

Satisfied with that thought, Xavier circulated throughout the room, perusing the players and the croupiers, remaining alert to any potential problems. Most of the players here tonight were familiar to him as regular attendees. Even the masked ones were familiar, although there were a few whose identities he'd not yet guessed.

A new woman caught his eye. He'd not seen her arrive and did not know in whose party she might be included, but there was something about her…

She dressed expensively in a gown of dark-green silk. Its sheen caught the lamplight and transformed the rather plain style into something elegant. Who was she and why she was here for the first time?

Xavier watched her.

And came more disturbed.

His brows knit as he walked closer to her. He knew her, did he not?

Xavier stood across the faro table from her, waiting for the puzzle pieces to sort themselves. She glanced up and her gaze held his for a brief moment. She quickly looked away.

He walked around the table and leaned towards her ear. 'May I have a moment to speak with you, miss?'

She bowed her head and allowed him to lead her out of the room.

He brought her to a private corner of the hallway and backed her against the wall. 'What the devil are you doing here, Phillipa?'

She glared at him. 'How did you know it was me?'

How did he know? The set of her shoulders. The tilt of her chin. Her smile. 'It was not that difficult.'

'Rhysdale did not recognise me.' That chin lifted.

'He does not know you as I do.' But he would not allow her to change the subject. 'Why are you here?'

She shrugged. 'To gamble. Why else?'

'Who is with you?' Her brothers were gone. And,

if they had not been, they would have had to answer to him for bringing their sister here.

'No one,' she said.

'No one?' She could not have come alone. 'How did you get here?'

She gave him a defiant look. 'I walked.'

Walked? 'Alone?'

She did not waver. 'Yes, alone.'

He seized her arm. 'Have you taken leave of your senses? You cannot walk about alone at night.'

'It is only a few streets.' She continued to stare into his eyes. 'Besides, Ned and Hugh taught me how to defend myself.' She lifted her skirt and showed him a sheathed knife attached to her calf.

As if she would have time to draw it, if a man accosted her. As if such a man could not easily grab it from her hand.

'And that makes you safe.' He spoke with sarcasm.

'There were plenty of people about and street lamps were lit along Piccadilly. It was like walking in daytime.'

He doubted that. He also doubted that she was there for the simple reason of gambling. 'Come,' he said. 'Let us talk in the supper room.'

The supper room served wine and spirits and a buffet supper. Designed in the style of Robert Adam, its décor was light and airy, the opposite of the game room with its darker colours. Chairs and tables covered with white linens were arranged for conversation. Along one wall stood a huge buffet table upon which were set out a variety of cold meats, cheeses, cakes and compotes. Patrons could help themselves to the food and sit at tables covered with white linen. Servants attended the room, providing drink.

The supper room was a needed respite from the high emotions in the game room, Xavier thought.

'Be seated. I'll get you something to eat.' He led her to a table set away from the few people seated in the room and made his way to the buffet.

To his dismay, Rhys was in the room, chatting with some gentlemen seated not too far away from the white pianoforte in the corner.

Xavier glanced back at Phillipa, whose posture had stiffened. She, too, had noticed Rhys.

Rhys excused himself and crossed the room to Xavier. 'I noticed we have a new woman patron.' He faced Xavier but his back was to Phillipa. 'What is wrong with her? She did not seem to be falling at your feet like other woman.'

Xavier's good looks did not matter one jot to Rhys. In fact, Rhys was perhaps the only person, besides Xavier's own family, of whom he could say such a thing. Rhys was no fool, though. He knew women were attracted to Xavier.

Xavier evaded the question. 'I am reasonably sure she is merely here for the gambling. Not the sort to cause trouble.'

Rhys laughed. 'I thought you'd met your match.'

Xavier shook his head.

Rhys put a hand on Xavier's arm. 'I have a favour to ask of you.'

During the war, Rhys twice saved Xavier's life. At Badajoz. At Quatre Bras. Xavier would have done the same for Rhys. 'What is it?'

Rhys glanced around. 'Take over the club for a few days, will you? The gentlemen with whom I was conversing have an investment that may interest me, but it would require a few days' travel.'

'Certainly,' Xavier agreed. 'What sort of investment?'

'Steam engines,' Rhys replied.

'Steam engines?' The machines that had caused such riots and unrest in the textile industry?

'Expanding their use. Making them smaller. Steam engines will do great things, you will see.' Rhys wanted another way to build wealth besides a gambling house. He'd never intended to make gambling his life.

Gambling and soldiering had enabled Rhys to survive after Rhys's mother died and Lord Westleigh abandoned him to the streets. Xavier, on the other hand, had grown up amidst luxury and the devotion of his parents and siblings. They made unusual friends.

Xavier nodded. 'If it looks to be a good investment, make certain I have a share.'

Rhys leaned forwards. 'If it is the sort of investment I expect, I may be asking you to take over the gaming house altogether.'

Run the gaming house? Xavier would do it. He delighted at doing the unexpected. Nearly everyone he'd ever met expected him to coast through life on his looks, but that was the last thing Xavier intended to do. He'd prove himself by skill, cunning, strength. Character. He'd already proved himself a good gambler, a brave soldier; he'd not mind proving he could run the best gaming house in London.

He glanced back at Phillipa. 'I'll take over the gaming house, if it comes to that, Rhys. But now I had better not keep this lady waiting.'

Rhys clapped him on the back and left the room.

Xavier brought two plates of food to the table where Phillipa waited.

'You must not have told him,' she said as he placed a plate before her.

'Told him?' Ah, she thought he would tell Rhys about her. 'Of course not.' He meant no one to know she'd come here. 'I am going to get you through this folly of yours without injury to your person or your reputation.'

'Reputation?' She made a disparaging sound. 'After what you told me about my father today, is not the whole family drenched in scandal? What does my reputation matter now?'

He signalled to a servant to bring some wine. 'Society has always known your father to be a gambler and a philanderer. His self-exile to the Continent will seem like an honourable act. Your family's reputation should stay intact.'

The wine arrived and Phillipa took a sip.

Her voice dipped low. 'No matter. I have no need to preserve a reputation. That is for marriageable young ladies or matrons concerned about children.'

He felt a stab of sympathy. 'You do not intend to marry?'

She glanced away. 'Do not be absurd. You know what is beneath this mask.' She turned back to him with a defiant gaze. 'So there is nothing to risk. If I am attacked on the street, what will it matter?'

'Do not pretend to be stupid, Phillipa,' he growled. 'A horror could befall you much worse than a cut on a face.' At Badajoz he'd seen what violence men could inflict on women.

She blinked. 'I know.'

He pushed the plate closer to her. 'Have a bit of cake and let us speak of other things besides horrors.'

She obliged him and he found himself fascinated by the small bite she took of the cake, of her licking a crumb off her lip. Her lips were a most appealing shade of pink.

'I am not really so much in the doldrums, you know,' she went on. 'I was merely trying to provoke you.'

He grinned. 'Poke me and I'll poke you back.'

They'd played that game as children. Much to his annoyance, as he recalled.

She pursed her lips. 'You had better not poke me. I poke back much better than I used to. I am no longer a little girl, you know.'

He could not help but let his gaze peruse her. 'I know.'

Her eyes flashed. 'Do not make a jest of me, Xavier.'

A jest? He was seeing her as a man sees a woman. 'You ought to know me better, Phillipa.'

'I do not know you at all now.' Her expression turned bleak. 'It has been a long time since we were children.'

'I have not changed.' He had changed, though. He'd once told himself he'd always look out for her, but he'd left her behind, a mere memory, as he grew to manhood and went to war.

'I have changed.' She lifted her chin again. 'I have become quite independent, you know.'

'Hence the excursion to a gaming hell.' He touched her hand, but quickly withdrew.

Her fingers folded. 'A gaming hell makes it sound so nefarious. It is rather staid, though. What a disappointment.'

He frowned. 'What did you expect?'

'Some debauchery, at least!' She laughed. 'I did not know what to expect, but my curiosity was piqued to see what my brothers thought would be the saving of our family. And of our village and its people. There are a great deal of counters being won and lost.'

'In gambling, the house always has the advantage. Rhys's success has been beyond everyone's expectations.' And Xavier vowed he'd make even more money from it.

Phillipa finished her wine. 'May I return to the tables, Xavier? I still have money left to lose.'

He didn't want to take her back to the game room. Not all the patrons of the place were gentlemen. She was too attractive—alluring, even—and she was alone. 'Rhys is in the game room.'

'Are you afraid he'll recognise me this time?' she asked.

'You should worry over it,' he countered. 'He might recognise you. Or someone else might.'

Her eyes shifted. 'No they won't. They have never looked at me long enough to recognise me in a mask.' She stood. 'I wish to return to the tables. I was getting accustomed to faro. I believe I will play some more.'

He had no choice but to stand. 'Very well, Phillipa.'

When they walked back to the doorway, she inclined her head towards the piano. 'Who plays for you?'

He shrugged. 'No one. It is left from the previous owner.' Who also ran a brothel here as well as a gaming house, but she did not need to know that. A young fellow played the piano and the girls sang and flirted with the men.

He escorted Phillipa back to the game room and left her at the faro table where he had found her.

'Campion brought you back?' One of the men gave her a flirtatious look. 'We despaired of ever seeing you again. Has the pick of the ladies, that one has.'

Xavier did not hear Phillipa's response.

He could not hover around her, though. He'd only call more attention to her. There were gossips in the crowd who would make it their business to discover who she was.

He would watch from afar, in case she needed assistance, and when she made ready to leave, it would not be alone.

He stepped in to the hall where Cummings attended the door.

No one entered or left without Cummings knowing of it. 'Do you recall the new woman who came earlier, the masked one in the dark-green gown?' Xavier asked.

Cummings nodded.

'When she is ready to leave, detain her and alert me. Do not allow her to leave until I speak with her.'

Cummings nodded again and, if he thought anything odd in this request, made no comment. But, then, Cummings rarely commented about anything.

'I thank you, Cummings.'

Xavier returned to the game room, glancing first to see that Phillipa still played at the faro table. He'd keep an eye on her as well as on the other gamblers, and he'd be ready to see that Phillipa arrived safely to her town-house door.

After Xavier left her at the faro table, Phillipa's very limited interest in gambling waned even further, but she persisted, merely to show him he could not drive her away.

One of the gentlemen who'd escorted her to the cashier and to the gaming room approached her. 'Are you enjoying yourself, ma'am?'

How unexpected it was to be called 'ma'am' as if she were a married lady.

Xavier glanced in her direction so she smiled at the gentleman. 'I am indeed. I even win sometimes.'

The gentleman laughed. 'That is the main purpose of coming here.' One brow rose. 'Or do you have another purpose in mind?'

By his very significant look, she knew he meant something of consequence. She was not sure, but it could be flirtation. How very unexpected, if so.

'The gambling attracts me, of course.' Why not simply ask him what he means? 'What else could there be?'

His eyes flitted over her person. 'I saw that Mr Campion singled you out for notice. Are you to be another of his conquests?'

Her smile stiffened. This was the second man to suggest such a thing. *'Another* of his conquests? Goodness! How many does he have?'

He slid Xavier a jealous look. 'He can have any woman he wishes.'

That did not precisely answer her question.

No matter. What difference to her how many women fell for the handsome Xavier Campion? What woman would not? She'd always known women found him irresistible.

For some odd reason, it bothered her to hear this man say so.

'Does he wish to claim you?' the man persisted.

Surely this was impertinence. Apparently impertinence was acceptable behaviour in a gaming house. And perhaps this gentleman did not think her a young lady worthy of respect.

That was why most of the women in the room wore masks, was it not? They would be scorned and their reputations ruined if their identities were known here. The masks protected them.

Ironically her mask merely assured that a gentleman would speak to her. He certainly would not have done if he had seen her face.

She turned back to the faro table. 'I do believe Mr Campion merely wished to welcome me to the house.'

The man bowed. 'I do understand.'

He understood? She wished she did. She'd intended to merely avoid his question. There was nothing to be understood.

He walked away.

She shook her head. If that man intended a flirtation, he gave up too easily.

She caught Xavier looking at her and, as she turned away from him, caught a woman glaring at her. Out of jealousy? Now this *was* a unique experience. A woman shooting daggers of jealousy at her instead of melting with pity.

All this was new. New people. New experiences. If she'd not consumed a little too much wine when with Xavier and if the hour were not so dreadfully late, her heart would be racing with excitement. She found it difficult to keep from yawning, though. Her mask itched and her feet hurt and she yearned to be between the cool linens of her bed.

She should leave.

Phillipa walked out of the room and cashed in her counters with the cashier. She'd lost money, but it hardly signified since the money simply went back to her family. She made her way to the hall to collect her cape and gloves. The same taciturn hall servant stood there.

And so did Xavier.

When the servant walked off to get her things, she faced him. 'Making sure that I leave, Xavier?'

'No.' He did not look pleased. 'I will walk you home.'

'That is not necessary, I assure you,' she responded. 'I am perfectly capable of walking by myself.'

'Regardless, I will walk you home.'

The servant brought her cloak and Xavier took it from him. He stepped towards Phillipa and placed it around her shoulders. The touch of his hands on her shoulders caused a *frisson* of sensation down her back.

She disliked being so affected by Xavier Campion. It made her think of how she'd felt dancing with him. The thrill of coming close to him, of touching him.

The servant opened the door and the cool evening air revived her.

Phillipa crossed over the threshold with Xavier right behind her. 'I do not need an escort.'

He fell in step with her. 'Nevertheless, I need to do this.'

She scoffed. 'Do not be absurd. You can have the company of any woman you like. One of the gentlemen told me so.'

His step slowed for a moment. 'Phillipa, if any danger should befall you on this walk home, I would never forgive myself for not preventing it.'

He sounded so serious.

'So dramatic, Xavier. I am not your responsibility.'

His voice turned low. 'At this moment, you are.'

It was very late. Three in the morning, at least, and she had never walked the streets of Mayfair at such an hour. Certainly not with a man at her side.

A man like Xavier.

But she must not think of him like that.

They crossed Piccadilly and as they headed towards Berkeley Square, their footsteps sounded a rhythm broken only by the echoing of a carriage or hackney coach somewhere in the distance. Other sounds—voices, music—wafted to her ears, only to fade quickly. She concentrated on the sounds, searching for a melody she might recreate on her pianoforte, a melody that would sound like the night felt. Cool, peaceful, empty.

'Are you talking to yourself, Phillipa?' Xavier asked.

She'd been lost in her music. 'Why do you ask?'

'Your lips were moving.'

She'd been playing the music to herself. How daft she must appear. 'I—I hear music in the sounds of the night. I try to remember them.'

'Music?' He could not hear the music, obviously.

'In our footsteps. The carriages.' She shrugged. 'The other sounds.'

He paused before responding. 'I see.'

Her mask irritated her face. She untied it and pulled it off, rubbing her scar before concealing her face with the hood of her cloak.

'I like music,' she explained. 'I have studied music and the pianoforte a great deal over the last few years.' Since that ball when she'd first danced with him. Of course, she'd never played 'The Nonesuch' again, though it had once been a favourite of hers. 'It is my greatest pleasure.'

'Is it?' He acted as if interested. 'I should like to hear you play.'

Such a polite thing to say. The sort of thing one says when pretending an interest that doesn't truly exist. Like choosing a dance partner as a favour to one's mother's friend.

'I play the pianoforte alone. It consumes my time.' She made it seem as if she preferred not to have an audience when she really longed to play for others, to discover if her compositions and her technique had any merit.

He stopped speaking for a half a street.

She regretted snapping at him. 'I think I spend too much time with my music. I think that is why I did not notice that my family was in distress.'

'You isolated yourself.' He sounded as if that would be a sad thing.

'Too much, perhaps,' she admitted. 'That is the main reason I decided to visit the Masquerade Club.'

'Could you not simply decide to attend balls and routs and musicales instead?' His tone disapproved.

She was invisible in such places. No one looked at her if they could help it. No one spoke to her if they could avoid it.

When she donned the mask this night all that

changed. 'Perhaps balls and routs and musciales are not exciting enough for me.'

His fingers closed around her arm and he stopped walking. 'Too much excitement can be dangerous. You must not play with fire, Phillipa.'

'Fire?' She laughed. 'What do you mean?'

'I mean that men will notice you at the gaming house. They will not expect you to be an innocent young girl.'

'Innocent girl? Young? I am three and twenty. Quite on the shelf.' But devoid of any experience, of that he was correct.

They walked again. 'You have had your excitement,' he went on. 'Go back to playing your music now.'

She was eager to return to her music room, to write down the notes she'd heard in the sounds of the street at three in the morning, the sounds of a gaming hell, of his voice.

But she could not be done with the Masquerade Club. She wished to see and hear more; she wished to experience more.

Too bad for him. 'I plan to return.'

'No!' he growled.

She lifted her chin. 'I fully realise you do not wish me around you, Xavier, but it is you who have insinuated yourself into my company, not the reverse.'

'You wrong me again.' He sounded angry. 'We are old friends, Phillipa. I owe you my protection as sure as if you were one of my sisters.'

'Once, perhaps, you were under an obligation to do me a kindness.' Her chest ached in memory. 'Not any more.'

A carriage clattered by and she forced herself to listen to the horses' hooves clapping against the cobbles, the wheels turning, the springs creaking.

She made it into music inside her head so she would not have to speak more to him, nor think about the thrill of him walking beside her, a sensation distracting in the extreme.

Would her old school friends still envy her as they'd once done when she'd danced with him all those years ago? Her friends were all married now. Some very well. Some very happily. She'd lost touch with most of them, although on the rare occasion her mother convinced her to attend some society event, she often saw some of them. Her most regular correspondence was with Felicia, who moved to Ireland when she married and never returned to England. Felicia's letters were all about her children, her worries about the poor and her fears of typhus. Felicia would probably not even remember when Phillipa had danced with the most handsome man at the ball. How trivial it would seem to her if she did.

They reached Davies Street and the Westleigh town house.

'Will someone let you in?' Xavier asked, walking her directly to the door.

She pulled a key from her reticule. 'No one will even know I've been gone.'

He took the key from her hand and turned it in the lock. As he opened the door, she stepped closer to slip in.

'Farewell, Phillipa,' he murmured, handing her back the key, standing so close his breath warmed her face. His voice felt as warm around her.

'Xavier,' she whispered back, unable to thank him for doing something she didn't want, battling a familiar yearning she thought she'd defeated years ago.

She closed the door quietly and set her chin. 'I will see you when night falls again,' she said, knowing he could not hear.

Chapter Three

The next day Xavier saw Rhys off to travel north to look into this steam engine venture. That night, as other nights, Xavier walked through the gaming room, watching to see if all ran smoothly. From the beginning of the Masquerade Club he'd assisted Rhys in this task. The croupiers and the regular patrons were now used to him, but he'd needed to earn their respect.

It was not unusual for other men to underestimate him. He knew their thinking—that a man with his looks could not possibly have anything of substance to offer. Soldiers in his regiment had scoffed at his capacity to lead them until he proved himself in battle. Even the enemy on the battlefield took one look at him and dropped their guard. He could still see the surprised faces of those who felt the sharp edge of his sabre.

Xavier always believed he possessed courage,

strength, cunning, but battle had tested it and proved it to him once and for all.

But he was done with war and fighting. He'd seen enough blood and suffering and death.

Xavier shook off the memories and made another circuit of the room. He paused at the hazard table, watching the men and women throw away fortunes with the roll of the dice, paying close attention to the dice, making certain they were not weighted.

Hazard, so dependent upon chance, had never interested him. To own the truth, even games of skill had lost their appeal. He'd demonstrated to the sceptics—and to himself—that he could win at cards. He possessed a tidy fortune to show for it.

Running the Masquerade Club was his latest challenge. Making it a success, in terms of popularity and profitability, was a game he intended to win. When Rhys returned, the house would be showing greater profits and more patrons than ever before.

Xavier knew he could be good at this. Hadn't he been the one to notice the irregularities at the hazard table, the ones that so involved Lady Gale and ultimately Lord Westleigh?

Good riddance to that man. Everyone was better off with him gone. Especially Lord Westleigh's family.

Especially Phillipa.

Lord Westleigh had been on the brink of ruining Phillipa's life.

She had changed from that waif-like little girl he'd vowed to protect at Brighton. He'd been nearly five years older than she, but after her injury that summer, he'd made himself her champion, doing his best to distract her from her scar and keep sadness and despair at bay. He'd repeated this charge every summer until his family no longer summered at Brighton.

He'd never forgotten her.

In 1814, when Napoleon had been banished to Elba and peace briefly reigned on the Continent, Xavier found her again and danced with her at one of the Season's balls. She'd seemed as light-hearted and gay as her many friends. And as pretty—if one ignored her scar. He'd looked forward to a second dance that night and a chance to spend more time with her, but she'd taken ill, her mother said. And he'd left for his regiment the next day.

Phillipa had changed in these last five years, though. She was remote. Guarded. As if she'd built a wall around herself, too deep and high to breach.

At least he'd seen her home safely last night. It had been foolish of her to come to the Masquerade Club alone. Still, he wished he could see her again.

Two men and a woman at the faro table parted and his wish came true.

There Phillipa stood.

She'd come back, even though he'd told her not to.

She glanced at him at that moment, straightening her spine defiantly. He acknowledged her with a nod.

He had a mind to march over, seize her arm and drag her out of this room, out of this gaming house and back to her home. Such a disruption would not be good for the house. And he certainly did not want to cause her undue attention.

He waited.

Finally she walked out of the room. He leaned over to one of the croupiers. 'I'll be right back.'

He caught up to her in the hallway. They were alone. 'Phillipa.'

She turned and held her head high.

'Are you leaving?' He would not allow her to walk home alone.

She did not answer right away. 'I am going to the supper room.'

He took her arm. 'I will come with you.'

When they entered the room, she strode directly to the buffet and made her own selections.

He asked one of the servants to bring wine to his table, selecting one far enough away that the other diners could not hear their conversation. The wine arrived before she left the buffet.

She turned and paused as if trying to decide

whether to join him or not. Tossing her head, she carried her plate to his table and sat down in silence.

He leaned towards her. 'What possessed you to return here, Phillipa? I told you not to.'

She sipped her wine. 'You *told* me I'd had enough excitement, as if you could know.'

'This is not a fit place for you.' How could he convince her? 'Not all who come here are gentlemen and ladies.'

'Enough, Xavier.' She glared at him. 'I will not be treated as if I am still seven years old. My half-brother made this a place ladies could gamble and so I shall gamble here. You cannot and will not stop me.'

She was right. He could not stop her. But he did have an obligation to her. He'd always had an obligation to her. 'Do you intend to come again?'

'Of course.' She smiled smugly. 'As often as I wish.'

'Name the nights you will come and the times. I will escort you to and from the place.' He could at least see she was safe on the streets.

'No!' she snapped.

'Why?' This was more foolishness. 'It is to keep you safe.'

She held his gaze with an obstinate look. Finally she said, 'Very well, but only if you agree not to tell Rhysdale.'

He'd never had any intention to tell Rhys. 'Very well.'

Their conversation became more companionable after that. She asked about some of the patrons and he told her frankly which men were gentlemen and which were not. She asked questions about the running of the Masquerade Club, about the collection of the money, especially for the card games. She asked about profits and the potential for losses.

She had a quick mind, grasping the workings of the place as quickly as did her brother Hugh.

After half an hour, she rose to leave. As they walked towards the door and passed the pianoforte, Phillipa ran her fingers over the keyboard. 'It seems a shame that no one ever plays. This is a pretty instrument.'

'It has a nice sound, as I recall.' Under Madame Bisou, the previous owner, music and raucous singing had filled the room for part of the night.

Phillipa looked at him with a careful expression. 'I will play for you, if you will allow me to.'

He cocked his head, thinking. It would keep her out of the gaming room, at least.

He gestured to the piano bench. 'Give it a try, Phillipa. Play whatever you like.'

She smiled. 'Not tonight. Tomorrow night.'

* * *

The next night Xavier met Phillipa outside her town house at the agreed upon hour. He walked with her through Mayfair, crossing Piccadilly to St James's Street and finally to the gaming hell. She headed straight to the supper room and the pianoforte.

He stayed to listen to her. If she was dreadful, he could stop her. Amateurs were often dreadful. Enough wrong notes, enough singing off-key and people would find another house in which to gamble. That would not happen under his watch.

Her first song he'd heard before—'I Have A Silent Sorrow Here', a song of unrequited love. The strings of the pianoforte and her voice resonated with emotion. She sang the song so beautifully it convinced him she had once loved a man who did not love her.

Who the devil was that man? That man who hurt her so? Was that what caused her to isolate herself? Had he made her bitter and unhappy?

The second song had a similar theme, although he'd never heard the tune before. Even more melancholic than the first, she sang of watching her beloved across a room and of being invisible to him.

He forgot about anything but the pain and sadness of her song, the emotion in her voice. He'd failed at his youthful vow to protect her. He'd not been there when this man wounded her. He clenched a fist. He'd like to find that fellow now.

She next played something light-hearted and he woke from his reverie. He glanced at the faces in the supper room. The people seated there abandoned their conversations. With rapt expressions, they all turned toward Phillipa.

The only way Phillipa would be a liability to the gaming house was if patrons abandoned the gaming tables to come hear her perform.

Xavier yearned to abandon his duties to stay to listen to her, but he'd already spent enough time away from the gaming room. He reluctantly left the supper room. In the gaming room the sounds were not melodic. Voices humming, dice rolling, cards shuffling. Although the sound of her voice and of the pianoforte sometimes broke through the din.

She did not stay long that evening, only a little more than two hours. As she promised to do, she sent word to him when she wished to go home. To escort her home would take little more than a half-hour. For that amount of time he could leave the club in the hands of Rhys's employees.

They stepped out into the cool night air.

Her spirits were so high, she seemed irrepressible. It reminded him of that long-ago ball.

'You enjoyed yourself tonight?' he guessed.

She almost danced down the pavement. 'I did. No one seemed disappointed in my playing.'

'You did very well.'

She did more than very well.

'Did I?' She skipped ahead of him and faced him while walking backwards. 'Do you truly think so?'

She pulled off her mask and the gas lamps illuminated her face, making it glow. Her happiness made her beautiful.

His heart swelled for her. 'I know little of music, but I enjoyed what I heard.'

She grinned and twirled around. 'That is all I wish!'

She chattered on about the songs she'd sung and played, reviewing her mistakes, assessing what went well. He liked listening to her. It reminded him of when she'd been a little girl and he'd been able to get her to happily chatter on.

In no time at all they reached her door and he put the key in the lock.

She reached up on tiptoe and kissed him on the cheek. 'Thank you so much, Xavier. You have made me very happy tonight.'

Her lips felt soft and warm.

He wrapped his arms around her and brought his lips within a hair's breadth of hers. He felt her breasts rise and fall against his chest, further tantalising him. Her eyes grew wide as her mouth opened in alarm.

Banking his impulses, he lightly touched his lips to hers.

When he released her, his breath came faster. 'I want you always to be happy, Phillipa,' he murmured. 'Same time tomorrow?'

She blinked up him, her brow puzzled. 'Same time tomorrow.'

He opened the door and she slipped inside.

It took him a moment to move away.

He'd appointed himself her protector, but perhaps his hardest task would be to protect her from himself.

For the next four nights Xavier met Phillipa at her town house and returned her home again. They walked side by side through the night with only the occasional gaslight or rush light to break through the darkness. There were few carriages in the streets and fewer still pedestrians sharing the pavement. They talked of her music and the patrons who attended the gaming house, traded stories of what transpired in the supper room and in the game room.

Xavier was careful not to touch her, at least not to touch her in the way he most desired. The old camaraderie from their childhood days might have returned, but what consumed Xavier's senses was the woman Phillipa had become. So graceful. So quick-witted. So passionate.

So unaffected by him.

How ironic that he should desire a woman who gave no sign at all of desiring him.

It was fortunate, he supposed, because this idyll could not continue indefinitely. When Rhys returned her performances would stop, and, Xavier suspected, Phillipa would have no more use for him. Still, he did not regret his decision to allow her to perform.

It brought her joy.

It even brought increased profits. People came to The Masquerade Club to hear her play and they stayed to gamble.

Could he contrive to see her when it was over? Would she receive him? Did he want to push himself on a woman who did not want him? God knew, he detested being pursued by someone he did not want.

This night she performed for two hours, as had become her custom, and sent word to Xavier that she was ready to leave. As they'd done on previous nights, they stepped out into the night air and began to share the night's events with each other. This night, though, when they crossed Piccadilly and made their way to the unlit streets of Mayfair, Xavier felt a change in the air. It was nothing more than an odd sound, an unfamiliar shadow, but the soldier in him went on alert.

When he and Phillipa reached Hay Hill, the hairs on the back of his neck rose and he could almost hear the drum beat of the *pas de charge*.

He stopped her and lowered his voice. 'Do you still carry your dagger?'

'Yes.' She caught his nerves.

'Pull it and hand it to me now.'

She did as he asked.

As soon as the knife was in his hands, three men burst from the darkness. One, stinking of drink, seized him from behind and dragged him into the Brunton Mews. Xavier twisted his way free and slashed the dagger at the man, slicing in to a tattered uniform. In his ears he heard the sounds of battle. Muskets firing. Cannons booming. Men and horses screaming.

But this was not battle.

Another man grabbed for his wrist and tried to wrest the knife from his grasp. Xavier whirled on him, kicked him in the groin and sent him sprawling.

The third man had Phillipa in his grip. Xavier strained to come to her aid, but the first man set on him again.

'We need money,' the man cried. No doubt he was a former soldier now driven to theft and violence.

'Leave us! Release her!' Xavier lunged at him, slicing the man's cheek and neck with his blade.

The man cried out and clapped his hand to his face. Blood dripped through the man's fingers and on to his uniform. Xavier turned away at the sight and saw the second man regain his feet. Xavier's thoughts were only on Phillipa.

She struggled to free herself. She gripped her captor's hair and pulled it hard, before stomping on the man's foot.

The second man went to aid the man fighting with Phillipa. Xavier launched himself forwards and seized the man's collar, pulling him away.

That man pulled a knife. 'Not so brave now, pretty boy.' He laughed. 'Give us your money.'

One more man underestimating him.

Xavier lifted his hands as if surrendering. 'I want no trouble.'

The man sneered in contempt and lowered his hands slightly, the chance Xavier anticipated. He let out a cry, so fierce and wild, the man shrank back. Xavier charged straight for him, his fist connecting to the man's chin. The man's knife dropped to the street.

Xavier slammed him against the wall of the building and put the dagger to his throat. 'Not so brave now, are you?'

'Don't cut me! Don't cut me!' the man pleaded.

Xavier snarled, 'Leave now and you leave with your lives.'

The man nodded in fear. 'We're leaving. We're leaving!' He raised his hands in the air and Xavier stepped away. The man sidled away and grabbed the arm of the man still trying to stop the bleeding of the cut to his face.

The third man now had Phillipa's reticule in his grip. She would not release it. His eyes widened when his companions ran off and Xavier advanced on him. Phillipa blocked the man's escape. He picked her up and thrust her aside.

She hit the pavement flat on her face, her forehead bouncing on to its hard surface.

She did not move.

'Phillipa!' Xavier ran to her.

Phillipa heard a man call her name.

She scented sea air and heard waves rolling on to the shore. She felt small and frightened and in pain. Her face hurt and she tasted blood.

She tried to move, but the wind had been knocked out of her. 'Phillipa!' the voice called again.

A man's hands turned her on her back. The darkness had melded into dusk and the air was briny.

'Wake up, my girl,' the voice said.

She opened her eyes and her vision filled with the

face of a man. A stranger to her, but she'd seen him before, in this exact way—or so it felt.

'Phillipa, wake up.' The face changed before her eyes, turning into Xavier's face.

She gasped.

'Are you hurt?' Xavier's hands were all over her, touching her arms, her legs, her torso. 'Did he hurt you?'

This was not at the seaside?

No, it was London. She and Xavier had been walking home. This was not Brighton. She was not a little girl. This was Xavier with her.

'I'm not hurt,' she managed.

She tried to sit up. His arms embraced her and lifted her to her feet. He held her against him. 'I thought you were hurt.' He held her tighter. 'I thought I had lost you.'

She remembered men jumping out of the darkness at them. She remembered fighting to be free.

But for a moment she'd been back in Brighton. She'd seen a different man lean over her. He appeared as real as Xavier appeared now.

She trembled. She'd seen something that was not really there.

Panic rose inside her, kept at bay only because of the strength of his arms. He comforted her. She was safe. Xavier held her.

He loosened his grip. 'I must get you home.'

Supporting her weight with one arm, he led her out of the mews, past Berkeley Square to Davies Street.

Her head throbbed as she remembered he'd had to fight off two men. 'Did they hurt you?' she asked. 'Did they get your money?' Her reticule still dangled from her arm.

His voice turned low and fierce. 'Not that miserable lot of ruffians.'

They reached her door and he embraced her again. 'I should have prevented that attack. We should not have been walking at this hour. I was wrong to agree to this.'

If he had not been with her, what would have happened to her? There had been three of them.

Her heart pounded, anticipating what would come next. He intended to forbid her to come to the Masquerade Club. He would stop her performances right when she was learning about how to make the music most entertaining. He would take it all away.

She could not bear it.

'Do not forbid me this, Xavier.' Her voice trembled and her head ached.

'It is not safe, Phillipa,' he insisted. 'You simply cannot take the risk.'

The hood of her cloak had fallen away, exposing

her disfigurement. She pulled it up again and put the key in the lock, turning it.

He covered her hand with his. 'Phillipa, do not come to the gaming house. Do not try it alone.'

She opened the door and turned to him. 'May I have my dagger back?'

He hesitated, but finally handed it to her.

'Thank you, Xavier.' Impulsively she threw her arms around him. 'You saved us both.'

To her surprise, he returned her embrace with one of his own. He held her against him so tightly it seemed as if he would never release her.

'Phillipa,' he rasped in her ear, as if wanting something more of her, but she did not know what.

She only knew she felt even more shaken when he finally released her and she hurried inside the house.

Chapter Four

Phillipa tossed and turned in her bed. If she drifted into sleep, her attacker returned, jarring her awake. Worse, in her dream, the attacker bore the face of the man she'd seen in her vision.

She must call it a vision. What else could it be? She'd seen something that did not exist. Not only *seen*, she'd actually *been* in another place, a place that smelled and sounded like the seaside.

Like Brighton.

Was she going mad?

She closed her eyes and made herself imagine the image of her real attacker. And then she purposely recalled the face of the phantom man. She could remember both, but remembering was not remotely akin to what she had experienced. Seeing the phantom face, feeling as if she were in another place, those were not mere memories.

Even now, safe in her home, in her bed, she trembled in fear. It made no sense to feel afraid now; she'd not been excessively afraid during the attack. Fear had not been a part of fighting off her attacker and refusing to give him her reticule. The terror had come when she fell and that phantom face appeared.

It had seemed so very real.

If it were not enough to worry about going mad, her head also hurt like the dickens. She rose from bed and, by the dawning light from the window, peered at herself in her dressing table mirror. Her forehead bore a nasty scrape.

Phillipa walked back to her bed and pulled off a blanket. She wrapped it around herself and curled up in a chair to watch the light from the window grow brighter.

Her maid entered the room quietly and jumped when Phillipa turned towards her in the chair. 'My lady!'

'I could not sleep, Lacey.' Phillipa stretched. 'I might as well dress, I suppose.'

Her maid helped her into a morning dress and stood behind her to pin up her hair as she sat at the dressing table.

The girl glanced at her in the mirror. 'What happened to your forehead?'

'It is nothing,' Phillipa answered quickly. 'I...I bumped into the wall by accident.'

The maid looked sceptical.

Lacey was younger than Phillipa and had been hired as Phillipa's lady's maid after the Westleighs arrived in London for the Season. How nice it would be if Phillipa could confide in her about how her injury came about.

'I'll just wear a cap today,' Phillipa said as the maid pinned up her hair. 'We need not mention my injury to my mother. No need to worry her.' A cap should hide the scrape well enough. Besides, her mother never looked at her too closely these days.

The girl nodded. 'Yes, miss.'

Once dressed, Phillipa went straight to her music room. She placed her fingers on the keys of the pianoforte and tried to release the emotions inside her. The keys produced dissonant, unharmonious sounds and her fear returned, as if her world were crumbling around her and she could not stop it, the same feeling she experienced when she fell.

Her music reflected the confusion inside her. No phrase complemented any other.

She became dimly aware of a rapping at the door, but she did not stop playing. Whoever it was would eventually go away.

Suddenly her mother stood before her, shocking her as much as if her mother had been a vision herself.

'Gracious, Phillipa! At least play a tune. This noise

grates upon my nerves.' Her mother pressed her fingers to her forehead.

Phillipa and her mother had barely spoken since the quarrel that sent Phillipa in search of answers about her family. And led her to Xavier. Now she could not speak of what she'd learned without revealing that she knew of the Masquerade Club.

Phillipa lifted her hands from the keys. 'As you wish, Mama.'

She softly played 'The Last Rose of Summer', reciting the words in her head—*Tis the last rose of summer, Left blooming alone; All her lovely companions Are faded and gone.*

She'd not felt alone since Xavier allowed her to perform at the Masquerade Club.

'When do Ned and Hugh return from wherever they are?' She knew her mother would not tell her, but it might make her leave the room before noticing Phillipa's bruise.

Her mother, still straight-backed and regal though in her fifty-fifth year, pursed her lips before answering, 'Please do not tease me about their whereabouts. I have no wish to have that discussion with you again.'

Phillipa continued to play *pianissimo*.

'Do you come to Lady Danderson's musical evening with me tonight?' Her mother's tone dripped with disapproval. No doubt she expected Phillipa to refuse.

She was correct 'I think not.'

Her mother swept a dramatic arm encompassing the pianoforte and half the room. 'Why not? I thought you loved music.'

Phillipa shot her a sharp look, but averted her eyes. No sense revisiting her mother's displeasure at her retreat from society. 'It is to be an amateur performance, is it not? Lady Danderson's daughters and other young ladies and gentlemen of her choosing?'

'It is,' her mother admitted.

'But she has not chosen me.'

Her mother cleared her throat. 'That is true, but…'

Phillipa stopped playing. 'I do understand it, Mama. The performers are eligible young people. She wishes them to show off to good advantage.' Phillipa did not need to explain to her mother that she would never show off to good advantage. Her mother would be first to agree. 'There is no reason for me to be there.'

'Well, there is the music,' her mother added.

Phillipa resumed playing and the final lines of the song came to her—*Oh! Who would inhabit this bleak world alone?* 'I would not enjoy it.'

'I will attend without you, then.' Her mother turned away and then swung back. 'Perhaps I will ask

Miss Gale if she will come with me. She is at least a sociable sort.'

Miss Gale was the young woman Phillipa's brother Ned wanted to marry. She was also the stepdaughter of Lady Gale, the woman carrying Rhysdale's child, the woman who also came masked to the Masquerade Club.

'Miss Gale will be glad of my company.' It was her mother's parting shot. She strode out of the room.

Phillipa's head suddenly ached, but she moved her fingers over the keys, barely pressing them this time, searching for a melody, any melody to erase this unrest within her.

Xavier waited for Phillipa that night at their appointed place, at their appointed time. This time, however, he waited with a hackney cab.

He paced the pavement, rather hoping she would not show up, yet yearning to see her, needing to know for certain that her injuries were minor. A blow to the head could be deceiving. What if she had been truly hurt, like that long-ago time in Brighton?

He'd have failed her again, that was what. And this time it would be his fault.

The jarvey leaned down from his perch atop the coach. 'How much longer, sir? My time is money.'

'I'll pay you for your time, do not fear.' Xavier paced some more.

Her town house door finally opened and a shadowy, cloaked figure emerged.

Phillipa.

She glanced towards where he stood near the coach, pausing briefly to put on her shoes before heading in his direction. She showed no sign that she knew it was he and looked as if she intended to walk past him.

'Phillipa,' he called out.

She drew back.

'It is Xavier.' He stepped in her path. 'I have a hackney coach.'

'Xavier?'

He opened the coach door.

She looked uncertain. 'You brought a hackney for me?'

'I feared you might try to walk alone.' *Or be too injured to make the attempt*, he added silently as he helped her climb into the coach.

She settled in the seat and pulled her cloak around her. 'I did not expect this.'

Xavier sat beside her in the close quarters of the coach's dark interior. He felt her warmth, inhaled the scent of jasmine that clung to her. Her face was shrouded by her mask, but he longed to see her for himself. Was she bruised? Did her injuries again show on her face?

'Have you suffered any ill-effects from last night?' he asked.

She did not answer right away. 'A scrape on my forehead and little headache is all.'

'That is all?'

There was something she was not telling him. He resisted the temptation to pull off her mask to see this scrape for himself. He also resisted the temptation to check her arms, shoulders, ribs, legs—all over her, as he had done the night before.

At the very least, he was tempted to hold her, like he'd done when she was a little girl and had been in need of his comfort.

The distance to the Masquerade Club made for a short walk and an even shorter ride. In no time the coach pulled up to the gaming house and they disembarked.

Xavier paid the driver generously. 'You'll earn that much again if you return in three hours.'

The jarvey grinned. 'In that case, I will, sir!'

Cummings opened the door, nodded to them both and took Phillipa's cloak.

'Thank you, Cummings,' Phillipa said, sounding more tense than other nights.

Xavier faced her. 'Give me your word you will wait for the hackney coach. Do not leave without me.'

'You have my word,' she assured him.

Xavier watched her climb the stairs to the supper room, but he was not perusing her for possible injuries. He was admiring her form and grace.

He glanced away and noticed Cummings regarding him curiously. Cummings turned and disappeared with Phillipa's cloak.

Xavier shrugged. Who ever knew what Cummings thought? Xavier crossed the hall in the opposite direction and checked in with MacEvoy.

'Our numbers continue to run high.' MacEvoy handed him the ledger where he kept count of the numbers of patrons attending and the amount of profits at the end of the night.

When Rhys returned he would look through the books and ask Xavier about the spike in patrons and profits. Xavier would tell Rhys about the *pianiste* who'd briefly performed in Rhys's absence.

He simply would not tell Rhys the *pianiste* had been Phillipa.

MacEvoy added, 'A woman asked for you.'

'Indeed?' Women often asked for him.

'Don't know her. She's wearing a mask. I told her you'd be back directly.' Most of the time MacEvoy recognised patrons, even when they wore masks. He knew the *pianiste* was the woman who'd called on Xavier that first day, but he did not know her real name.

Unless he had asked Cummings. She'd announced herself to Cummings. Both Cummings and MacEvoy probably knew Phillipa's identity. Xavier would have to deal with that.

'Thank you, Mac.' He returned the ledger to MacEvoy.

Xavier's next stop was the gaming room. He wound his way around the room, stopping to chat with patrons or the croupiers. He stepped to the side and surveyed the room, looking for signs of potential trouble. A reckless loser. Or an angry one. Or, a gaming hell's worst trouble—cheaters.

A masked woman approached him. The woman who'd asked for him, he surmised.

'Hello, Xavier.' Her voice was low and lustful.

'Ma'am.' He was usually as skilled as MacEvoy in recognising patrons beneath their masks, but she was new to him.

She laughed. 'Do you not know me?'

He smiled. 'I make it a practice not to know anyone wearing a mask.'

Except Phillipa.

She touched his arm. 'You must know me!'

He had no idea.

'It has been an age. Ten years. But I have never forgotten you.' Her fingers squeezed his arm in too familiar a manner.

Ten years? A dampening feeling spread over him.

Yes. He knew her suddenly. She'd nearly ruined her marriage, her reputation and the good name of his family when last he'd encountered her.

'But I do not know you,' he said, untruthfully. 'The mask disguises you. Your identity is safe here, I assure you.'

'Xavier.' Her tone turned sharp and her fingers dug tighter. 'You would not forget me.'

Indeed he would not.

He'd been barely eighteen. She'd been two years older and unhappily married. She'd pursued an affair with him with all the force of a regimental attack.

And now she was back.

He was careful to remain no more than civil. 'I assure you, ma'am. Those who choose anonymity may be secure in it.' Illusory though it was. 'I will not know you.'

She pulled him over to a corner of the room and pulled down her mask. 'It is I. Daphne. Lady Faville. Surely you remember me.'

She had not changed. Same pale, unblemished skin. Same flaxen hair and wide-set blue eyes. A perfect beauty.

He put her mask back in place. 'Of course I re-member you, my lady.' He remembered her desper-ate loneliness and her belief that an affair with him could alter her unhappiness.

'My lady?' She sounded as if she would cry. 'Can it not be Daphne and Xavier between us?'

'No, it cannot.' He softened his expression, but glanced around the room. 'Is Lord Faville here with you?'

Her eye sparkled. 'Did you not hear? He is dead.'

'I am sorry to hear it.' He really ought to peruse the newspapers more carefully. 'My condolences.'

She waved a hand. 'I am out of mourning. I have attended some of the Season's parties, hoping to see you. Then I learned you were here.'

She'd come looking for him. This was not good.

She smiled. 'There is no one to stop us now.'

Xavier gritted his teeth. 'Daphne, I am stopping it. You caused a great deal of trouble and pain to my family as well as nearly ruining your good name and your marriage—'

Her eyes lit up. 'You called me Daphne!'

Oh, good God.

'Enough of this.' He held up a hand. 'You are wel-come here. To play the tables, or cards or refresh yourself in the supper room, but what is past is over.'

He strode away and did not look back.

* * *

In the supper room Phillipa played only pieces that were so well practised she need not look at her music. If the patrons recognised that she was not challenging herself to play her best, they showed no indication.

She knew the exact moment Xavier entered the supper room, if not by her senses alone, by the way other women's heads turned in his direction. She glanced at him, too.

He stood near the door, arms folded across his chest, listening to the simple tune she played. His handsome face was composed—such a contrast to how he'd looked fighting their attackers.

Strong and fierce.

He did not stay long. He never stayed long, but she also sensed the moment he left.

The gentleman who'd met her that first day entered the room, looking gloom-faced. He sat near the pianoforte, drink in hand. He was one of her admirers. There were several men who always listened to her play and spoke pretty words to her.

Imagine. Several men, none of whom would give her a second glance if they first saw her scar.

The idea usually amused her, but not this night when other faces flashed through her memory. The men who attacked her. The man in the vision.

* * *

After performing for an hour and a half, Phillipa's head ached. She rose from her bench and those in the room, the gentleman included, clapped their appreciation.

She curtsied to them. 'Thank you. Do go gamble. I will play again after a brief respite.'

The patrons who left the room at that point were unlikely to return once they were deep in their cards or dice, but it did not matter. The more men and women gambled, the more improved her family's finances would be.

A gentleman she had not seen there before approached her. 'Excellent performance, ma'am.'

Was this to be another admirer? 'Thank you, sir.'

He inclined his head in response. 'I did not expect to hear such excellent music. I confess I did not know of the fine entertainment when learning of the Masquerade Club.'

'You flatter me.' The flattery she received here always surprised her.

'Nonsense. I speak the truth,' the gentleman said.

Like most of the men who attended the club, he did not wear a mask. His face was pleasant, as was his manner. It put her at ease.

He bowed. 'Allow me to present myself. I am Mr Everard.'

'How do you do, Mr Everard,' she responded. 'You have not been to the Masquerade Club before?'

'It is my first time,' he admitted. 'I have especially enjoyed the music.'

'Not the gambling? There are several tables and games to enjoy.'

He shook his head. 'I never gamble. I am a man of business, you see, and I believe it is not a good thing to risk money on cards or dice.'

Had her father's man of business possessed the same philosophy? Had the man warned her father against gambling the family fortune away? Perhaps her father simply ignored him. Xavier might know.

'Surely you did not come here just to hear me.'

'I confess I did not.' He smiled. 'Although I might have done so had I known of your excellent music. I am here in the capacity of escort.'

'Escort?'

'I was my lady's husband's man of business until his death, but I will say no more, else risk revealing her identity.' He looked wistful. 'Suffice to say I try to serve her in whatever way she needs me.'

'How very generous of you.' Phillipa glanced towards the servant attending the supper room. 'If you will excuse me, my throat is very dry. I need to ask the servant for something to drink.'

He raised his hand. 'Tell me. I will order it for you.'

'Some sherry would be very nice.'

He crossed the room to speak to the servant.

The gentleman who assisted her the first day rose from his chair and walked over to her still carrying his drink. 'I see you have another admirer.'

'One more is always welcome.' She'd learned to banter with gentlemen.

He lifted a hand and counted on his fingers. 'Mr Campion is certainly an admirer. This new gentleman...and me, of course. How many more?'

Phillipa sat down at a nearby table. 'Do not talk nonsense. I think you are peeved for some reason. Perhaps you have lost too much at cards and now you are seeking distraction at my expense.'

He rubbed his forehead. 'How very astute. You are right, of course.' He looked genuinely contrite. 'Forgive me. I have lost a great deal of money and I am very uneasy about it.' He gestured to one of the chairs. 'May I join you for a moment?'

Such a request was commonplace to her here. 'As long as you behave properly.'

'Agreed.' He sat.

Mr Everard hurried over, carrying a wine glass. 'Please forgive me. My lady is here.'

'Thank you for the sherry, Mr Everard,' she called to the already retreating figure.

Everard hurried to the doorway where a masked lady stood.

Phillipa's eyes widened. She'd expected a stooped-over dowager, not this elegant creature in a gossamer confection of a gown that seemed to glow from the candlelight of the chandeliers. Her blonde locks shone equally as brightly as she gracefully stepped into the room, immediately greeted by Mr Everard.

The gentleman seated with Phillipa cocked his head towards the doorway. 'That is Lady Faville, the great beauty. I recognise her even with the mask.'

She glanced at him in shock. 'You should not tell me who she is!'

He shrugged. 'I know. I know. Supposed to be anonymous. But it is quite easy to guess who is under a mask.' He regarded Phillipa. 'I have not the least notion who you are, however.'

Of course he had no notion. 'You have likely never met me before.'

'Likely not.' He smiled and extended his hand. 'I am Mr Edward Anson.'

Anson? Oh, Goodness. She'd once met John Anson, the heir of Earl Wigham. One of her schoolmates had married him. This must be his younger brother.

She accepted his hand.

He released it and glanced back at Lady Faville.

'What a shame she wears a mask. Her beauty is truly extraordinary.' His tone turned reverential. 'She married Viscount Faville for his title and fortune. I believe there was some scandal attached to her shortly after she married. I don't recall what precisely, but it involved another man. All hushed up very quickly.' He took a sip of his brandy. 'The Viscount kept her on a short leash after that. She can take her pick of any man now, though. Faville had the courtesy to die on her. Left her very well off.'

Phillipa watched Mr Everard pull out a chair for Lady Faville. The woman had certainly caught Everard's affections. The poor man. A beautiful, wealthy widow of a viscount was way above the touch of a man of business.

She sipped her sherry and felt her senses heighten. Xavier had returned.

'There is Campion checking on you,' Anson said.

Xavier stood in the doorway, perusing the room. His gaze did not seek out Phillipa, however, instead riveting on Lady Faville. He quickly backed away and disappeared into the hallway.

Anson finished his drink. 'I wonder if I discouraged him.'

'I wish you would not say such things,' Phillipa snapped. 'I dislike it very much.'

He sobered. 'My apologies once more.'

* * *

Phillipa returned to the pianoforte and began 'Bright Phoebus', a song much happier than she felt. Her audience had thinned, as she'd expected, with more comings and goings of those left.

The reputedly beautiful Lady Faville departed after a time, but Mr Everard remained. Presumably, the lady returned to gambling. Anson also left, but Phillipa hoped he'd gone home and not stayed to risk losing more. Xavier appeared briefly. Was he checking on her welfare? Her heart warmed with the idea.

After she finished she stopped in the ladies' retiring room. Lady Faville was also there.

'I wonder if you would help me,' the lady asked. 'My dress has come apart on the shoulder seam and I cannot pin it in place.'

'Certainly,' Phillipa stepped forwards to do the task.

'I pulled at a thread and all the stitching came apart. Can you imagine?' She handed Phillipa some pins. 'How my lady's maid overlooked the problem, I cannot say.'

Phillipa worked one pin through the fabric.

'You are the songstress,' Lady Faville went on.

Phillipa would have rather been recognised as the *pianiste*. 'Yes, I am.'

'You have a lovely voice,' she said. 'And you play beautifully.'

'Thank you.' Phillipa held the extra pins in her teeth.

'This wretched mask is such a bother.' The lady pulled it off. 'Don't you hate wearing a mask?'

'No. I prefer it, actually.' Phillipa placed the pins so they would be secure, but not show.

'I think I will go without a mask.' The lady paused for a moment. 'Tell me. Do you know Mr Campion well?'

The question took Phillipa completely off guard. 'I know him, certainly. I—I play the pianoforte here most nights.'

'Do you know if he has any attachments? He's been out of society of late and I have seen or heard nothing about him.'

Phillipa worked on the last pin. 'I do not know of his personal affairs.'

Lady Faville's voice turned to a wistful whisper. 'I knew him long ago.'

Phillipa lifted her hands from the dress and stepped back.

And saw Lady Faville's face.

She saw an angel. Skin so pale and smooth it appeared other-worldly. Beautiful azure eyes. Full lips the tint of summer roses.

No wonder Mr Everard was smitten and Mr Anson prosed on about the woman's beauty.

Lady Faville touched her gown's shoulder. 'Oh, you have done a marvellous job.' She glided over to the mirror and smiled. 'It is perfection! I am so grateful.'

Her smile made her even more beautiful.

Phillipa could hardly speak in the presence of such physical perfection. 'My pleasure,' she managed.

The lady looked at herself in the mirror. 'I wonder if I need the mask.' She turned to Phillipa. 'What do you think? I am a widow. Widows are allowed certain licence, are they not?'

Phillipa lowered her gaze. 'I would not presume to advise you.'

'I believe I will forgo it!' she said brightly. She gave Phillipa another dazzling smile. 'Thank you again. I am indebted to you.'

Phillipa waited a few minutes before following the beauty out of the retiring room. She was shaken. For the second time in two days she could not explain her reaction to a face. The first one was certainly imaginary, but Lady Faville was all too real.

With a glance towards the door, she turned back to the mirror and lifted her mask.

The contrast between her image and Lady Faville's face caused sheer pain.

She put her mask back in place and shook herself

as she walked to the hall. It had been years since she'd so directly compared her appearance with another woman's. Years since envy had so plagued her. She'd worked very hard to accept what could not be changed and to be grateful for what she did possess. Talent and musical skill.

Ever since the attack—and her vision—her emotions had been in disorder. She'd been in such excellent control of herself before last night.

No longer.

Cummings brought her cloak and Xavier's hat and gloves.

A moment later Xavier strode into the hall. 'Forgive me. I was detained.'

'I only just got here,' she responded.

Xavier took the cloak from Cummings and placed it around Phillipa's shoulders. She pulled up the cloak's hood and waited while he donned his hat and gloves.

Cummings opened the door for them.

'Goodnight, Cummings,' she said.

The servant nodded.

As they stepped out into the street to await the hackney coach, Phillipa felt a shiver up her spine. The night strongly resembled the previous one, which had started out so comfortably. She'd not been comfortable since, and now the whole experience repeated itself in her mind's eye. Including the vision of the man's face.

She'd seen him before, she was certain, but the only memory she could retrieve was the one of the vision.

The coach pulled up and Xavier helped her inside. When he sat next to her, she felt his warmth, inhaled the scent of bergamot that would forever make her think of him. She removed her mask and, covering her face with her hood, thought of Lady Faville.

'With the hackney coach you no longer need to come with me,' she said into their silence. Neither of them had spoken heretofore.

It seemed as if he needed to rouse himself from his thoughts to answer her. 'I will escort you, hackney coach or no.'

Why inconvenience himself in this way? She could only suppose he felt some obligation to her family. Fancied this was his duty.

Like dancing with her.

When the coach reached Hay Hill, near where the attack took place, he put his arm around her and held her close. She blinked away tears. He might escort her out of duty now, but he was still her childhood friend, comforting her when she became sad.

And she selfishly thought only of herself. Never mind that she interrupted his duties at the gaming house. Never mind that she'd caused him to be attacked by ruffians. She wanted to perform her music.

She did want to perform her music. She wanted it so badly she would have braved the streets alone and risked another attack, just for this chance.

He held her the rest of the way to the town house and walked her to the door. They'd not spoken a word.

She wanted to wish him goodnight, to thank him for his kindness, but words would not come. She took his hand and he squeezed hers in return. With his other hand, he cupped her cheek—the scarred one—and leaned his forehead on to hers.

The moment was brief, but Phillipa's heart raced as if she'd run from the Masquerade Club to here.

She hurriedly opened her door and slipped inside.

Chapter Five

Xavier returned to the hackney coach and rode it back to its stand on Piccadilly. He paid the jarvey and walked the rest of the way back to the gaming house.

Phillipa had been very quiet this night. So had he, but taking her in his arms when they passed the scene of the attack had shaken him nearly as much as the attack itself. He wanted to hold her and never let anything hurtful happen to her again.

He hadn't wanted to leave her this night. When they reached her door, he wanted to follow her up the stairs to her bedchamber. He wanted to show her the delights that sharing a bed offered, delights that would erase the pain in her eyes, the pain that had not been there before the attack.

Instead he must return to the gaming house, which he dreaded.

Daphne would still be there, no doubt, waiting for

him, like a spider waits for a fly to become ensnared by its web.

He could not deny her beauty, beauty that had almost seduced him when he'd been eighteen. She had dazzled him. Tempted him.

And ultimately got him sent away to the army. That had been the agreement with Lord Faville— send Xavier away or Faville would drag his family's name through the mud.

Xavier's father had purchased a commission for him and the army had made him into the man he was today. Xavier would not have wished it to be any other way.

As soon as he walked into the gaming room again, he saw her there. For the rest of the night, Daphne's eyes followed him wherever he went.

To Xavier's dismay, Daphne, no longer wearing a mask, returned to the gaming house again and again. The newspapers quickly reported that the lovely widow, Lady F—, had developed a new passion for gambling at the Masquerade Club.

The gossip brought in more patrons than ever.

Daphne's man of business, a non-gambler, escorted her each time. As far as Xavier could tell Daphne had several fawning admirers, but she seemed to have no friends. Certainly no women friends. The women who attended the Masquerade Club turned away or shot daggers at her with their eyes.

He felt sorry for her, but only enough to keep him from speaking too sharply to her. Each night Daphne found some opportunity to speak with him. He was cordial, nothing more. She made no more presumptions about him.

Phillipa, too, attended the gaming house. Although she seemed more recovered from their attack, her initial exuberance about performing had disappeared.

Gone, too, was the ease between them. He missed it.

She was still determined to perform and for that he was grateful. At least he could be with her. He would see her tonight. And Daphne, too, he supposed.

But first he must appear for dinner at his parents' town house.

He'd received the invitation the previous day. He'd neglected them, he had to admit. He trusted that they wanted merely to see he was in one piece, rather than bearing some bad news for him. Bad news did not wait for a dinner invitation.

He was a bit late when he knocked on their town-house door.

'Good evening, sir.' The footman grinned widely as he took Xavier's hat and gloves.

'How are you, Buckley?' Buckley was a long-time retainer for the Campions.

'No complaints, sir. Thank you for asking.' He bowed.

Xavier gave Buckley a conspiratorial look. 'And my parents? Anything I should know?'

'They are in good health, if that is what you mean.'

Xavier touched the man's arm. 'Be sure to get word to me if that changes. They are not likely to tell me.'

'I will, sir.' He inclined his head towards the drawing room. 'I dare say they are waiting impatiently for you.'

'I had best hurry.'

Xavier opened the drawing room door and both his parents sprang to their feet, welcoming him with loving embraces.

'We had about given up on you,' his mother said, hugging him tightly.

'Not I.' His father clapped him on the shoulder. 'I told her you would come late.'

The butler appeared to announce dinner, also greeting Xavier warmly. He and his parents headed straight for the dining room.

The meal passed pleasantly, filled with news about his older brothers and his sisters and their assorted children. He was the youngest of four boys, with two older sisters and two younger ones. Every one of his brothers and sisters was married. All his brothers were occupied in what his father deemed worthy occupations. It took a great deal of the meal to fill him in on everyone, from his eldest brother to the youngest niece.

When dessert arrived their attention turned to him as he knew it eventually would.

'You cannot spend your life running a gaming house,' his father said after lamenting Xavier's lack of direction.

'I do not intend to,' Xavier assured him. 'I am merely assisting Rhys.'

'I do like Rhys very much.' His mother took another bite of custard. 'But I cannot like that he runs a gaming house. It isn't at all the thing.'

'I agree,' Xavier assured her. 'It is only temporary.'

Rhys already had bigger plans. He'd be in manufacturing, if not of steam engines, then something else. He'd make a fortune and prove himself to the father who sent him penniless into the street.

Xavier's desire to succeed was equally as strong as Rhys's. He did not want a factory, though.

At least his mother and father could be grateful for that. Owning a factory would probably be less genteel in their eyes than a gaming house.

His father took a sip of wine. 'I admit that I am

glad you have given up the army. You know I never wanted that life for you. So dangerous. Kept you far away, as well.'

His father did not have to add that Xavier had been sent to the army because of Daphne and her husband's threat.

Xavier winked. 'Well, do not ask me again to read for the law or to join the church—'

His father held up a hand. 'I know better.'

Xavier wished to avoid a heated exchange with these dear people. He loved them too much.

His father brightened. 'How about farming? We can help you purchase a pretty estate—'

Xavier interrupted him. 'I have money enough to buy land. I do not need yours. Perhaps I will end up doing exactly that, but farming is suffering since the war. So much is changing. It may not be the wisest course.'

It would be the simplest one. Become a gentleman farmer, overseeing others doing the actual work.

Where was the challenge in that?

Xavier finished the custard Cook had prepared especially for him. 'Do not worry over me. I will manage something.'

He did not remain long after that. He kissed his mother, shook hands with his father and walked out of the town house feeling unsettled. It was just turning dusk and on this mild night the streets were still busy, the shops still open.

Xavier trusted that he'd know when the right opportunity came his way. It must spark his interest. It must test him in some way, make him more than he was right now.

He walked on Piccadilly past St James's. As always happened, women turned to look at him. A few streets over in Covent Garden, the women would openly proposition him. He would not walk that far.

He reached the new Burlington Arcade and stepped inside. What a grand idea Cavendish had to make this property into an arcade of shops. It was said Cavendish had built it to prevent oyster shells, bottles and other refuse from being thrown into his garden. No matter the reason, the shops employed many workers. Having employment was precious in these difficult times.

He walked past shop after shop. Lace makers, hosiers, milliners. Shoemakers, watchmakers, umbrella-makers. Even a music-seller.

On impulse Xavier entered the music-seller's shop.

'Music for pianoforte. Whatever is newest and best,' he requested of the shopkeeper.

He purchased 'Bid Me Discourse', a song written from Shakespeare's poem *Venus and Adonis*.

Bid me discourse, I will enchant thine ear,
Or, like a fairy, trip upon the green,
Or, like a nymph, with long dishevell'd hair,
Dance on the sands...

Would it please Phillipa? He hoped so.

He walked out of the shop and noticed the beadles in uniform, standing tall, watching over matters, making certain the rules were enforced. Cavendish had recruited them from his former regiment, the Tenth Hussars. A clever way to provide work for at least some of the former soldiers whose regiments were disbanded and who were left to fend for themselves.

Xavier left the arcade and headed back towards St James's and to Rhys's gaming house. He passed former soldiers on the street, wearing their old uniforms for want of other clothing. Some begged. Some were filled with too much drink.

One man leaned against a building, his eyes watchful. His face bore a still-healing cut on his cheek and neck, the cut Xavier had inflicted.

The man nodded towards Xavier. 'Spare a penny for a soldier?'

Xavier advanced on him and the man's eyes widened.

'Do you remember me?' Xavier asked in a low, deep voice.

The man lowered his gaze. 'We should not have done what we done to you and the lady. No forgiving that.' He touched the cut on his cheek. 'I got what I deserved.'

'Why did you do it, then?' Xavier demanded.

'Too much drink, sir. Our bellies were filled with gin.' The man looked ashamed.

Xavier eyed him. 'You were hungry?'

The man nodded.

'Are you hungry now?'

The man nodded again.

Xavier reached into his pocket and drew out several coins. He dropped them into the man's hand. 'Meet me right here tomorrow at noon.' He pointed to the coins now in the man's open palm. 'There will be more of that tomorrow.'

The man looked from the coins to Xavier. His eyes narrowed. 'How do I know you won't bring the Watch with you?'

Xavier held his gaze. 'You don't. But I'll tell you this. I was in the East Essex. I was in the battle, too.' He did not need to tell the man which battle. They both knew he meant Waterloo.

The man bowed his head respectfully. 'I will be here tomorrow when the clock strikes twelve.'

* * *

That night, as before, Phillipa crept down the stairway in her stocking feet and quietly let herself out the town house door. After stopping to put on her shoes, she walked quickly and confidently to the corner where she knew Xavier would be waiting with the hackney coach.

He greeted her as she walked towards him. 'How are you, Phillipa?'

He never complained about accompanying her, yet she knew she inconvenienced him in a myriad of ways.

'Very well, Xavier,' she responded as he helped her in to the coach. 'And you?'

'Tolerable.' He sat next to her.

'Just tolerable?' Perhaps she inconvenienced him once too much.

He waved a hand. 'Nothing dire. I dined with my parents tonight.'

'I hope they are in good health.' She had not seen Lord and Lady Piermont since her mother's ball.

How long ago that seemed.

'They are in perfect health. As is everyone in the family. The Campions are a hearty lot, you know.'

There were eight Campion children. When she'd known Xavier in Brighton, the oldest sons had been at Oxford. She'd hardly glimpsed them during those summers. Xavier's younger sisters were near her age, but it had been Xavier who'd singled her out for friendship.

He still acted her friend even with the trouble she caused him.

'What made dinner with your parents merely tolerable?' It was rare he talked about himself, she realised.

Even in the dim light of the carriage, she could see him smile ruefully. 'As you might imagine, my parents wish me settled. They would prefer I occupy myself in ways other than helping to run a gaming hell.'

'It is not a hell, surely!' It seemed quite tasteful to her, not dark and dangerous.

'No, it is not a hell. But it is not what they would choose for me.'

'Of course they would not choose that for you.' The aristocracy did not run gaming houses. Her brothers had got Rhys to do it for them. 'My parents would not choose for me to play the pianoforte in a gaming house either. That is, my mother would not. I doubt my father would trouble himself to give it a thought.' But she was talking about herself again. 'I do not think we should be confined to society's expectations. The question should be, are you happy doing what you are doing?'

He grinned at her. 'Phillipa Westleigh. I did not know you espoused such an enlightened philosophy.'

She turned away. 'Now you are making a joke of me.'

He put his fingers under her chin and turned her back. 'Perhaps a little, but, believe me, as vexing as you've been, wanting to walk the streets alone, I admire your determination to do what you most wish to do.'

She looked into his startlingly blue eyes. 'I have you to thank for it, Xavier. You provided me this opportunity to perform my music and my songs in front of an audience. It has been a joy for me and I thank you.'

His eyes darkened. 'Show me your gratitude.'

'Show you?' She was puzzled.

One corner of his mouth turned up. 'With a kiss.'

She felt the blood rush to her cheeks.

He averted his gaze. 'I am teasing you.'

Of course. He'd meant it as a jest. What could be more amusing than the scar-faced lady kissing the man once called Adonis by her friends?

He placed his hand over hers. 'I almost forgot.'

This gesture of affection confused her more. 'Forgot what?'

He stroked her hand with his thumb. 'I purchased a piece of music for you today. The store clerk assured me it is quite new, so you are unlikely to have it already.'

'Xavier.' Her throat tightened. 'Thank you.'

Impulsively, she touched her lips to his.

He held her and prolonged the kiss, a wondrous sensation of soft flesh somehow firm and strong against hers. She felt the kiss throughout her body, filling her with yearning.

The driver rapped against the side of the coach and they jumped apart. Phillipa's heart pounded so hard she thought Xavier must be able to hear it.

'I guess we have arrived,' he said, his voice thick.

He climbed out to help Phillipa and pay the driver. They entered the house and, as usual, Cummings took her cloak.

Xavier touched her hand again. 'I will come to listen to you when I am able.'

She nodded, but she was still under the power of the kiss and everything else seemed unreal.

Checking to make certain her mask was in place, she made her way to the supper room where the tables were filled with patrons waiting only to hear her sing and play.

Mr Everard sat at a table close by the pianoforte. That meant the beautiful widow, Lady Faville, was here again. She'd been at the gaming house every night Phillipa had performed.

Not to listen to Phillipa, though.

Mr Everard nodded a greeting as she sat on the bench.

She smiled.

In front of her sat a new music sheet with a brief note written in pen on its cover—

For your pleasure,

X

Her fingers trembled as she opened the cover and scanned the first pages.

These lyrics caught her eye:

Love is a spirit all compact of fire,

Not gross to sink, but light, and will aspire.

Phillipa took a deep breath. She must never aspire. No matter the kiss, which surely was part of his jesting with her. She'd come perilously close to aspiring after one dance, after one Season. No more.

She glanced over to the door and saw Xavier…with Lady Faville upon his arm. Xavier, tall and dark, his blue eyes fringed by dark lashes. Lady Faville, dainty and light in contrast. They were so beautiful, so perfect, she had to look away, only to notice that all eyes were on the stunning couple. Lady Faville seemed to bask in the attention. Xavier looked as if he'd not noticed. He escorted Lady Faville to Mr Everard's table.

Poor Mr Everard appeared stricken.

You also must not aspire, Mr Everard, Phillipa thought.

To her surprise, Xavier stepped away to stand at the back of the room.

Phillipa put the sheet of music he'd given her behind her other music and selected another song to play.

She sang:

*Her hair is like a golden clue
Drawn from Minerva's loom.
Her lips, carnations dropping dew,
Her breath a perfume...*

The room applauded when she finished. Lady Faville beamed.

Xavier bowed his head and rubbed his forehead.

Lady Faville remained in the room when Phillipa stopped playing to take her usual respite about halfway through her time there. The lady leaned towards Mr Everard and said something to him. He immediately jumped up and hurried to the buffet. To fill a plate for her, Phillipa supposed.

She straightened her music and rose, flexing her fingers.

'You play beautifully,' Lady Faville said to her. The

lady smiled and patted the chair next to her. 'Please do sit with me a little. I've asked Mr Everard to fix us both some plates of food and to order you something to drink.'

Phillipa had no choice but to sit. 'That is kind of you...and Mr Everard.'

Lady Faville tossed him a fond glance. 'He is such a dear. I do not know how I would cope without him.' She turned back to Phillipa. 'I believe I told you I am a widow.'

'You did, indeed.' What possible reason could this woman have for inviting this conversation?

The lady glanced around the room again. 'This club is finely decorated, would you not say?'

Phillipa could easily agree. She especially loved this room, decorated in the Adam's style, all pastels and carved plasterwork.

Lady Faville did not give her time to say so, however. 'I suspect the décor was influenced by Mr Campion. I understand he has been at Mr Rhysdale's side throughout everything. All the rooms show such refined taste. I quite did not expect it. But seeing how involved Mr Campion is in the running of the house, I just attribute it to his influence.'

Phillipa's hackles rose. How dare she assume her half-brother would have no taste if not for Xavier?

She immediately smiled inwardly at herself. She

certainly had accepted Rhysdale into the family if she felt like flying to his defence.

She tried to keep her tone neutral. 'I presume you have never met Mr Rhysdale?'

Lady Faville laughed. 'Goodness, no. How would I?' She looked down at her wine glass and twirled it absently by its stem. 'I also understand that Mr Campion escorts you to and from the gaming house.'

'Yes, he does.' Now she understood why Lady Faville had sought her out.

She supposed everyone knew that she came and left in Xavier's company. She'd been attending the Masquerade Club for so many nights, it would certainly have been noticed. But this lady would have had to deliberately seek out this information.

Lady Faville continued to fiddle with her glass. 'When you so generously helped me with my dress, you did not leave the impression that there was any…attachment between you and Mr Campion.' She glanced up and looked earnestly into Phillipa's eyes. 'Because I would not for the world come between a woman and her—her—*paramour.* If there is one thing I respect above all other things it is the *love* between a man and a woman.'

Phillipa held the woman's gaze. Inside her Lady Faville's words felt like a daggers stabbing her heart, but she did not know why she should feel so.

Except for the kiss.

She found her voice. 'Why do you ask me such a question? I do not know you and your question is of a very personal nature.'

Lady Faville coloured slightly. 'Oh, I am being presumptuous, am I not? It is merely that I do like you excessively. I wish us to be friends. And I would not in the world do injury to a friend.'

This was sincerely said, but Phillipa felt wary. Perhaps it was her own envy of the woman that made her doubt.

Lady Faville reached over and touched Phillipa's mask. 'I assume Mr Campion has seen the face beneath this mask and has fallen desperately in love with you.'

Phillipa lowered her gaze. Xavier had indeed seen beneath her mask.

Lady Faville went on. 'I think you should remove your mask and let all the gentleman admire you.'

Could the woman be mocking her? How could she know of Phillipa's disfigurement? No one here knew her except Xavier and she did not wish to believe he had talked of her to anyone.

He certainly had seen beneath her mask, though. How could he not compare her scars to this lady's perfection?

Phillipa resisted the urge to touch her marred face.

A servant brought her a glass of sherry. She lifted the glass and took a sip before answering Lady Faville. 'The mask suits my purposes.' She took another sip and met Lady Faville's eye deliberately, smiling enigmatically. 'I can tell you that Mr Campion and I are…friends.'

Let her stew on that!

A tiny line appeared between the beautiful lady's eyes.

Phillipa glanced away for a moment and noticed that Mr Everard stood with two plates of food, watching them. Lady Faville nodded to him slightly.

He immediately brought the plates to the table. He served his lady first.

She beamed at him. 'Oh, you have picked all I could like.'

His expression softened and his hand shook as he placed the second plate in front of Phillipa. 'My lady thought you would enjoy some delicacies.'

'Thank you, Mr Everard,' Phillipa said.

The poor besotted man.

Mr Everard bowed. 'I will leave you to your conversation.' He looked pointedly at Lady Faville. 'I remain at your disposal, ma'am.'

'You are a treasure, sir,' the lady said.

Mr Everard backed away.

Lady Faville smiled at Phillipa again. 'Did he not do a fine job of selecting treats for us?'

Phillipa selected a piece of cheese. 'He seems quite devoted.'

'Devoted.' Lady Faville nodded. 'That is such a lovely word to describe him.' She shook her head as if ridding herself of Mr Everard. 'But we were talking of Mr Campion, were we not?'

'You were,' agreed Phillipa.

A determined look came into Lady Faville's eyes. 'I assumed that because Xavier—I mean Mr Campion—escorted you here every night that it meant there was a relationship of a personal nature between the two of you.'

'A friendship of a personal nature,' she said enigmatically.

Just as she pretended to be worthy of the flirtation the gentlemen of the Masquerade Club sometimes engaged in with her, Phillipa could pretend she and Xavier were lovers, that she could indeed be a rival to this ethereal creature.

Phillipa knew better, though. Xavier was merely an old family friend, now forced by her to act in a protective role.

She should not step in the way of what might make him happy.

But she still could not resist creating these implications. 'I do not assume that you and Mr Everard have a relationship of a personal nature. He escorts you to and from the Masquerade Club, does he not?'

Lady Faville's eyes widened in surprise. 'Certainly he does, but—' She blinked. 'Oh, I comprehend your meaning. Your connection to Mr Campion is more in the nature of employer and worker!'

No, that was not what she wished to imply at all. Xavier was not her employer. He'd given her a gift— *For your pleasure*, he had written. He was a friend.

He'd returned her kiss.

Phillipa pretended to attend to her food and to enjoy the sweetmeats and other confections Mr Everard had brought her.

Lady Faville leaned closer. 'I must confide in some-one! I am only here at the Masquerade Club because of Mr Campion. We—we were lovers once, but I was married and nothing could come of it. I needed to be certain that no one stood between us. You are so clever and so lovely that I feared his affections were engaged and I had for ever lost my chance with him.'

Lovers? Lovers?

The word was a new dagger to impale her, but it should not matter to her. It should not.

'I cannot be your confidante, my lady. It is not my place—'

Lady Faville gripped her wrist. 'Oh, but you must. I do not care if you are below me—'

Below her? Phillipa was an earl's daughter.

'I confide in my maid, as well.' Lady Faville smiled patronisingly. 'But you *know* Mr Campion. You will understand and you may be able to help.'

Phillipa raised her brows. 'A low person like me? A mere *pianiste*?'

Her sarcastic tone was lost on the lady. 'He must talk to you when he brings you here and takes you home. Has he ever mentioned me?'

Phillipa had talked to him more than he'd talked to her. Might he have confided in her about Lady Faville if she had given him the chance?

'He has not mentioned you to me,' Phillipa answered honestly.

Lady Faville's face fell, but she quickly recovered. 'But you will tell me if he speaks about me? I know you will!' She clasped Phillipa's hand. 'We are friends now.'

Phillipa pulled away. 'It is time for me to perform.'

'Of course.' The lady smiled. 'And it would be a delight to listen to you. But I should put in an appearance in the gaming room, should I not?'

Phillipa rose and returned to the pianoforte. She began with a tune she'd written herself. It was about a sailor's return from the sea and into the arms of the woman who waited faithfully.

A happiness she would never know.

The music, as always, filled her spirit and drove all else away. She abandoned herself to it, so much so that she blinked in surprise when the audience applauded. When the time drew near for the hackney coach to arrive, she announced the last song, one of farewell. It was a composition of hers with which she ended each performance. She had written the first notes of the song not long after that first Season ball when Xavier danced with her.

A few minutes later she waited for Xavier in the hall. She'd already donned her cloak with her new piece of music tucked safely in a pocket.

Xavier came from the gaming room. He strode up to Phillipa, close enough that no one else would hear him. 'I cannot ride home with you, Phillipa.'

This had never happened before. 'Is there trouble?'

He glanced up to the gaming-room door. 'There might be if I leave. Shall I send someone else with you? Or do you trust our hackney coachman? I will pay him extra to see you safe to your door.'

'I will be entirely comfortable with the coachman,' she assured him.

He took her arm. 'I'll see you to him and explain matters.'

Phillipa glanced up and saw Lady Faville watching them from the landing. Would he end his night with her? she wondered.

Outside the hack awaited and Xavier quickly explained matters to the jarvey before turning back to help Phillipa into the coach.

Phillipa took his offered arm, but did not immediately climb into the coach. 'Remember I will not be coming tonight.'

He nodded. 'You'll be missed.'

She settled in the seat while he closed the door. Before the horses moved, she leaned out the window. 'I forgot to thank you for the music. I should have it ready to perform when next I come.'

He smiled. 'I will look forward to hearing it.'

When the coach pulled away, Phillipa sat in darkness, alone, uneasy, but not fearful. She missed Xavier. Their brief rides alone in the dark hackney coach were precious, she realised. And unique. Even without her mask, her face was obscured.

She was not so far removed from that silly girl she'd been in her first Season, when she'd momentarily believed in impossible dreams. Even now she clung to the slimmest straws, spending mere minutes with him, performing and knowing he could hear her play, hear her sing.

How long could she keep this up?

When Rhysdale came back it would be over. He would ask questions about the *pianiste* Xavier allowed to play and Xavier would tell his friend who it was behind the mask.

She would return to her music room and her reclusive existence, and some day she feared she would read in the *Morning Post* that Xavier Campion had married Lady Faville.

Perhaps that day she would compose a mournful funeral dirge.

Chapter Six

Xavier kept his appointment with the former soldier who'd attacked him and Phillipa. As he walked to the appointed spot, the soldier already waited. The man looked watchful and wary.

And much too thin.

He shifted nervously from foot to foot as he watched Xavier approach. 'I am here, sir. As you wanted.'

Xavier extended his hand to shake. 'Good day to you. I am pleased you came.'

The man haltingly accepted Xavier's hand. 'You said there would be more money. What must I do for it?'

'Perhaps nothing,' Xavier responded. He was unsure himself why he asked for the meeting. He had no plan. Xavier clapped the man on the shoulder. 'I am famished. Let us make our way to Bellamy's Kitchen. Would you fancy a pork pie?'

The man was the very picture of hunger, but he had pride. 'I might, if you are buying.'

'I'm buying.' Xavier extended his hand again. 'I am Mr Campion, lately a captain in the East Essex.'

'Jeffers.' The man was more willing to shake hands this time. 'Tom Jeffers, sergeant. From the 42nd.'

'You lost many men in the battle.' Almost three hundred if Xavier's memory served him.

'It was a bad business.' Jeffers's voice turned thick. He rallied. 'But we had Boney running in the end, eh?'

'That we did,' Xavier agreed.

The battlefield of Waterloo gave them common ground. Those who fought there were a select group. Only they could know what a day of death and honour it had been.

They chatted more about the battle until reaching Bellamy's, a place frequented by members of the House of Commons. Xavier found a table where Jeffers's battered uniform would not stand out against more elegantly dressed men.

They ordered pork pies and ale and talked more about the war. Jeffers finished his pie very quickly and Xavier ordered him another.

'What did you do before the war?' Xavier asked.

'I'd just finished an apprenticeship as a cabinetmaker. Should have looked for work instead of listening to those tales of adventure the recruiter told us.'

'A cabinetmaker?'

'That's the right of it.' Jeffers took a big gulp of ale. 'Was pretty good at it, too, if I don't say so myself.'

'Have you looked for work here?' Surely such a skill would be valuable.

'No one's hiring. I'm too old, they say, and not enough experience.' He stared into his ale. 'If they'd give me a chance, I'd show them.'

The tavern maid came up to the table and leaned provocatively over Xavier while pouring more ale. 'Anything else you have a fancy for?' she asked.

'Bread and cheese,' Xavier said without expression.

After she walked away Jeffers's gaze followed her. 'I'd say she had a fancy for you.'

Xavier shrugged.

'I'll wager that happens a lot to a pretty fellow such as yourself,' Jeffers said.

Xavier hated being called pretty. 'Often enough.'

'Lucky bloke,' muttered Jeffers.

Other men always considered him lucky. After all, men such as Jeffers endured much worse. He knew that. But his looks did affect his life, much like Phillipa's scar affected hers. It was all a matter of degree.

'I have an idea,' An idea that formed itself as Xavier

spoke. 'Could you run a shop? Make furniture?' Now here was a new challenge.

Jeffers's jaw dropped. 'What is your meaning?'

'Exactly as I said.' Xavier took a sip of ale. 'If you think you can open a shop, I'll finance you.'

Jeffers turned pale. 'I do not understand you. By the right of it, you should hand me over to the magistrate. I attacked you and your lady. I should be in Newgate for it.'

'You should. But I have a whim.' If Cavendish could create an arcade of shops, perhaps Xavier could open one shop…and make some employment for his fellow soldiers who, like he, came back from war with nothing to do. 'Do you know other men with your skill? You could take on others.'

'Others? I dare say I can find others,' Jeffers rasped.

'Excellent.' Xavier dug into his pocket and took out a purse. 'I'll pay until the shop is profitable, then you pay me a portion.' Not unlike how Rhys arranged the gaming house.

They talked on, about what steps to take. First find a shop to let, then purchase wood and tools. The proposition became more expensive as they spoke, but Xavier did not care. The more he thought of this plan, the more certain he became.

Was it a risk? Certainly. But it was also a new way to test himself. Could he turn men like Jeffers away from a life of crime and create a successful business at the same time? He was determined to do it.

Xavier parted company with Jeffers. As the man walked away, he stood taller, prouder. Xavier smiled.

He almost laughed aloud. The last thing he ever expected to become was a shopkeeper. That was worse in the eyes of the *ton* than running a gaming hell. Cavendish might have pulled it off under the guise of a whim, but he was the brother of a duke.

Phillipa's words came back to him. *I do not think we should be confined to society's expectations.*

He was certainly taking it to heart.

What she would think of his impulsive offer? He'd made it to one of their attackers, after all. Would she understand why he'd done it? She'd become more subdued since the attack. Although she did not speak of it, he suspected she was not entirely recovered.

He would not mention this to her. At least not right away.

Xavier missed Phillipa that night. He found himself listening for strains of the pianoforte to rise above the din in the gaming room. When he entered the supper room, his gaze immediately turned to where the pianoforte sat. He expected to see her there, masked and mysterious, charming the patrons with her music and her voice.

Unfortunately, Lady Faville was present and he was convinced she'd not given up her pursuit of him. She was clever enough not to plague him too much, though. Still, she found some opportunity to talk to him each night, some moment when he could not avoid her.

Like the night before when she'd appeared in the hallway the exact moment he made his way to the supper room. Others were in earshot when she asked him to escort her there, so he could not refuse.

She divided her time between the supper room and the gaming room, never wagering much, but always attracting a great deal of attention from the men, each very willing to partner her, to assist her, to teach her how to play.

She basked in the attention, the admiration, as if she could not exist separate from it, as if she were nothing but how she appeared to others, as if her beauty was all she was worth.

That she was a beauty was indisputable. When he'd been eighteen she'd been a young man's dream, so lovely it hurt to look at her. He'd been smitten.

Until he realised it was his looks that held the most appeal to her. And finer elements of character, like being faithful to her husband, paled in comparison to what a beautiful couple she and Xavier would make.

He'd not bedded her at eighteen. Of that he was grateful, and grateful, too, for a husband wise enough to send temptation away from his obsessed young wife.

Xavier left the gaming room to check on the supper room, and a moment later she appeared by his side, looking as if she merely wished to pick some delicacies from the array of food available.

'Where is your songstress, Xavier? Have you let her go?' Daphne's tone, always sweet, grated on his nerves.

He frowned. He did not wish her to plague Phillipa. 'She does not play every night.'

'It is not the same without her, is it?' She sighed and tossed a glance towards the pianoforte. 'I confess, I miss her immensely. We've become great friends, you know.'

He would not wager on that.

She kept him there chatting for a time longer before he could escape without appearing to the others to deliberately cut her. Someone might remember the trouble she caused him all those years ago. He did not want those rumours resurfacing.

He went next to check on MacEvoy in the cashier's room. Cummings remained always a shout away from MacEvoy, should he need him. For that matter, either of the former soldiers was well able to take care of any nonsense, but if any trouble brewed, Xavier wanted to be aware of it.

When he stepped into the hall a familiar gentleman handed Cummings his hat and gloves.

'General Henson?' Henson had been at Waterloo. Xavier met him in Brussels before the battle and, before that, at Salamanca, another ghastly but triumphant battle. Xavier always had the sense he'd met Henson somewhere before that, but he could never place where.

The general swung around. 'Campion, is it not?'

'Yes, indeed, sir.' He nearly stood at attention, but instead extended his hand. 'A pleasure to see you here.'

Henson shook his hand. 'Good to see you, Campion. Just returned to town and heard of this place. Honest games, they say.' The man seemed in an uncommonly good mood. 'I heard Rhysdale runs it.'

'Indeed he does, sir,' Xavier answered.

Henson clapped him on the arm. 'Friend of yours, I recall. Brave fighter. Done very well for himself. Who would have guessed his fortunes would have turned in this direction?'

Rhys had not been a typical officer like Xavier, a younger son whose choices might include the clergy, the law, or the army. Rhys made his way in life through gambling. Perhaps Henson did not know that Rhys purchased his commissions with his gambling winnings. Rhys's skill and bravery on the battlefield earned him his promotions.

'Rhysdale always does well,' Xavier told him. 'He is out of town at present and I am running the place for him. I will show you to the cashier.' He led the way.

They entered the cashier's room and MacEvoy immediately stood.

Xavier gestured to him. 'General, MacEvoy here was also in the East Essex. Cummings, too, whom you met in the hall.'

Henson shook MacEvoy's hand. 'Good to see soldiers like you, MacEvoy.'

'Sir!' MacEvoy responded.

MacEvoy went on to explain how matters worked at the gaming house, how those who came in masks—ladies, mostly—could only receive credit or write vowels if they revealed their identities.

'Having the ladies here is quite refreshing, I must say.' Henson purchased his counters.

Henson was not married, as Xavier recalled. Perhaps he was in town to find a well-dowered wife, like many an officer without a regiment.

'Certainly it has contributed to Rhys's success,'

Xavier responded. 'I'll show you to the gaming room, if you like.'

The general shook MacEvoy's hand again before they left him.

As they walked to the gaming room, Xavier said, 'I lately encountered one of your infantrymen. Tom Jeffers. Do you remember him? He was a sergeant.'

'Ah, yes!' The general nodded. 'Jeffers. A fine sergeant. He was one of the men who carried Moore from the battlefield.'

General Sir John Moore died from wounds at the Battle of Corunna and was much mourned by his men. Sir Arthur Wellesley had had big shoes to fill when he took Moore's place as the Commander of the British army in the Peninsula—no one knew then that Wellesley's victories would result in him becoming the Duke of Wellington.

'A good man,' Henson went on. 'Hope he is doing well.'

'Matters are improving for him,' Xavier said.

They chatted a bit about the great numbers of former soldiers who were out of work and suffering, before reaching the gaming room.

It did not surprise Xavier to see Daphne hovering near the doorway.

She smiled. 'Have you brought someone new for us, Xavier?'

Xavier gritted his teeth. She'd been lying in wait for him. 'Lady Faville, may I present to you General Henson.

Henson bowed. 'Charmed, my lady.'

She lifted her hand for him to clasp. 'I am delighted, General.'

Xavier stepped back and out of the room, but not before seeing a disappointed look in Daphne's eye.

Phillipa had not slept well, even though she'd not gone to the Masquerade Club the night before. The visions of the mysterious man's face had abated, but now her mind filled with the memory of Lady Faville on Xavier's arm.

It should not matter. *Could* not matter. She must be content with being able to perform her music for others. That was the gift Xavier had given her and all she could expect from him.

Besides the piece of music he'd purchased for her.

And the kiss…. She'd practised Xavier's music all the previous day and had already committed it to memory.

Tired of tossing and turning, she rose and summoned her maid to help her dress. She might as well eat breakfast and she fancied a walk outside in the sunshine, a visit to the shops, perhaps.

She entered the dining room and saw her mother

seated at the table, sipping a cup of chocolate and looking through the mail.

Her mother looked up at her entrance. 'Goodness! You are up early. How are you this morning, my darling girl?'

Her mother was in uncommon good spirits. Perhaps her father's absence was the cause. It was certainly reason to celebrate.

'I woke early,' Phillipa responded. 'It is early for you, too, is it not?'

Her mother smiled. 'It is, but I feel quite well, none the less.'

Phillipa chose her food from the sideboard and sat adjacent to her mother.

A footman appeared. 'Chocolate, m'lady?'

'That would be excellent, Higgley.'

He poured her the last of it from the chocolate pot. 'Shall I bring you more, Lady Westleigh?' he asked.

'Do, Higgley,' her mother responded as she picked up an envelope to read the address.

When he left the room, Phillipa asked, 'Have there been any letters from Father or Ned or Hugh?'

Her mother's smile faded. 'I had a letter a few days ago. They arrived at their destination and all is well.'

'And will you tell me now where they are?' Would her mother say they had arrived safely in Brussels?

Her mother waved a dismissive hand. 'On the Continent.'

This was more information than her mother had given before. '*Where* on the Continent?' she pushed.

Her mother put her cup down hard on the table. 'Do not plague me with this! It is men's business and you need know nothing of it. There is absolutely no cause to worry.' She fussed with the collar of her morning dress. 'I—I do not know the half of it myself. They tell me nothing, you know.'

She knew more than the half of it, Phillipa thought. It was useless to pursue, however.

Her mother went on. 'I thought I would call upon Lady Gale and Miss Gale this morning. Will you come?'

Lady Gale was the woman carrying Rhysdale's child and the woman who had come masked to the Masquerade Club. Miss Gale was betrothed to Ned. She had not given them much thought when meeting them before, but now that she knew of their interesting connection she could admit to being curious about them.

'I believe I will. I have a need to be out of doors. The walk will do me good.'

Her mother beamed. 'I am glad of your company.'

Phillipa and her mother stepped out after noon to make their call to the Gale house. The day was warm and sunny enough to carry parasols. It had not been the family habit to spend the summer in London. Indeed, it was unusual for any of the aristocracy to be in London in summer, but Parliament remained in session and, though the company had thinned, there were still plenty of social engagements to interest her mother.

And now Phillipa knew that their stay in London could also be attributed to the family's financial woes.

Her mother opened her parasol. 'I do wish you would wear one of the hats I had made for you. They are so flattering.'

Phillipa wore a hat, just not one contrived to cover her scar. 'Mother, I like this hat. The others make my face itch.'

It had been so long since Phillipa had ventured out in daylight that she looked upon everything with fresh eyes. The lovely green of the trees and grass, the creams and reds of the houses, were vibrant compared to the various shades of grey she and Xavier had walked past.

They crossed Mount Street and passed Berkley Square and Gunter's Tea Shop where several people gathered outside to cool themselves with pistachio or elderflower ices. Her mother nodded a greeting to people she knew, who never quite looked Phillipa in the face. At least at the gaming house people looked at her. Because her mask concealed her.

They turned on to Curzon Street and strolled to Half Moon Street where Lady Gale and her step-daughter lived. Phillipa sounded the knocker and tried to remember when she'd last made calls with her mother. She'd not come to this house before.

The butler opened the door to them and announced them to Lady Gale and Miss Gale. Both women stood at their entrance.

Lady Gale stepped forwards. 'How good of you both to come.' She turned to her butler. 'Tucker, we will have some tea, I think.'

'Very good, ma'am.' He bowed and left.

Miss Gale rushed over to them, her hands extended. 'Lady Westleigh, I am so happy to see you!' She clasped her future mother-in-law's hands and turned to Phillipa. 'What a treat to see you, as well, Phillipa!' The girl could not quite look at Phillipa for more than a moment.

'We thought it past time to see how you both are faring,' Phillipa's mother said.

They sat, Phillipa's mother and Miss Gale together on a sofa. Phillipa took a chair near Lady Gale.

'Have you any news from our dear Ned?' Miss Gale asked.

Her mother answered, 'He wrote only to say they had arrived and all was progressing well.'

Phillipa assumed her mother's vague reply was for her benefit. Why should all this be a secret from her?

'Have you any letters from Ned?' Phillipa asked Miss Gale. 'Did he write you from where he is?'

'Brussels?' the girl chirped.

Miss Gale was so easily led.

Phillipa could feel her mother stiffen. 'Yes, Brussels.'

'He did write me a very sweet letter about how he hoped to be home very soon.' Miss Gale sighed.

Phillipa persisted. 'How much more does he need to accomplish in Brussels?'

Miss Gale jumped into the snare. 'He said he and Hugh would leave the moment your father is settled in suitable lodgings.'

'I see.' Phillipa stole a glance towards her mother, who sat with pursed lips.

But not for long. 'Did you enjoy the musicale we attended?' her mother asked Miss Gale.

'I did,' the girl responded brightly, her blonde curls bobbing as she inclined her head towards her stepmother. 'Celia does not attend the social functions in her state and Grandmama is not available.'

'Oh?' Phillipa feigned surprise and turned to

Lady Gale 'Are you and Miss Gale's grandmother not well?'

Lady Gale put a hand on her abdomen. 'I am very well. Celia's grandmother has recently moved to Bath where she has many friends and should be very happy.'

Phillipa's mother frowned.

Just one more secret to bring out in the open. 'Were you ill, though?'

Miss Gale, of course, answered. 'She was ill at first, but the doctor said all women are at the beginning. All is fine now. In fact, I have asked Celia and Rhysdale to say their vows when Ned and I do. We'll have a double wedding! Will that not be wonderful?'

'It will indeed.' Phillipa smiled at her mother. 'Do you not agree, Mama?'

'Yes. Yes,' her mother responded in a testy tone, but simpered towards Miss Gale. 'You must attend more functions with me, my girl. My daughter refuses all invitations.'

Miss Gale glanced at Phillipa and her expression turned sympathetic. 'I do understand.'

The tea arrived and the conversation turned to the other invitations her mother had received and which should be accepted. Miss Gale wisely ceded all decisions to Phillipa's mother.

Obviously her mother approved Ned's choice of a

wife. Miss Gale was pretty, malleable and hungry for approval.

Phillipa stared into her tea cup and thought of all the secrets kept among them. Her father's transgressions, his whereabouts, Lady's Gale's interesting condition. The best-kept secret might be hers, though. None of them knew she ventured out at night and played the pianoforte at a gaming house.

Lady Gale leaned towards her. 'You play the pianoforte, do you not?'

For a moment Phillipa wondered if Lady Gale somehow knew her secret, but more probably her mother had mentioned it to Miss Gale that Phillipa closeted herself with her music all day. Miss Gale likely told all to her stepmother.

'I do play,' she admitted.

If it were not for secrets, she could ask Lady Gale about her experience at the gaming house, if people treated her differently when she'd worn a mask.

Chapter Seven

That night Xavier stood by the wall in the supper room while Phillipa played 'Bid Me Discourse', the music he'd purchased for her.

If he were able, he'd stay the whole time she performed. She played and sang with skill, but also with passion. He not only heard the music, he felt its emotion though her.

'Bid Me Discourse' showed Aphrodite's enchantment by Adonis. She saw only Adonis's physical beauty. Daphne shared Aphrodite's misconception.

Appearances could obscure the truth of a person. He'd realised as much since he'd been a young boy. His face and his physique were the least important things about him. He had strength, courage and prowess. He had determination. When he'd finally joined the East Essex regiment, he'd had the chance to prove his true self. Phillipa's true self—her beauty, her sensibility, her complexity—was revealed through the performance of her music.

He'd seen flashes of this true self in her childhood. The intensity with which she examined a flower. The unanswerable questions she asked that showed an understanding far beyond her years—and his, at the time. The empathy she showed to those less fortunate than she.

'It is better to have a scar than to be poor and hungry, is it not?' she said to him once when they'd given coins to a mother begging for her two unfortunate children.

It was indeed.

They were an odd pair in those childhood days, both trying to overcome the handicap of their faces.

Neither had done too badly, he thought as he watched her fingers move confidently on the keyboard.

Still, he wished that he could have prevented the marring of her face back then and saved her the struggle to acceptance.

Phillipa finished the song.

...By law of nature thou art bound to breed,
That thine may live when thou thyself art dead.
And so, in spite of death, thou dost survive,
In that thy likeness still is left alive.

Xavier would not mind seeing a little girl such as she had been, one who could grow up without the pain of disfigurement. But, as for himself, he would not wish his face on any son.

He clapped appreciatively after the last chord was played. She looked directly at him and smiled.

'Wasn't that lovely?' a woman's voice piped up. Daphne, grabbing the attention to herself.

Cummings appeared at the doorway and gestured to him. Xavier crossed the room to him and followed him into the hallway.

'MacEvoy says come talk to him,' the man said.

Xavier hurried down the stairs to the cashier's room. 'What is it?'

'Those fellows in masks you worried about the other night are back,' MacEvoy said. 'I'm thinking they are up to no good.'

'You were right to tell me,' Xavier responded. 'I believe I'll spend some time in the gaming room.'

MacEvoy grinned. 'My hackles tell me that is a grand idea.'

Xavier sauntered into the gaming room and immediately saw the two men that worried MacEvoy. They'd found two partners for whist and were making a grand show of being deep in the cards, but something about their manner rang false. Xavier alerted a couple of the croupiers to the men and tried to keep a close eye on them without seeming obvious.

General Henson strolled up to him. 'Your house seems busy tonight.'

'It is,' responded Xavier.

The general remained next to him, as if wanting more conversation.

Xavier decided to confide in him. 'See those two fellows there?' He gestured to the men.

The general turned in that direction. 'I do.'

Xavier's voice deepened. 'I believe they are trouble.'

'You do not say?' The general nodded. 'I will watch them.'

It did not take much time for Xavier to see the sleight of hand. 'We have a pair of Captain Sharps, sir.'

He made his way to the table and grasped the arm of the man dealing the cards. 'One moment, gentlemen.'

He pulled a card from the man's sleeve.

The man and his partner bounded to their feet. The man Xavier grasped knocked over the table. A shout rose from the gamblers. Women shrieked. The man tried to shove Xavier away, but Xavier did not let go.

The second man tried to make it to the door, but

the general blocked his way and one of the croupiers seized him.

Xavier and the card sharp careened against another table, scattering the players, cards and counters. Fists flew.

Phillipa heard shouts and screams coming from the gaming room. She'd seen Cummings summon Xavier. Something was wrong. She jumped from her bench and ran from the room.

When she reached the door to the gaming room, a dishevelled Xavier dragged a man, nose bleeding, from the room. Others held a second man.

The second man made an attempt to get away and, in the struggle, careened into Phillipa. She lost her balance and, as she fell, felt the aura of her vision.

No! It was gone. She'd been certain it was gone. It must not return. She did not wish the loss of her mind in this public place.

But strong arms steadied her, preventing her fall. She breathed a sigh of relief and lifted her gaze to thank the man.

She froze.

An older gentleman held her, but his face was that of the man in the vision.

'Nothing to fear,' the man said. 'I've got you.'

She blinked, but his face did not change. He was

real. This was the man in her vision, but this time he was real.

'Who—who are you?' she managed.

He released her and bowed. 'Allow me to present myself. I am General Henson and you must not be alarmed by this commotion. Campion spotted some men cheating at cards and he made short work of them.'

She barely heard. Cheaters? 'Why are you here?'

He looked puzzled for a moment, but immediately assumed a kindly expression. 'I came for a little gambling, is all.'

The grey hair was wrong. It had been black in her vision. But the face was the same. *The same.* A few more lines, perhaps, but the same face.

'Have you come to gamble?' he asked conversationally. 'I would be pleased to escort you into the gaming room. It should be straightened up by now. I assure you, all the excitement is over.'

'No, I—I wanted to speak to—to—Mr Campion.' Her voice sounded shrill.

If he thought that odd, he made no indication. 'I suspect he will be busy for a time. Is there somewhere you would like to wait? I will be honoured to convey your request to him. Whom shall I say asks for him?'

She almost spoke her name, but caught herself. 'Say his *pianiste*.'

He smiled. 'So you are the *pianiste* I have heard so much about? I came last night for the first time, having heard the Masquerade Club had both gambling and fine music. You were not here.'

She could not absorb the compliment.

Lady Faville appeared. 'What was the commotion?' she asked Phillipa, but then noticed the general. 'Oh, General Henson. How nice to see you again. When our Miss Songstress ran out, I wanted to follow, but dear Mr Everard convinced me to stay. You do recall Mr Everard, do you not, General? You met last night.'

'I do indeed,' he answered.

Mr Everard stood behind Lady Faville, but addressed Phillipa. 'You should not have dashed out, miss. You might have encountered danger.'

'She had a brush with it,' Henson said. 'Nothing of consequence, but it has upset her, I think.'

Lady Faville's eyes widened. 'What happened?'

General Henson explained about the men caught cheating and, while Lady Faville listened and asked questions, Phillipa backed away and returned to the supper room. It was abuzz. There had been a fight, they said. Xavier had overpowered the culprit. A big fellow, they said. Imagine. A man who looked like Campion overpowering a man like that.

Phillipa had seen him fight. Xavier had taken on three men the night they were attacked.

And once again the man in her vision appeared to her.

This time he was real.

She asked the servant to bring her a brandy. Mere sherry would not do to calm her nerves this night. She retreated to a table far in the corner and, after the servant set the glass in front of her, she picked it up and took one sip, then another. Her hand shook.

She closed her eyes and tried to make sense of it all.

The man was real...

'Phillipa?'

She opened her eyes and Xavier stood before her.

It had taken Xavier some effort to find Phillipa tucked away at this corner table. Reaching her had been even more difficult. The patrons delayed him, asking questions about what transpired in the gaming room.

She looked grateful to see him.

He sat. 'Were you injured?'

She shook her head.

'What possessed you to come to the gaming room, Phillipa?' He put her hand in his. 'It could have been dangerous.'

She averted her gaze. 'I feared for you.'

He squeezed her hand. 'Foolish girl. I have plenty of men to come to my aid, if necessary. Think of Cummings. What man could be a match for him?'

'I was not thinking. I heard the sounds—' Her brow furrowed and she looked at him with an uncertain expression. 'May we talk alone? I know it is presumptuous, but could we talk in Rhys's drawing room, perhaps?'

He immediately stood. 'Of course.'

Only a few people slowed him down with questions and comments as he led her through the room and out into the hallway. When they started up stairway to the drawing room, he glanced back and saw Daphne staring at him from the supper-room doorway.

Xavier leading a woman up to Rhys's private rooms? What conclusion would Daphne make? He did not care. His worry was for Phillipa. She seemed unsteady under his touch.

They entered the drawing room and he brought her directly to the sofa. 'You are shaking, Phillipa. Are you certain you are not injured?'

'It is not that. Really.' She pulled off her mask and rubbed her scar. 'I could not stand the mask another minute.'

There was more to it than the mask.

He walked over to a cabinet and brought out a bottle of brandy, pouring one glass and handing it to her before pouring another for himself.

He sat next to her on the sofa. 'Tell me what happened.'

She took another sip of brandy and reached out, almost touching his face, but withdrawing her hand. 'First, tell me if you are hurt. There was a fight, they said, and I saw the other man's bloody face.'

His skin yearned for her touch, but he spoke as if nothing had affected him. 'That fellow had the worst of it. He should not have tangled with me.' He took her hand, relishing the warmth of it. 'It is all over now. They will not be back.'

She nodded and slipped her hand away. He took a gulp of brandy. His desire for her surged, but this was not the time.

Eventually she spoke. 'There was a gentleman— he kept me from falling. General Henson. Do you know who I mean?'

He nodded. 'I know the general.'

She turned away. 'I am fearful you will think me mad.'

'Mad?' He could never do so.

'I saw the general before.' She took another sip and swallowed. 'That night we were accosted by the three men. One man knocked me down and—and—suddenly I was someplace else. Someplace that smelled like the sea. When…when you helped me up, your face was a different face. It was that face of that man. The general.'

His face was another face?

'It was a vision.' Her voice cracked. 'I had the vision again. Several times. Falling. Smelling the sea. Seeing the face. It was always as though I was in a different place, but only for an instant.' She pressed her finger to her forehead. 'I do not understand it.' She waved a hand. 'In any event, the visions stopped and I thought them gone, but when I lost my balance it almost returned. This time, I saw the general. The real one, I mean.' She took a breath. 'I am certain it was the general's face in my vision, but now he looks older.'

Xavier's brows knitted.

She put her hand to her scarred cheek and turned away. 'You do think me mad.'

'No. No. I am trying to make sense of it.' He pulled her hand from her face. 'Are you certain it was a vision? Perhaps it was a memory.'

Because the pieces fit.

'If it was a memory, I would have remembered it!' Her voice rose. She glanced away again as if in thought. 'It was *familiar*, though. As if I ought to have remembered it.'

'Maybe it was a memory about your fall.' She'd smelled the sea. That could have been Brighton.

'My fall?' She looked confused.

He touched her scar. 'Listen to me. I know of soldiers who have memories of battles so vivid they think they are there again. This could be a memory. What do you remember of that event? When you fell at Brighton?'

She put her palm where his fingers touched. 'I was running up stone stairs and I fell. Or I must have fallen. My mother said I fell. I remember running up stone steps and falling. That is it.'

She did not remember it all, but Xavier did.

It had been dusk in Brighton and he'd been out poking around at the base of the sea wall. Sometimes people dropped things from the top of the wall, while they were gazing out to sea. He'd found coins, a watch, all sorts of treasure.

He heard the sounds of a quarrel. A man and woman, mere shadows at that time of day. He saw the man hurry away and the woman rush after him. And, then, there was the little girl—Phillipa.

He should have stopped her. The steps were too steep, too slippery to run up at that pace. Instead, he just watched. And saw it all.

The woman was Phillipa's mother. Lady Westleigh. The man. Could it have been General Henson?

'Do you remember a man being there when you fell?'

'No one was there,' she insisted. 'My mother found me and picked me up and carried me home.'

'Do you remember that?'

She shook her head. 'Do you think the general was there?'

Xavier had never seen the man's face, but he'd worn a coat that might have been an officer's coat.

'My mother would have told me if a man was there.' She touched her scar again.

Would it help if he told her? He wanted to.

He could not tell her, though, not when he'd sworn a promise not to.

He'd given his word.

Phillipa pressed her fingers against her temple. 'I do not know what to think.'

Could her vision be a memory? It could not be the hallucination she feared, because General Henson was real. One could not conjure up a person and then discover he was real.

It must be a memory.

Xavier handed her the glass of brandy. 'Drink the rest. It will calm you.'

She took it and did as he told her.

The clock on the mantel struck the hour.

She picked up her mask. 'I should return to the supper room. People will think it odd that I am not performing.'

He stilled her hand. 'You are under no obligation to perform. You may stay here and rest until it is time for the hack to arrive.'

She had another hour. 'No, I'll play. The music will help.'

She put her mask in place.

'I'll tie the ribbons for you.' His voice turned low and soft.

What a marvellous voice he possessed. It could soothe. It could menace. It could make heat rush through her.

His fingers did the job of securing her mask gently but competently and his warm hand slid to the bare skin of her neck. 'There.' He rose from the couch and extended his hand to help her up.

This time his hand felt strong and secure. 'I'm certain everyone will wonder where you are,' Phillipa said, to cover up the silly emotions he aroused in her.

Emotions that nearly betrayed her long ago when she'd fancied herself in love with him.

He left her at the doorway of the supper room.

She entered the room and all heads turned to her. 'I am back,' she said to them in a cheerful voice. 'Do you wish me to play?'

Several voices called out their assent and she sat

down on the bench to the pianoforte and quickly looked through her music for something she could manage in her shaken state.

Something joyful, she thought, to raise everyone's spirits.

Lady Faville approached her. 'Are you feeling better, Miss Songstress?'

The appellation surprised her. 'Yes. I am quite recovered.'

The lady's full pink lips turned up in an angelic smile. 'Was it not kind of Mr Campion—Xavier—to allow you some time to refresh yourself.' Her smile faltered a bit. 'I assume that was why he took you out of here. He is nothing if not the kindest of men.'

Phillipa supposed everyone knew she'd gone with Xavier to the private rooms, but surely they would think nothing of it. They thought her in the employ of the Masquerade Club, so it should not feel odd for the manager to speak to her alone.

But it rankled that Lady Faville commented upon it. 'Yes. I was shaken up by all the excitement, and—and almost falling.'

'Did you almost fall?' Lady Faville asked with a mere touch of scepticism.

'I did,' Phillipa assured her. 'And the general caught me.'

'How exciting!' cried the lady. She turned solicitous again. 'As long as you did not hurt yourself. I would have been desolate if my new friend were in-jured in any way.'

New friend. Even if it was merely Phillipa's envy that prevented it, she could not ever consider this creature a friend.

'Thank you,' she said tightly and turned to her music.

Chapter Eight

The next morning Phillipa resolved to ask her mother about her accident all those years ago. If it had been possible that there was a man present, surely her mother could tell her.

Phillipa had slept late, exhausted by the night before. She missed her mother at breakfast and could only hope she had not yet gone out.

She checked her mother's bedchamber first, but she was not there. She started down the stairs and spied Mason below.

'Mason, where is Mother, do you know?' she called down.

The butler looked up. 'In the drawing room, m'lady, but—'

'Thank you!' She was near the drawing room. She knocked quickly and opened the door. 'Mama—' she began, but stopped short.

Quickly rising from the sofa was a gentleman.

General Henson.

Her mother spoke as she, too, rose. 'Phillipa! How good it is you have come. I want you to meet this dear old friend of mine.'

Dear old friend?

She stepped forwards and tried to look calm. What was he, of all persons, doing in her mother's drawing room?

Her mother took Phillipa's hand and pulled her closer. 'Phillipa, may I present my dear friend, General Henson.' Her mother gave the general a fond look. 'Alistair, my daughter.'

'This is Phillipa?' The general smiled as he had smiled the night before. In the better light of day, the lines of his face were more apparent. 'I cannot believe you are grown up.'

Phillipa's heart pounded painfully. 'Did you know me when I was a child, General?' she asked, remembering in time to extend her hand.

He clasped it in a fatherly way. 'I saw you when you were little more than a tot, my dear.'

He, of course, noticed her scar, but did not seem surprised about it. He must have known about it, but she had been much older than a tot when the accident happened. She'd been seven years old.

'I do not remember you,' she said. Although, apparently, she did.

He exchanged a glance with her mother. 'No reason why you should.'

'The general invited me for a drive in the country,' her mother broke in. 'Does that not sound delightful?'

The man looked apologetic. 'I would include you in the invitation, but, alas, my curricle is a small one.'

'Do not concern yourself,' Phillipa replied. 'I have much to do today.'

'My daughter spends her days playing the pianoforte.' Her mother's tone was disapproving, of course.

'Does she?' The general smiled in delight. 'What a worthwhile occupation.'

'How do you know my mother?' Phillipa asked. 'I do not recall her mentioning you.'

'We met in B—' He stopped himself. 'We met long ago through—through other connections. For most of the time until now I have been off fighting wars.'

'Well, enough of that,' her mother said with false cheer. 'We ought to leave, Alistair, if we are to return in time for me to dress for the opera.'

'As you wish.' He gave her mother a warm glance, but turned back to Phillipa. 'Will you do me the honour of allowing me to escort you to the opera as well as your mother? Your mother has graciously invited me to join her in her box.'

'Thank you, but I rarely go out.' Perhaps she should go. Find out more about this general. And her mother.

Her mother took the general's arm and led him to the door. She turned her head back to Phillipa. 'If you do not wish to come, Phillipa, be so good as to send a note to Miss Gale, inviting her to come with us. Do it quickly so she will have time to send a reply.'

'Yes, Mama.'

She watched them leave, her mother happier than she'd seen her in years.

Phillipa might have spent her time in near seclusion, but she was not so green a girl not to guess that her mother's relationship with General Henson was not merely friendship.

Had he been there, the day she was injured? If so, why had her mother not said so?

After her mother and the general left the house, Phillipa paced in the music room. She could not play a note, let alone compose one, although she forced herself to write to Miss Gale.

She wanted to talk to Xavier. He was the only person with whom she could discuss this latest of events, finding the man in her vision seated with her mother in the drawing room.

Time passed much too slowly, though. She might indeed go mad if she had to wait until the middle of the night.

Why wait? She could call upon him. She'd done

so once before, although she'd thought she would be calling upon Rhysdale. Calling upon one's relation, even one born on the wrong side of the blanket, would not cause too many questions, but calling upon a single gentleman could not be proper.

She did not care. She was not an *ingénue*. At twenty-three, in her situation, she was solidly on the shelf. Who would care what she did?

And her mother was not at home to question where she went or why.

She summoned her maid to help her don a walking dress and, before leaving her bedchamber, had the girl find a straw hat with so much netting her mother would have been pleased to see her in it. When she stepped out into the fine day, her face was well shaded from anyone recognising her as well as from the sun.

She walked as quickly as she could without attracting notice. As she neared the spot where she and Xavier were attacked, she slowed her pace. Anxiety fluttered inside her. She'd not walked this route since that night. Once there, the events returned to her mind, but without the darkness, the area held no lingering menace. She paused, wondering if the vision would recur.

It did not.

When she tried to recall the face in the vision, she saw only the man who'd been seated with her mother, who'd caught her when she almost fell.

She reached the door to the Masquerade Club, its innocent appearance striking her anew. She sounded the knocker and Cummings opened the door.

She almost greeted him by name. 'Lady Phillipa to see Mr Campion, please.'

'Not here,' the footman said.

'Oh dear.' She'd not considered this.

He stared at her for a moment. 'At the Stephen's Hotel, mayhap,' he finally said. It was an impressive string of words for the close-mouthed man. 'Doesn't come 'til later.'

The Stephen's Hotel was not far and it was still early enough to walk back by Bond Street. She could stop by the hotel and ask for him. It was a brazen idea, but very unlikely that anyone would know about it.

'Thank you,' she said.

Cummings nodded and closed the door.

Only after she set off for Bond Street did she realise how odd it was for Cummings to give Xavier's direction. Had Cummings recognised her? As more than the woman who had called upon Rhys that day?

She shook her head. She could not worry about that at the moment.

* * *

She hesitated once more as she approached the door of the Stephen's Hotel. Surely it was not what a lady would do, to enter this establishment that catered to army officers. She took a deep breath and opened the door, stepping in to a sparsely decorated hall. There was a desk behind which a clerk stood.

The man looked up and his brows rose.

She approached him. 'I would like to see Mr Campion, if I may.'

He looked askance. 'He would wish to know who calls.'

She had not thought that far in advance. 'Tell him his *pianiste* calls.'

'Very good, ma'am.' The man gestured to an open door on his right. 'Would you care to wait in the drawing room?'

Phillipa thanked him and hoped no one else would be in the room. Luckily she was alone amidst the assortment of chairs and couches arranged for conversation. The curtains were drawn and, although the room had more the air of a gentleman's library, fresh flowers on the mantel and on the tables made it somewhat cheerful.

The idea of coming here seemed suddenly foolish. How much could it have mattered to simply wait to talk to him that night?

A man's voice sounded in the hall and Phillipa hurried to the doorway, expecting to see Xavier.

It was not Xavier.

It was General Henson, obviously sneaking a giggling woman through the hall.

Phillipa's mother.

Xavier quickly put on his coat and ran a hand through his hair as he descended the stairs, trying not to appear too eager for the clerk's sake.

She'd come alone, the clerk said. What could have possessed her to do so? He could only think that something bad had happened.

The clerk was again behind his desk by the time Xavier crossed the hall to the drawing room. When he walked through the doorway he saw her.

She simply stood, gazing blankly towards the door.

He hurried to her. 'Phillipa, what is it? Has something happened?'

God help that it not have happened to Rhys. Or Lady Gale, Rhys's lover. Or any member of her family. He could think of no other reason she would come to him here.

She did not answer.

Unless something had happened to her.

He lifted the netting away from her face. 'Phillipa! Talk to me.'

She blinked. 'Oh, do forgive me.' She was pale as chalk. 'I am quite speechless.'

He gripped her shoulders. 'What happened?'

She shook her head as if not believing her eyes. 'I just saw General Henson. In the hall. The real General Henson. Not a vision.'

He softened his touch and his tone, but did not cease holding her. 'The hotel caters to army officers.'

'I know.' Her voice was breathless. 'There is more. My mother was with him. They obviously came from his rooms.'

That must have been a shock.

His fingers slipped down her arm and grasped her hand. 'Come. Sit.' He led her to a sofa. 'You could not have known that before you came here.'

She smiled wanly. 'I did not, but it was why I came, none the less.'

She told him of encountering General Henson with her mother in her mother's drawing room. Of her mother professing to know him many years ago. Of the general saying he'd seen her when she was a tiny girl.

'But, this is the thing.' She touched her scar. 'He showed no surprise at seeing my scar. People are always surprised the first time they see my scar. So he must have known about it. He must have seen me— and Mama—after it happened.'

Henson must have been the man on the beach that night. Nothing else made sense.

'I think they were lovers,' she said firmly. '*Are* lovers, still. They obviously have become reunited.'

'General Henson has not been in town long, I think.' He realised he still held her hand. He released it. 'Does it upset you to discover your mother has a lover?'

'Goodness, no.' She laughed. 'If any woman deserves a lover, it is she. My father certainly gave her more trouble than care or devotion.' Her eyes narrowed. 'Were you thinking I should have a fit of the vapours? I assure you I have acquired some knowledge of the world.' She gestured to her face. 'When nobody looks at you, much can be observed.'

He felt a stab of pain for her.

'It surprised me to see them, that's all.' She glanced away as if witnessing them again. 'My mother was as giddy and silly as a girl in her first Season—' She cut herself off and turned back to him. 'I am the one who feels silly, coming to you like this.'

He met her gaze. 'I confess, I feared something much more serious brought you here.'

From the window, the sun's rays dusted her chocolate-brown eyes with flecks of gold. Her lips were moist and tempting. Her skin, too, was luminous and so smooth he itched to touch it—

He stopped himself. Why was it he'd only found one instance to kiss her? Every other time the desire overcame him, she was too overcome with emotion.

He contented himself to savour her beauty. What a pity people did not look at her. Or if they did, they saw only her scar.

Her eyes darkened and she lowered her lashes. 'It was foolish of me. I simply needed someone to tell about General Henson and my mother. There was no one else but you.' Her lashes fluttered. 'It should have waited until tonight.'

He almost touched her again. 'I do not mind it, Phillipa.'

She fussed with the netting on her hat and covered half her face. 'It is the sort of thing one runs to one's lady friends about, I suppose, but I've lost touch with most of my school friends and the others live far away.'

'You have hidden yourself away,' he said.

Her chin rose. 'I have been busy with my music. It has been my passion.'

He did indulge himself and touched his finger to her chin, but it was as he used to do when they were children and he wanted to tease her about the faintest cleft in her chin. 'You've achieved impressive results.'

Her eyes widened and she leaned back. 'Why,

thank you, Xavier. I have longed to hear words of approval for my music.'

He was puzzled. 'You hear such words every night you play, do you not?'

She released a breath. 'They do not know who I am.'

'Should it make a difference?' He noticed a stray curl escaped from her bonnet.

'The daughter of an earl is not supposed to perform music. At least not in a gaming house. At a musicale, perhaps, but there everyone who plays is deemed marvellous.' She lowered her voice. 'I do not think you would lie.'

'I would never lie to you.' Withhold information, perhaps, but never lie.

'This is all of no consequence.' She waved a hand. 'The vision must be a memory, as you have said. General Henson must have been there when I fell. My mother would not tell me such a thing, if he had been her lover. What do you think?'

'It seems plausible,' was all he could say.

'I would so much rather have a memory than see things that were never there.' She leaned against him like she used to do when they were playmates. 'This seems so much like it used to be in Brighton. You were always my friend and confidant.'

He put his arm around her and enjoyed the moment of comfortable closeness with her.

'I must go.' She sat up straight again. 'I presume too much, taking up your time like this with my nonsense.'

She rose from the sofa.

He stood as well. 'Wait a moment. I'll get my hat and walk you home.'

'No,' she said quickly. 'I came on my own. I can leave on my own.' She shook her head. 'Besides I do not want my mother to see you. She might be home by now. I do not wish to endure her questions.'

He nodded.

She started for the door but turned back to him. 'Thank you for being so kind, Xavier. I truly did need a friend to talk to about this.'

'I am your friend, Phillipa,' he responded. 'I have always been.'

She smiled, but did not meet his eye. 'Good day.'

He did not want her to leave. 'I will see you tonight.'

'Yes. Tonight.'

She turned back to the door, but suddenly ran back to him, throwing her arms around him in a big hug. She would have pulled away just as quickly, but he held her there, against him, and inhaled the jasmine scent of her, relished the warmth of her.

He released her and she hurried away. He stepped to the window to watch her walk briskly away. She stopped suddenly and pulled the rest of the netting back over her face.

And he again felt a stab of pain for her.

Without hat or gloves, he stepped to the door to follow her home and make certain she arrived safely.

That night she sang songs about forbidden love.

Still thinking about her mother, Xavier surmised. He felt even closer to her than before, even closer than as children, the sort of closeness a man wants with a woman he craves.

He stood at the back of the room, his usual place, watching her as her long, elegant fingers moved over the pianoforte keys and her voice rang out with emotion. He wished she could remove her mask so he could see the emotion on her face as she played.

Her music was full of life because she'd put her whole life into it. It made him sad for her, but also appreciative of her considerable achievement.

He could listen to her for hours, but ought to spare only a few minutes more before attending to the gaming room.

Daphne sidled up to him. 'I did not know you had such an…appreciation of music, Xavier.'

She ruined the moment for him. 'You do not know me, Daphne.'

She was undaunted. 'We have become bosom bows, your Miss Songstress and me. Did you know that?'

'I believe you have said as much before.' But he doubted it. He inclined his head towards Phillipa. 'Does she know it?'

Her lips pursed for a moment, but she turned them up in a smile. 'You will make me laugh, Xavier, and then I will interrupt the music.'

He straightened. 'I cannot remain here and talk to you. I must return to the gaming room.'

He walked away from her without a second glance.

Later when he came to collect Phillipa for the ride home in the hackney, Daphne stood with her, chattering away. It was difficult to see Phillipa's reaction under her mask.

When they were in the coach, he perused her. 'Have you befriended Lady Faville?'

She did not answer immediately. 'She befriended me.'

He shook his head. 'Why?'

She stiffened. 'Is it so difficult to believe someone would befriend me?'

'Not in the least,' he assured her. 'But someone like her—'

Phillipa drew away from him. 'Because she is so lovely?'

'You know I do not mean that.' This was merely causing tension between them. 'I was surprised, that's all. She is not the sort to make friends.'

He dropped the subject and so did she, but they rode in uncomfortable silence the rest of the short journey. He felt like kicking himself. He ought to have let her talk of her mother and General Henson.

The hackney pulled up a few doors down from the Westleigh town house and Xavier helped Phillipa from the carriage. Just as they both stood on the pavement, the Westleigh town house door opened and a man emerged.

Xavier and Phillipa stood in the shadows away from the hackney coach's lamp.

General Henson walked past them.

Chapter Nine

The next day Phillipa rose early to catch her mother at breakfast.

By rights Phillipa ought to confront her mother about her affair with the general, but she didn't have the heart. Her mother deserved some happiness, after all.

But Phillipa's memory of General Henson and its apparent attachment to her injury were another matter. So when she descended the stairs and entered the dining room it was with a determined step.

Her mother was already seated there.

'You are up early,' they said in unison.

'I could not sleep,' they answered together.

Her mother laughed, a sound Phillipa had so rarely heard in recent years.

She turned to the buffet and picked out a piece of bread and jam.

Her mother spoke. 'I rose early so I could go to the

shops.' Her tone was defensive. She was lying. 'I plan to shop all day, so I am certain you would not wish to keep me company.'

A wave of tenderness for her mother washed over Phillipa. 'I do not, but who do you take with you? Your maid? Higgley?'

Her mother lifted her nose. 'If you must know, General Henson will accompany me.'

'Again today?'

Her mother crossed her arms over her chest. 'Yes. Again today. I have not seen him in very many years—'

Phillipa held up a hand. 'I meant no criticism, Mama.'

'Oh.' Her mother relaxed again.

'There is something I wish to ask you, though.'

Her mother tensed again. 'Not more about your father and brothers, if you please. I am done talking about that with you.'

Phillipa chewed and swallowed a piece of bread. 'Not that,' she assured her. 'I wanted to ask you what you remember about the time I fell. When my face was cut.'

Her mother glanced away. 'Whatever for?'

'Curiosity.' She took a breath. 'Tell me about it again.'

Her mother rose and fussed at the buffet. 'Must I? It was a terrible event and I dislike remembering it.'

'Please, Mama. Just tell me again.'

'There is nothing to say.' She sat again. 'You went outside without permission and I found you on the beach. You'd fallen. That is all.'

'What was I doing out there?' Phillipa had never thought to ask this before.

Her mother threw up her hands. 'I do not know. You went out. You confessed not to remember. It was a terrible shock to find you all—all bleeding and insensible.'

Why had her mother gone out to find her? She'd never thought of it before, but her mother sent servants for tasks like that.

Her heart pounded. 'Was anyone else there, on the beach when you found me?'

'No.' Her mother's eyes darted away. 'Enough of that, now. The whole terrible event is best forgotten. I will not say another word about it.'

Phillipa persisted. 'Is there anything you can tell me now that you withheld from me as a child? I do wish to know.'

Her mother busied herself with her food. 'Nothing. Unless you wish to hear a hideous description of the skin hanging off your face.'

'Spare me that, Mama.' Her mother was being deliberately cruel.

'You would do better to forget about the past. You need to rejoin society.' Her mother straightened in her chair.

This was an old, familiar lecture.

'You are an earl's daughter,' her mother went on. 'For that reason alone, you are a desirable catch for any respectable gentleman, no matter what your age and your—' She stopped. 'No respectable gentleman would be unkind to you, because of—' Again she closed her mouth.

The word her mother refused to speak was *scar*.

'There is a ball tonight,' her mother said. 'You should attend.'

Phillipa glanced down at her plate. 'No, Mama.'

'Very well.' Her mother stood. 'I will take Miss Gale with me.' She flounced out of the room.

Phillipa rested her head in her hands. Such an attack by her mother had only one end. To force Phillipa's retreat.

There was something her mother did not wish to speak of and that something had to do with her accident. These secrets were killing her.

General Henson must have been there. Her memory told her so. Why could her mother not simply admit it and explain what really happened?

* * *

Over the next two days there was no opportunity for Phillipa to confront her mother again. Her mother spent every spare minute with General Henson. Phillipa surmised he spent at least part of the night in her mother's bed even though she and Xavier never saw him leave again. She held her breath entering the house in the wee morning hours for fear of bumping into him on the stairway.

Phillipa encountered another worry. Her maid had discovered that she was sneaking out at night. Luckily the girl was loyal. And ambitious. Phillipa paid her well for her silence.

Since General Henson was with her mother, he did not show up at the Masquerade Club. However, Lady Faville was always there.

Soon, though, it would all end. Each night that passed brought her closer to the time when Rhysdale would return. That would be the end of her performing.

The end of her time with Xavier.

It broke her heart.

This night as Phillipa took her seat at the pianoforte, she forced herself to be happy for the moment and not think of the future.

Lady Faville and the steadfast Mr Everard sat at their usual table. She supposed she would have to endure another *comfortable coze*, as Lady Faville called it, where Lady Faville would prose on about her devotion to Xavier and her determination to marry him.

Whenever Lady Faville stood next to Xavier, Phillipa was struck anew at how perfect they looked together, that contrast of light and dark. Mr Everard saw it too, she noticed. She could see it in his eyes when he looked at the beautiful pair.

Lady Faville gave her a little wave and Phillipa started playing. She chose the happiest piece she could think of. Not one of her compositions, which all tended to more wrenching emotions, but 'La De Belombre', an old composition for harpsichord she liked because it challenged her fingering.

Xavier listened through the whole song before leaving. Phillipa always knew when he was there.

After he left, she played in waves, happy music drifting to songs of love lost or lovers' deaths, then back to something joyous or frivolous.

At the end, there was gratifying applause. She stepped away from the pianoforte and chose her refreshment, taking it to the table in the corner that gave her some privacy.

Until Lady Faville approached her, that is. 'You did very well this night, Miss Songstress.'

This lady's approval held no importance. 'Thank you.'

Lady Faville sat without being invited to. 'Does Xavier not look handsome tonight? More handsome than usual, do you not think?'

To Phillipa he looked wonderful every night. 'He is a very well-looking man.'

Lady Faville laughed. 'You are always so careful not to say too much.'

That was perceptive of her, more perceptive than Phillipa would have given her credit. 'I must be discreet.'

With this lady, Phillipa played the employee. It was what Lady Faville and most of the patrons wished to think of her. An employee would be careful what she said about an employer or his designated manager.

Lady Faville leaned across the table. 'Has he said anything about me? Did you talk to him about me?' She was forever wanting Phillipa to convince Xavier of her regard and she hoped Xavier would tell Phillipa of his admiration.

In truth, Xavier talked so very little about himself that she truly did not know from his lips how he felt about the lady. Most of the gentleman preened and strutted around Lady Faville, but Phillipa did not ever see Xavier doing so. A man as handsome as he had no need to do so.

'I cannot presume to talk to him about you,' Phillipa told her for what seemed the hundredth time. 'And our conversations are not such that he would mention any patron.'

Lady Faville gave her a sceptical smile. 'You know I do not credit that. You do not tell me all.' She released an exaggerated sigh. 'I do not know what kind of friend you are, to hold back what is so important to me.'

She was no friend at all, Phillipa thought. 'I am holding back nothing.'

Except, perhaps, that she wished Lady Faville to leave her alone. It was painful to Phillipa to be the lady's confidante, to hear of her intent to marry Xavier, to know the wealthy young widow would be a prize any man would covet.

Lady Faville put a hand on Phillipa's arm. 'I know you will say nothing to me, but I do count on you to be my very dear friend.'

Sometimes Lady Faville was so charming that Phillipa could almost like her, but it was difficult to like someone who had everything you lacked.

* * *

She'd almost finished her final set when Xavier returned. His presence disturbed her in a pleasurable way, making her both self-conscious and bold in her piano playing.

When she was done, he walked her down the stairs. 'The piece before your last one, was that one of your compositions?'

It had been the bagatelle she'd laboured over for so many hours and days. 'Yes, it was.'

He shrugged. 'It reminded me of the gaming room somehow.'

She stopped. 'Do not say it. That is precisely the sound I was attempting to recreate.'

He grinned. 'You accomplished it.'

She felt like skipping the rest of the way.

When they sat in the hackney coach and she pulled off her mask, she asked him about his night, if there were any problems in the gaming room.

'One fellow lost too much,' he told her. 'I feared for him; he was so despondent.'

He'd told her stories of men who'd lost fortunes and killed themselves. Her father lost a fortune and merely tried to cheat his way out of it.

'What did you do?' she asked.

He turned to her, his features muted in the dark coach. 'I gave him a loan.'

'Will Rhysdale approve of that?' she asked.

'I have seen him do the same from time to time,' he responded. 'But I did not use his money.'

She knew what he would say. 'You used your own money.'

He shrugged. 'I did.'

Her breast swelled with pride for him. What a fine thing to do.

How was she ever going to give up knowing him, talking to him every day?

She promised herself that she would savour every moment at the gaming house and with him. She would hold every moment in her heart and never let go of them.

The hackney coach pulled up to its usual place on her street, but before Xavier opened the door, he took her hand. 'I enjoyed your performance tonight, Phillipa.'

Before she could speak, he pulled her into his arms and kissed her. It was a short kiss, but one that took her breath and left her weak.

He opened the door and Xavier jumped down to help her out. 'Goodnight, Phillipa. Sleep well.'

She kept hold of his hand. 'Goodnight, Xavier. I will see you tomorrow night.'

He pressed her hand tighter before letting go. She turned to walk the short distance to her town house, but had gone no more than two steps when two men jumped from the shadows.

Xavier grabbed her arm and pulled her behind him.

'Phillipa, do not hide from us,' a familiar voice said. Her brother Ned.

'Who is this with you?' Hugh, her other brother, demanded.

The jarvey called down, 'Need assistance, sir?'

Xavier walked over to him and paid his fare and his tip. 'You may go, Johnson, I'll be walking back tonight.'

'After I'm done with you, you won't be able to walk,' Hugh said.

'You'll do nothing of the sort!' Phillipa cried.

The coach pulled away.

Xavier held her arm again, but spoke to Hugh. 'Hugh, it is Xavier. I can explain this.'

'Xavier!' Hugh was taken aback. 'What the devil? You are the man carrying on with my sister?'

'It is not what you think,' Phillipa broke in.

Xavier still kept hold of her. 'May I suggest we not discuss this in the street?'

'Come. All of you,' Ned ordered.

Xavier held Phillipa's hand as they followed him to the town house.

Her brothers were back from Brussels. The ending she dreaded had come without warning.

This had been her last night to perform her music. Her last night with Xavier.

What a blasted mess, Xavier thought as he followed Ned into the town house. They walked directly to the drawing room where Lady Westleigh was seated.

Where was General Henson? Hiding in a closet somewhere? In Lady Westleigh's dressing room, perhaps?

'We found her, Mama,' Ned said.

'And the man.' Hugh, with a disgusted expression on his face, gestured in Xavier's direction. 'Xavier Campion.'

The countess's brows rose when she saw him. 'Xavier Campion!'

He bowed. 'Lady Westleigh.'

'I cannot believe this of you.' She shook her head in dismay. 'Your mother is my friend.'

'Mama,' Phillipa cried. 'You must allow me to explain.'

'Explain?' Ned faced her. 'We come home in the dead of night and discover you are not in your bed. Your maid, after much coercion, finally confesses that you leave the house every night after everyone retires. You return three hours later.'

Three and a half hours, to be more precise, Xavier thought.

'And it is Campion you were sneaking out to see.' Hugh glared at him. 'Taking liberties with my sister.'

'Liberties!' Phillipa cried. 'He took no liberties.'

Except that he'd just kissed her, but he could not regret that.

'Listen to her explanation,' Xavier demanded.

'Very well.' Lady Westleigh leaned back in her chair.

Phillipa spoke. 'I have been attending our gaming house. The Masquerade Club.' She held up her mask that had been gripped in her hand all this time. 'I play the pianoforte there and I sing.'

'You sing?' Hugh shot back. 'Like a common—' He did not finish.

'The gaming house?' Ned cried. 'You were not supposed to know about the gaming house.'

'I was not supposed to know many things of great import to our family, apparently.' Her chin rose.

Hugh swung towards Xavier. 'Rhys told her, didn't he? What business was it of his? Just because he joined the family did not give him the right.'

Xavier shot him a quelling look. 'I told Phillipa. Not Rhys. Rhys knows nothing of this. He is not even in town.'

Lady Westleigh tossed him a very worried look. 'Precisely what did you tell her—?'

'About Father,' Phillipa cut in. 'About our debt

and how Rhys helped our family, only to have Father cheat him and challenge him to a duel. About how Ned and Hugh took Father to Brussels where he agreed to stay.'

'Good God, what didn't you tell her?' Hugh said.

There was more he didn't tell her. Couldn't tell her.

'See, Mama, I have not fallen apart.' Phillipa raised her arms. 'I learned all this and I still stand before you, the same as always. I have attended a gaming house and performed music there and I remain in one piece. I am unfazed by your secrets. I did not need to be protected from them. I do not need protection from anything.'

She was strong, Xavier did admit, but not without need of protection. What might have happened to her if she'd been alone when they were attacked?

'You obviously needed protection from Campion here.' Hugh leaned into his face. 'What the devil is wrong with you, Campion? You can have any woman you want. Why trifle with my sister? Were you bored with the pretty ones?'

Xavier seized Hugh by the front of his coat. 'Do not insult her. Do you heed me?'

He pushed Hugh away and Hugh lowered his head. 'I didn't mean it that way. Not how it sounded.'

Phillipa swung towards Hugh. 'Xavier has been a perfect gentleman towards me. He escorted me to and from the gaming house, because he knew I would walk there alone if he did not.'

Ned glared at her. 'Phillipa, you cannot spend time alone with any man in the middle of the night. If this becomes known, your reputation will be ruined.'

'That is a laugh, Ned.' She pointed to her face. 'What do I need a reputation for?'

Ned turned haughty. 'Well, I, for one, will not have the lady to whom I am betrothed besmirched by your loose morals.'

'Stubble it, Ned.' Xavier wanted to strike him. 'Your sister has not displayed loose morals—'

'Listen to me,' Phillipa broke in again. 'I wanted an adventure and I have had one. Xavier made certain I was safe while doing so. It is ended. It is over. No one else knows. Leave it. There is nothing to be done.'

Ned seemed to consider this.

Even Hugh settled down somewhat. 'He did not seduce you?'

'He did not,' she answered.

Xavier reined in his temper. Matters were calming down. Ned and Hugh were beginning to see reason.

Ned blew out a breath. 'I suppose…if no one knows…'

'Let it be as Phillipa desires,' Xavier said.

His attention shifted to Lady Westleigh, who'd developed a very calculating look in her eye.

'I must return to the Club,' Xavier said. 'I am usually gone only a few minutes.'

He slid a regretful look at Phillipa.

She nodded her approval. 'Leave, Xavier,' she said. 'It is over. There is no harm if no one knows, and who would tell?'

Not Cummings or MacEvoy, Xavier would see to that.

He bowed to Phillipa and to Lady Westleigh. 'I bid you goodnight, then.'

Lady Westleigh rose. 'Not so hasty, young man.'

He stopped and turned.

She looked like a player holding the winning cards. 'It is of no consequence that you did not steal my daughter's virtue. Or that no one will know you carted her off in the middle of the night. You still behaved very dishonourably. You have compromised Phillipa and you know what honour dictates you do.'

Yes. He understood very clearly.

Lady Westleigh intended to manipulate him into marrying Phillipa.

'No!' Phillipa cried. 'No, you cannot do this, Mama. It is not fair.'

She had never foreseen this, never even dreamed it could happen.

She turned to Xavier. 'Do not listen to her.' She

swung back to her mother. 'This is wrong, Mama. You must not require this of him.'

'Must I not?' Her mother actually looked smug.

'Mother,' Ned began. 'Perhaps this is not the thing to do.'

Her mother's eyes flashed. 'Of course it is the thing to do. Mr Campion knows what honour requires of him, do you not, Mr Campion? He must marry her.'

Phillipa could not bear it. To ruin his life like this? It was all her fault. 'Xavier, do not heed her. My family will say nothing. No one will know. No reputation will be ruined. There was no harm done.'

He turned to her mother and brothers. 'Allow me to speak with Phillipa alone.'

'No.' Her mother straightened her spine. 'Call upon us tomorrow. We will discuss the particulars.'

Her mother acted as if the decision had been made.

He glanced at Phillipa, who nodded her assent.

'I'll call tomorrow.' He bowed.

Phillipa watched him walk away through the doorway until she could see him no more.

She whirled back to her mother, angrier than she had ever been in her life. 'How could you do this to him?'

Even Ned spoke up. 'Mother, maybe it would be better to hush this up.'

'Xavier doesn't want to marry her,' Hugh added.

Her mother stood. 'Go to bed, all of you. We will discuss this in the morning.' She started to the door.

Hugh rubbed his hands. 'I'm not going to bed. I'm going to the Masquerade Club. Someone should check on things if Rhys is not there.'

Ned looked wary. 'I had better go with you. The last thing we need is you getting into a dust-up with Xavier. Then there will be talk.'

'Leave him alone,' Phillipa said to their departing backs. 'He deserves none of this.'

Her mother patted Phillipa's arm as she also passed. 'Do not concern yourself over Xavier, dear. Think of this as good fortune.'

Good fortune? It was disaster. Cruelty. Pain.

She was left alone in the room, but it took several minutes until she could make herself walk to her bedchamber.

As soon as she opened the door, her maid cried, 'Oh, m'lady, I did not mean to tell them. I tried not to, but your mother was so insistent. And then she tricked me and made me say what I promised I would not say.' She reached into her pocket and took out a purse. 'Here is the money you paid me to be quiet.'

'Keep it, Lacey,' Phillipa said in a weary voice. 'I do not hold you to blame.'

'Oh, thank you, m'lady.' The girl bobbed. 'I am ever so grateful.'

'Just help me out of this dress and into bed.' Phillipa rubbed her face.

A few minutes later she was between her bed linens and her maid had gone. Her head and her heart ached.

One thing was certain. She would not allow Xavier to be coerced into marrying her. No matter how much her mother connived.

Chapter Ten

Xavier was glad for the walk to the Masquerade Club. He needed the physical exertion and cool night air.

Those cursed Westleighs. He was angry with the lot of them.

Except for Phillipa. How could they treat her so shabbily? Had they given any care to what she did before this? Perhaps if they had shown some interest in her, some support of her music, she would not have had to venture out on her own and put herself in peril.

Xavier knew he'd done what he must. She would have braved the streets alone had he not escorted her. He certainly did not regret allowing her the chance to perform. Not when it brought her such joy.

Honour might dictate that he marry her, but honour be damned. It must be what Phillipa wanted, not what suited the rest of them.

He'd speak to her alone. She alone must decide. By God, he'd marry her if that was what she wished, but only if it was her wish. Not her mother's. Not her brothers'.

Not even his.

Xavier knew what he wanted. He wanted to whisk Phillipa away from them. All of them. He wanted to find a myriad of ways to give her the joy she'd found performing her music. Because it was not only she who had found joy in this interlude. He had, as well.

But she must want it. She must choose.

He reached the town house and sounded the knocker. Cummings opened the door to him. Xavier left him his hat and gloves and went straight to MacEvoy, who informed him that nothing eventful had come to his attention.

He left MacEvoy and went next to the gaming room.

As soon as he walked in the room, Daphne was beside him.

'Did you get our lovely Miss Songstress back to Covent Garden?' she asked in her dulcet-toned voice.

He faced her directly. 'Daphne, I have no patience for your nonsense tonight. Tell Mr Everard to take you home.'

For an instant she looked as if he'd slapped her and he was sorry he'd taken out his ill temper on her.

'That was unkindly said,' he spoke more softly. 'I apologise for that, but you should spend your time elsewhere.'

A determined gleam appeared in her eyes. 'I know what I want, Xavier.'

'No, Daphne. Your happiness is not with me.'

Ned and Hugh walked in and Xavier left Daphne without another word.

'What now, gentlemen?' He braced for more insults to their sister.

Ned's expression was conciliatory. 'We simply came to see how the place is faring.'

'I have not managed to burn the place down yet,' Xavier answered. 'Do you want to see the books?'

'It seems a good place to start,' Ned replied agreeably.

They had started back for the door when Hugh leaned over to Xavier. 'Who is that beautiful creature?'

Xavier did not need to look to know of whom Hugh was speaking. 'Lady Faville. She's taken a fancy to gambling.'

'Lady Faville,' Hugh repeated quietly. 'I've never seen her before.'

Xavier took them to MacEvoy, where they glanced through the ledgers. Did they notice the rise in prof-

its while their sister was here? Afterwards, they re-
tired to the supper room.

When they walked past the pianoforte, Xavier
glanced at Phillipa's music.

Should he send her music home with Ned and
Hugh? In truth, it was too precious to trust them
with it. They did not even seem to notice the pianoforte that had been so important to their sister.

He led them to a table and ordered brandy.

'All looks well here,' Ned remarked.

'Rhys did not tell us he would be away. You cannot blame us for worrying,' Hugh added. 'Our family fortune is at stake.'

'I do not blame you for seeing to your investment.'
Xavier blamed them for their treatment of their sister.

The brandy was served.

Ned took a sip and nodded approvingly. 'Sorry
about this business with our sister.'

Hugh peered at him with narrowed eyes. 'You had
better be telling the truth. If I discover you trifled
with her—'

Xavier gave the younger Westleigh a severe look.
'You'll do what, Hugh? Make me marry her? Bloody
my face? I would relish the opportunity for you to
try.'

'Do not tempt me,' Hugh countered.

Xavier went on as if Hugh had not spoken. 'Or will

you merely insult your sister several more times? I ought to call you out for the things you said about her.'

Hugh looked genuinely surprised. 'What did I say?'

'That she was not one of the pretty ones. That her singing was common.'

'Xavier is correct,' Ned said. 'That was not well done of you.'

Xavier turned to him. 'And you accused her of loose morals. Tell me why she deserves such talk from her brothers?'

Ned looked chastened; Hugh, about to lose his temper again.

Until Daphne walked in and sat with Mr Everard. Hugh's gaze riveted on her, as well as the gazes of several other men in the room.

'When does Rhys come back?' Ned asked, changing the subject.

Xavier tasted his brandy. 'I do not know. Soon, I expect.'

Hugh dragged his attention back. 'Ned merely wishes to know when he will be able to get married.' He laughed. 'I have a capital idea. The three of you can be married together. Three at once.'

'No.' Phillipa would despise such a thing, even if she did agree to marry him. 'And nothing is decided.'

Ned leaned forwards. 'I think Phillipa had the right

of it. There is no reason for you to marry her. If no one knows about her—her activities here—we can all go on as before.'

Xavier took another drink. 'It must be as Phillipa wishes.'

The next morning at breakfast, without her brothers present, Phillipa tried to reason with her mother.

'Please, Mama. Surely you see the sense in this. If we say and do nothing, all will go on as before. If I marry Xavier, then there will be talk.' She shuddered at the thought. 'A man of his appearance marrying a disfigured woman like me? No one would talk of anything else.'

'That sort of gossip is of no consequence.' Her mother was almost cheerful this morning.

Phillipa's voice rose. 'It would be wrong to force Xavier to marry me.'

Her mother made a gesture for her to speak more quietly. She inclined her head towards the servants' door.

'Do not be ridiculous, Mama.' Phillipa leaned back in her chair. 'The servants know. Or will do so soon.'

'Only when I am ready for them to know,' her mother said.

Phillipa lowered her voice. 'Why would you insist upon my marrying Xavier when I do not wish to?'

Her mother continued to eat her food, talking between bites. 'Because it secures your future, Phillipa dear. You have been hiding in your music room. That is no way to achieve a proposal of marriage. This is a godsend.'

'Mama!'

Her mother's expression turned stern. 'You have been apprised of the state of our family's finances, Phillipa. Much as I have tried to shield you from this distress, you may as well know that you have no dowry. Any money meant for you is gone.'

She had not known that part of it. Had even her dowry been squandered by her father?

Her mother went on. 'I have very little money left, as well. There is nothing to leave you when I am gone. You are a burden to this family now, and if you do not marry you will for ever be a burden.'

A burden. What cruel words.

'But if you marry Campion—' her mother smiled '—you will have a household of your own. Pin money of your own.'

'I am to marry for money?' Phillipa scoffed.

Her mother waved away her words as if they were an annoying fly. 'There are worse reasons to marry. And you know you are marrying a good man. We have known his family since before you were born. No one ever gossips about them—' She glanced away.

'Well, there was the one time, but that problem was quickly dispatched—'

What on earth did she mean?

Her mother smiled again. 'The Campions have a respectable fortune, and it is said that Xavier has his own money. From an uncle or aunt or somebody.'

'So I *am* to marry for money,' Phillipa muttered.

Her mother pursed her lips. 'My dear daughter, he is the perfect husband. He is rich. He comes from a decent family and he has been brought up to be an honourable man. He will treat you well.' She pinned her with her gaze. 'Need I go on?'

'But he is also a friend.' Phillipa felt as if her insides were in shreds. 'A friend you would have me treat quite shabbily. He has been kind to me, but he cannot regard me as a wife.'

Xavier was the sort of man who would offer, though. For honour's sake. He should not be punished so for what had been her instigation.

'Do not turn romantic on me, Phillipa,' her mother scolded. 'It will be a good marriage for you. You will see.'

'But what about him?' Phillipa cried. 'What about Xavier? You cannot saddle such a man with me. A—a man of his looks and his character. He does not deserve it.'

Her mother smiled. 'Then he should not have been running around with you in the middle of the night.'

It was no use to argue with her.

'I will not do it, Mama,' she whispered. 'I will not marry him.'

Her mother glared at her. 'You will marry him or I will make certain you regret it.'

It mattered not what revenge her mother intended. 'I will not marry him.'

She loved him too much.

Xavier presented himself at the Westleigh town house at the appointed time. The solemn-faced butler announced him to the family.

When he entered the drawing room, his eyes immediately found Phillipa. Her features were pinched and her posture taut, as if wanting to flee.

Lady Westleigh had enthroned herself in an armchair. Ned and Hugh stood at her side, like pages.

Xavier bowed to Lady Westleigh, but quickly straightened. 'I will see Phillipa alone.'

Lady Westleigh met his eye. 'I think not.'

He'd not yield the power to her. He gave her a look his soldiers once knew—he'd brook no argument. 'I will see Phillipa alone.'

He'd wrestled with the matter overnight, getting no sleep at all.

In honesty, he wanted to marry Phillipa—if for no other reason than to keep her away from this family. But also to find a way to give her joy.

In that, his motives were unchanged from their days in Brighton.

Except he also wanted her as a man wants a woman.

Lady Westleigh huffed. 'There is nothing for you to discuss together, because you will marry her.'

Phillipa leaned towards him. 'Do not heed her, Xavier.'

'Phillipa,' her mother warned.

Xavier's hands curled into fists.

'Now, Mother.' Ned's tone was quelling. 'Let them talk together—'

'Be quiet, Ned,' Lady Westleigh snapped.

A knock at the door silenced them all. The butler appeared again. 'General Henson, my lady.'

'Alistair!' The lady brightened. 'Do show him in.'

General Henson stepped into the room, but stopped as if he'd not expected to see them all gathered there. 'My dear lady. Forgive me. I interrupt you.' He noticed Xavier with even more surprise and nodded. 'Campion. Good to see you.'

'General.' Xavier said. Who else would show up? Lord Westleigh?

The general bowed to Phillipa. 'Lady Phillipa.'

She merely nodded.

Ned and Hugh exchanged puzzled glances.

Lady Westleigh simpered. 'Alistair, you have walked in on a—a family meeting, but do come forwards. I would be delighted to introduce you to my sons.'

The introductions were made as if this were the most ordinary of social occasions. The general acknowledged an acquaintance with Hugh from when both were in the Peninsula and the two of them spoke of mutual acquaintances.

Ned glanced at his mother, brows raised.

She gave him a patient smile. 'Ned, dear, General Henson and I are very old friends. We happened to meet again in town and he has been good enough to act as my escort on occasion.'

And as her lover, Xavier thought, but Ned and Hugh would work that out soon enough. Their mother's intimate manner towards Henson spoke volumes.

'I am very happy to be reacquainted with you all. My gracious, you were mere boys when last I saw you.' The general gazed from one to the other. 'But I will interrupt you no further. I take my leave.' He walked up to Lady Westleigh and clasped her hands. 'I shall return, my dear.'

He left and the room fell silent.

Hugh finally spoke. 'Mother! What the devil?'

Lady Westleigh lifted her head regally. 'I do not

approve of such language, Hugh. My friendship with the general is my affair. Not yours.'

Hugh laughed scornfully. 'Affair. Interesting choice of words, Mother.'

'What of my friendship with Xavier?' Phillipa broke in. 'Is that not *my* affair, Mama?'

The lady responded with sarcasm. 'Affair. Interesting choice of words, Phillipa.'

Phillipa's face turned red.

'Enough!' Xavier shouted. He turned to Phillipa. 'Where can we talk?'

'Here, if they will leave,' she responded.

Lady Westleigh hesitated a moment before she stood. 'Oh, very well. Ned. Hugh.' She spoke to them as if they were in leading strings. 'Come with me.'

Phillipa's mother and brothers closed the drawing-room door behind them and she was alone with Xavier.

He looked even more handsome in the light of day, as tall as her brothers, but perfectly formed and in a coat that fit him like a second skin. He'd stood tall when facing her mother, and now, gazing at her, he seemed perfectly in control.

'Do you wish to sit?' He gestured to the sofa.

She shook her head.

He waited, giving her time to speak first.

She took a breath. 'This is all nonsense, Xavier.

My mother does not believe you truly compromised me. She sees this as a grand opportunity for me to snare a husband and secure my future.'

'I surmised that.' He looked directly into her face.

She wished he would glance away. 'We must stand up to her. If we do, this will all pass and things will be as they were.'

His intense blue eyes bored into her. 'Is that what you want? For things to be as they were for you?'

She lowered her gaze, fearing he would see all the way to the grief she felt at losing the Masquerade Club and the nightly time they shared. 'I always knew it was a temporary adventure.'

He lifted her chin with his finger and she was forced to look at him again.

'What if we did marry, Phillipa?' He spoke *sotto voce*. 'What if things do not have to return to what they were? I am willing if you are.'

How dare he use a voice so deep and soothing, like the rumble of the lowest pianoforte keys? How dare he say he was *willing* to marry? Such words were daggers disguised as jewels.

She turned her head from his touch. 'Do not toy with me, Xavier.'

'I am not toying with you. I want this, if you do.'

Now he was merely being honourable.

She touched her scar and moved near the window where she knew it would show in stark relief.

'No!' She lifted her hand. 'You cannot want it.'

Adonis with a scar-faced wife? How he would be pitied. How soon before he would pity himself?

His face was no less impossibly handsome even as he frowned. 'What if I told you I did want to marry you?'

She touched her scar. 'I would not believe you.'

'Why do you not believe me?' he asked.

'Why?' It hurt more that he pretended to want her. 'Because everything I've done has forced you into involving yourself with me. Whether it was dancing with me or escorting me or letting me perform. None of it has been by your choice—'

'Dancing?' He looked puzzled.

Of course, he would not remember the dance. It loomed large only in her memory.

She felt tears sting her eyes. She blinked them away. 'I will not marry you, Xavier. I refuse.' She gathered all her courage and met his eye. 'I do not want to marry you. That is the end of it. There is no more to be said.'

She could not stay a moment longer without bursting into tears. She forced herself to stand straight and to stride with a purposeful gait towards the door.

'Phillipa?' She heard his voice behind her, but she opened the door.

Her mother and brothers waited in the hallway outside the room. She walked past them.

'Where are you going?' her mother cried. 'We are not finished.'

'I am finished.' She did not stop.

Hugh dashed after her and seized her arm, a look of concern on his face. 'What happened in there, Phillipa?'

She shrugged out of his grasp. 'Xavier made an offer of marriage and I refused him. That is all.'

She reached the staircase and started to climb.

Her mother came after her, calling to her from the foot of the stairs. 'Come back here, Phillipa! If you leave it this way you will regret it. I will make you rue the day you threw away such an opportunity. You will have nothing without it! Do you hear me? Nothing!'

Phillipa did not answer her mother. She did not slow her pace. She did not turn back to see if Xavier also watched her walk away.

She merely climbed the stairs and retreated to her music room even though she was empty of music.

Xavier watched her walk past her family and climb the stairs. He watched until she disappeared on the upper floor.

He felt as if he'd been run through with a sabre.

He'd been prepared for her refusal; he'd not been prepared for the pain of it.

Although he ought to have known.

He'd been attracted to her, especially from the moment he'd witnessed her perform. She'd no longer been the little girl to whom he felt a responsibility; she'd turned into a woman who captivated him.

And his interest had never been returned.

Would people not laugh to know that he, to whom it was reputed that women flocked, could not get the one woman he wanted?

She thought him a friend and nothing more.

Hugh strode over to him. 'What the devil did you say to her?'

Xavier would not allow that hothead to see his wound. 'I offered marriage and she refused. She made her desires very clear. It is time to drop this.'

Ned spoke up. 'I agree. The best thing to do is forget this happened.'

Hugh scoffed. 'She's daft.'

'She is foolish and ungrateful.' Lady Westleigh pursed her lips before turning to Xavier. 'It is my turn to speak with you alone, sir.'

'Don't rail at him, Mother,' Ned said. 'He's done the right thing.'

His mother glared at him.

Ned seemed not to heed her. 'I beg your leave. I am off to call upon Miss Gale, who does not even know I have returned. I tell you we are done with this. Time to move on to other matters.' He extended his hand Xavier. 'This was a bad business, but we will put it behind us and act as before.'

'Certainly.' Xavier shook his hand. He'd never look at Ned in the same way, however.

'Go, if you must,' his mother snapped at Ned. 'Xavier, come in here.'

Xavier returned with her to the drawing room. She sat in her chair and gestured for him to sit, as well.

'I'll stand, ma'am.' His parents taught him well how to remain respectful, but he'd stand his ground all the same.

'I will make Phillipa change her mind,' she told him. 'And I'll hold you to your proposal of marriage.'

'Leave Phillipa be, ma'am.' He spoke firmly. 'She knows her own mind. Her wishes need to be respected.'

Lady Westleigh huffed. 'She knows nothing. She is determined to hide herself away with nothing but a pianoforte. What sort of life is that for her?'

He held her gaze. 'Give your daughter credit to know her own mind.'

She crossed her arms and raised her head defiantly. 'I will do what is best for my daughter.'

He opened his mouth, ready to threaten to spread talk about her affair with the general, but what good would that do?

He lowered his voice. 'Let go of this now.' He bowed. 'Good day to you, Lady Westleigh.'

He turned to walk away, but she called him back. 'There is another matter I wish to discuss with you.'

He looked over his shoulder. 'That is?'

'You told my daughter a great deal of family business. It was not your place to do so.' Her tone was scolding.

He faced her again. 'I do not apologise for it. She deserved to know.' This whole family sold Phillipa short.

'It was not your place,' she repeated, emphasising her words. 'However...' she paused, still giving him a haughty look '...tell me what else you told her.'

'What else?' He did not know what she meant.

She leaned forwards and her expression turned to worry. 'Did you break your word to me? You gave me your word all those years ago in Brighton. Did you break it?'

'Did I tell her the truth about her accident, do you mean?' He held something over this woman's head that was much bigger than an illicit affair, but he could not use it. 'I did not break my word.'

Lady Westleigh leaned back in her chair and suddenly looked very old. 'That is good. That is as it should be.'

'Was it General Henson on the beach that day?' Xavier asked.

She sat up straight. 'Why? Why do you ask me that?'

'Because I thought I remembered him as the man who was there,' he lied. It was Phillipa who remembered him.

'Do not say a word of this to her. Do you hear me?' She avoided his question, but her manner gave him the answer. 'You are honour-bound to keep your word.'

'I will keep my word,' he assured her. 'But you should tell her of that night. She needs to know it.'

'I'll be the judge of what she needs to know.' She waved him away. 'Leave now. I will get a message to you if Phillipa comes to her senses.'

He did not argue further, merely bowed again and left.

Chapter Eleven

Xavier walked back to the Masquerade Club, quiet at this time of day. Cummings and MacEvoy were nowhere to be seen and only the sweet scent of baking, wafting up from kitchen, revealed anyone was in the house.

He walked through the rooms still disordered from the previous night's gamblers. By the time the doors opened that night, every room would be cleaned and made ready for play. He straightened chairs here and there in the gaming room and made his way to the supper room.

All the plates, cutlery, and glasses had been cleared away the night before. Some of the tables were bare of their cloths, making the usually elegant room appear bereft.

Mimicking how he felt inside.

He felt the loss of Phillipa.

No longer would this room fill with melody. No

longer would he hear Phillipa sing or the applause of others who recognised her worth. He glanced at the pianoforte. Her music still rested there, as if waiting for her to bring it to life.

He walked over to the instrument and gathered the sheets of music. Perhaps in time he could return them to her. In the meantime, he'd keep them safe.

August drifted to September and Xavier pressed on, helping with the Masquerade Club and checking Jeffers's progress on the cabinetry shop.

Jeffers exceeded Xavier's expectations. The soldier quickly found a storefront, a place with a workshop behind it and room for men to build furniture. Jeffers located the shop in Cheapside. It was a good location to sell furniture priced for the merchant class, rather than aiming for the elite of the *ton*. Jeffers procured the wood and in no time simple tables and chairs, and chests were on display in the front of the shop. Three other former soldiers who were skilled carpenters were hired. They'd all been maimed in the war. One man lost a leg, another an eye. The third reminded him of Phillipa, although the scars on his face came from burns suffered at Hougoumont. Jeffers was scarred, as well, but from Xavier's knife the night of the attack. He, too, was a reminder.

This venture seemed so ensured of success that

Xavier was on the lookout for more challenges. There were all sorts of goods that might be manufactured and sold. They'd already found men to start a candle shop and Jeffers was keeping an eye out for other soldiers who might be able to do skilled work.

These ventures functioned much like Rhys's gaming house. The men ran the shops and he, like the Westleighs, provided the investment.

It was still not enough for Xavier.

He was restless.

Rhys had returned a fortnight after Phillipa's last night at the Masquerade Club and Xavier told him about her having performed her music there. Once Ned knew, Rhys was bound to find out. He told everything, except about the attack, and Phillipa's visions of General Henson. He told about Ned and Hugh discovering them. About his offer of marriage and her refusal.

'But you did not trifle with her.' Rhys did not accuse, merely stated a fact.

'You know I would not.' That was also a fact.

Rhys had leaned back in his chair, still regarding him. 'Phillipa took a risk, coming here night after night. At least no harm came of it.'

Except to Xavier. And Phillipa.

'I am not so certain,' he'd admitted to Rhys. 'Check on her for me, if you can, would you?'

Rhys had contact with the family, especially with Ned and Hugh, who kept an eye on the gaming house. He called upon Lady Westleigh with Lady Gale and Miss Gale to discuss the wedding. He'd never seen Phillipa, but when he enquired, Lady Westleigh always assured him she was in good health.

Ned and Hugh said the same thing.

Xavier never felt easy, though. He needed to see for himself.

He would get the chance at Rhys's wedding, the double wedding with Ned and Miss Gale.

The day of the wedding came quickly, about three weeks after Rhys returned. Both Rhys and Ned procured special licences so that they could marry in the privacy of the Westleigh town house. Because of the scandal Lord Westleigh had created—and Lady Gale's obvious condition—Lady Westleigh declared that the weddings should be as private and unobtrusive as possible. There would be no guests, only family.

Xavier was an exception. Rhys asked Xavier to stand up with him. Another exception was General Henson, who, according to Ned and Hugh, had become a fixture in the Westleigh home, constantly to be found at Lady Westleigh's side.

Xavier knew Phillipa would be present at the wedding. He was eager to see her, to see for himself if she was in good health. If she was content. He also hoped to restore some of the *bonhomie* between them, to be friends again.

He missed her. He missed her more than he'd ever missed his family when he'd been off to war. He'd not expected this intensity.

Without her he had lost the music in his life.

The morning of the wedding Xavier and Rhys walked the distance to the Westleigh town house. At Lady Gale's request Rhys had spent the night before at the Masquerade Club.

'I spent so much time away from her, I could not see this one more night away,' Rhys said.

'But it was what she wanted, was it not?' Xavier responded.

'That is so.' Rhys smiled. 'Which is enough to explain why we are walking across Mayfair this morning.'

'Will this steam-engine venture take you away from her in the future?' Xavier asked.

'Undoubtedly.' Rhys sounded regretful. 'I am convinced it will secure our futures, however.'

Xavier was happy for Rhys. Soon he'd have a wife and a child and a business with a future. Quite a feat for a bastard son left alone on the streets to fend for himself.

And Xavier, whose upbringing had provided him everything he could want and a loving family to boot, had lost what he wanted most.

Phillipa.

Xavier turned off that train of thought. 'I confess I am surprised you agreed to this double wedding. Do you feel so much a part of that family?' Lord Westleigh had been Rhys's father, but Rhys had never been accepted by the family, not until they needed his help to deliver them from financial ruin.

'I no longer resent and despise them,' Rhys admitted. 'Lord Westleigh, perhaps, but not the others.' They crossed Charles Street. 'The wedding decision was Celia's. Her stepdaughter wanted it and Celia was most anxious to please the girl. There'd been such a breach between them since—since the news of the baby.'

'Miss Gale seems incredibly young, do you not think?' Lady Gale's stepdaughter could not be more than nineteen.

Rhys gaped at him. 'And you are so old? You're not yet thirty.'

Xavier felt old, however.

They reached the Westleigh town house and were admitted to the drawing room where they'd once waited together for the Westleighs' ball to begin, where he'd danced with Phillipa. It also was the room where Phillipa had refused to marry him.

The furniture in the room had been placed against the wall so that a space was opened for the wedding ceremony. In a corner a trio of musicians were setting up. A nearby table held wine and glasses and vases of flowers stood on almost every other surface.

The butler poured them sherry, a drink not nearly strong enough for Xavier.

'How are you faring?' he asked Rhys after the butler left.

Rhys finished his sherry. 'Eager to have it done. It has been a very long time since I have belonged to anyone.'

It reminded Xavier he ought to call upon his parents.

They would be shocked at what he was up to. Virtually becoming a shopkeeper. On good days his mind whirled with possibilities to employ other craftsmen. His goal was to employ as many former soldiers as he could. The fewer such men he could see on the street, the better.

How was Phillipa spending her time? Was she composing music?

He turned his thoughts away from her and from music he would never hear.

He examined the room. The last time he'd stood in this room he hadn't noticed if Lady Westleigh had replaced the portrait of her husband that dominated this room with one of her own. But her portrait was certainly on display now. Unless he missed his guess, it was by Gainsborough. The artist had painted her against a wild landscape and a cloud-filled sky when she'd been young and beautiful.

He could see Phillipa in the image.

At that moment the door opened and Phillipa entered, wearing a lovely day dress of green-and-white stripes that shimmered in the light and accentuated her slim figure. In fact, she looked thinner than when he last saw her. Her hair was a cascade of curls that appeared to be held in place with a feather headpiece. One feather of the headpiece brushed her cheek and obscured her scar.

It did not hide the fact that she looked pale.

She hesitated when she saw the two of them, but recovered and briskly approached Rhys with a smile. 'Once again I am the first in my family to greet you. You make a handsome bridegroom, Rhysdale.'

Rhys took her extended hands and kissed her cheek. 'I am a happy one. It is good to see you, Phillipa.'

She turned to Xavier, but did not quite look at him directly. 'Xavier. How nice of you to come.'

He bowed. 'Phillipa.'

She looked ill! He wanted to ask why, but knew women better than to make such a remark on a day when one's appearance was important.

Footsteps sounded outside the door. 'Higgley, find her! If she has left, I shall be very vexed.' Lady Westleigh entered, but turned back to the door. 'Never mind, Higgley. She is here.' She quickly surveyed Phillipa and gave a little approving nod.

Xavier felt Phillipa stiffen in response.

But Lady Westleigh did not see. Instead she put on a smile and swept over to Rhys. 'Rhysdale, how good it is to see you. You look in excellent health. This is a very special day, is it not?'

Rhys bowed. 'I am pleased you think it special on my behalf, my lady.'

She inclined her head towards Xavier. 'Xavier,' she said, adding a significant look in her daughter's direction. What was that about?

He bowed. 'My lady.'

The butler appeared at the door. 'General Henson,' he announced.

Lady Westleigh's expression brightened. 'Alistair!'

She stepped forwards to greet him. He took her hand and clasped it in a fond gesture. 'My dear lady, what an honour it is to be invited to such a happy event.'

'Nonsense, Alistair.' She covered his hand with

hers. 'You know how I value your friendship. You must be at my side.'

Xavier glanced at Rhys, who returned a comprehending look. He'd told Rhys about the general and Lady Westleigh.

A visibly nervous Ned entered with the clergyman and introductions followed. The servants filed in and Lady Westleigh sent the butler out to tell Hugh and the brides that all was ready. The clergyman stood at the far side of the room, holding his Book of Common Prayer. The musicians started to play, a Haydn piece, one Phillipa played often on the pianoforte.

He glanced at her, but could not see her expression.

'Stand by Reverend Peck, gentlemen.' Lady Westleigh waved a finger at Rhys and Xavier. 'The two of you on one side. Ned, you stand on the other. Quickly now, before they come in.'

The butler opened the door and the two brides walked in, escorted by Hugh.

Xavier watched Rhys's face as Lady Gale—soon to be Mrs Rhysdale—approached. Rhys adored her so strongly, Xavier felt it in the air. If he reached up, he fancied he could touch it. He was happy for his friend and envious. There was no doubt in his mind that these two people each knew—and loved—the essence of the other.

The ceremony began.

'Dearly Beloved. We are gathered together here in the sight of God, and in the face of this congregation...'

Vows for Miss Gale and Ned went first, then Rhys and Lady Gale.

Rhys looked into his beloved's eyes. 'I, John, take thee, Celia, to my wedded wife, to have and to hold from this day forward, for better for worse, for richer for poorer, in sickness and in health, to love and to cherish, until death us do part...'

Xavier glanced over at Phillipa, whose gaze was averted, as if she were deep into her own thoughts. Was she thinking that this could have been her wedding?

He was.

Very quickly the minister came to the end, 'I now pronounce that they be Man and Wife together, in the Name of the Father, and of the Son, and of the Holy Ghost...'

With those words it was done. Rhys and Celia's lives had changed. So had Ned's and his wife.

All that was left were a few sonorous prayers and then the congratulations. Champagne was served and the musicians started playing again.

Xavier walked up to Rhys and his new wife. 'You make my friend very happy, Madame Fortune.' He used the name the patrons gave her when she had gambled at the Masquerade Club.

She laughed at that. 'I think you should call me Celia after all we've been through.' She threaded her arm through her husband's. 'Or Mrs Rhysdale.'

Rhys put a hand on Xavier's shoulder. 'Call her Celia. She is too beautiful to be Mrs Rhysdale.'

General Henson's loud voice filled the room. 'This is a fine day. A fine day!'

Rhys leaned towards Xavier. 'He is acting as if he is the man of the house.'

Xavier nodded. 'Lady Westleigh looks ten years younger when she looks at him.'

'Well, I am certainly not going to judge either one of them,' Celia said, touching her abdomen. 'We all must seize our happiness when we can.'

Xavier was willing to seize it, if he ever saw a chance for it.

At least he'd tried once.

Hugh came up to them, champagne glass in hand and a frown on his face. 'I feel like planting him a facer.' He inclined his head towards the general. 'He's quite taken over our mother.'

He moved on to speak to the butler before any of them could respond.

The servants left the room and Hugh returned to the wine table.

Xavier noticed Phillipa standing alone, listening to the music being played quietly in the corner.

He walked over to her. 'Do they play well?' he asked.

She looked surprised to see him. 'Well enough.' She turned back to the musicians.

'The ceremony went well.' He could not think of anything better to say.

'Yes, it did.' Her voice held little expression.

He listened to the music with her until the violinist, flautist and violoncellist finished their piece and turned to a new page of music.

She walked away just as the musicians began to play 'I Serve a Worthy Lady'.

The butler announced the wedding breakfast.

Lady Westleigh sat at the head of the table. The general, of course, was at her side. Xavier was seated between Ned's wife and Phillipa, which he thought was a cruel touch on Lady Westleigh's part.

There was no speaking to the new Lady Neddington, who was too enthralled with her new husband, and Phillipa showed no signs of wishing to converse with him.

He noticed she made a show of eating, pushing her food around the plate without actually consuming it. No wonder she was getting thin.

He very much wished they could regain at least a piece of their friendship. Perhaps be cordial to each other. He searched his mind for something to say to her that would serve that purpose.

He remembered the sheets of music she'd left at the Masquerade Club. 'I have your music, Phillipa,' he told her. 'Forgive me for not returning it to you. I will have it brought to you tomorrow, if you desire it.' Perhaps he would deliver it himself.

'There is no need.' She stared at her plate.

'No need?' He did not understand.

'I do not play music any more,' she said.

Not play music? 'Why not, Phillipa? What about your pianoforte?'

'I no longer have a pianoforte.' She faced him directly and her eyes seemed like walls, closing her off from him. 'Mama had the pianoforte removed.'

'Removed?' He could not believe his ears.

She resumed toying with her food. 'Mama has this notion that, if she makes my life miserable, I will somehow bend to her will.'

'She took away your pianoforte.' This was cruelty in the extreme. 'Because you refused my proposal?'

Her voice trembled. 'She said she is done indulging me.'

Xavier lost his appetite as well.

* * *

Phillipa speared the piece of lobster with her fork and brought it to her mouth, not for wanting it, but to have a reason not to say more to Xavier. She'd not meant to tell him about her pianoforte, about her music.

It had been difficult to see him, especially during the ceremony, listening to words that might have been spoken between them.

If her mother had got her way.

Her mother was still furious at her for refusing Xavier. Taking away the pianoforte had been done in a fit of temper, but her mother would not back down from that decision. To be deprived of music was like being starved of sustenance. Hearing the trio play had been more gratifying than witnessing the marriages of her brothers. She devoured every note.

Now the musicians had packed up their instruments and departed, and again she was empty inside.

No one spoke to her about music. The servants certainly would not mention it. Her brothers seemed to have forgotten about it. Initially they had argued with their mother on her behalf, insisting she return the pianoforte to Phillipa, but her mother sold it. Phillipa would never get it back. After a few days, Ned and Hugh became involved in other matters and that was the end of her music.

Captain Henson stood with glass raised. 'I propose a toast. To the happiness of these two fortunate couples.'

Phillipa's mother joined in. 'To their happiness!'

Phillipa dutifully drank, but anger bubbled up inside her. Logic told her that her mother deserved a man who truly cared for her, but at the same time Phillipa resented that her mother possessed what never could be hers—a man who loved her.

Phillipa always felt the vision pushing forwards when the general spoke. Or when he came to dinner. Or arrived to take her mother to some social event.

Xavier spoke to her. 'I cannot decide if he is encroaching or merely greatly attached to your mother.'

She longed to talk about it with him. He was the only one who knew everything.

Her throat tightened. She pretended to keep eating.

She'd not been wrong to refuse him, she told herself again. A man so perfect could only be unhappy with an imperfect wife.

When the breakfast was over, Phillipa slipped away while the couples were busy saying their goodbyes. She was certain no one would notice. She returned to her bedchamber and tried to play in her head the music she'd heard that day.

And erase the image of Xavier Campion from her mind.

Chapter Twelve

Two days later the house was so quiet Phillipa thought she would go mad. If she'd had her pianoforte she would have loved such a day. She would have filled the air with music.

Her mother now spent all her spare time with General Henson. Ned and Adele were on their honeymoon trip, and Hugh had gone to the country, to Westleigh House, to oversee the harvest. Phillipa had begged her mother to allow her to go with him—there was a pianoforte there—but her mother refused and Hugh would not counter their mother's wishes.

Phillipa was alone with no way to fill the days.

Out of desperation she turned to needlework. And to winding her music box over and over.

Higgley knocked upon her door. 'A gentleman to see you, Lady Phillipa.'

Her spirits drooped lower. 'Who is it?'

'Mr Campion.'

She knew even before he spoke the name. What other gentleman would call upon her? 'I will see him in the drawing room.'

She looked at herself in the mirror. She wore an old dress and an old cap and looked her very worst. She changed nothing.

Instead she wound the music box once more and closed her eyes as it played. Unfortunately the tune it played was 'Plaisir D'amour'.

The pleasures of love lasts only a moment.
The pain of love lasts a lifetime.

She closed the box and left the room.

The door to the drawing room was open and she paused for a moment.

He stood at the window. Even in profile, he could take her breath away. His coat and pantaloons were superbly cut, fitting him well, as did all his clothing. His dark hair was slightly longer than fashionable and untamed.

She stepped in to the room. 'Xavier?'

He turned to her and did not speak for a moment. 'Good day, Phillipa.' He seemed to scrutinise her. 'Are you in good health?'

That was a way of saying she looked so dreadful she must be at death's door.

She waved a hand and crossed the room to a chair. 'I am well enough. Why are you here?'

She might as well force him to the point.

He sat in a chair near her. Too close for her comfort. Surely now he could see the dark circles under her eyes and the lines etching her forehead.

And her scar.

'It is about your music.'

Of course. He'd said he would bring her music.

'You should not be without your music.' He leaned towards her. 'It is plain to see that you are not doing well without it. I propose to give it back to you.'

'*Propose* to give it back? Have you not brought it with you? You said you would.' Although what could she do with it besides hide it from her mother?

'I do not mean your sheet music,' he said.

Then what did he mean? 'Do not say you have purchased a pianoforte. My mother will be rid of it.'

'Your mother will have no say. The music will be all yours.'

'Stop talking in riddles, Xavier.' She pinched the bridge of her nose. Must she get a headache, too?

'Marry me, Phillipa.' His voice dropped. 'Reconsider and marry me. Do so and you may work on your music to your heart's content.'

His words were stabs of pain. 'We have been through this before.'

He held up a hand. 'No. Not this. When you refused me before you could not think your mother would take away your music. Marriage to me will restore it and more. I promise I will buy you the finest pianoforte to be found in all London.'

She could not believe her ears. 'I should marry for a pianoforte?'

He smiled. 'Why not? Other women marry for a title or wealth, why not marry for a pianoforte?' He turned serious again. 'You can perform at the Masquerade Club, if you wish, and I promise to help you sell your music. I already showed one piece to a music seller. He agreed it was good. He gave me a list of music publishers here.'

Her head whirled. He'd done all that for her?

He went on. 'You ought not to be deprived of what you most love. Your music.'

'But that is not your doing.' She knew where the blame rested. 'It is mine. And my mother's.'

'But I have the power to fix it.' He touched her hand. 'We can put it in the settlement papers, if you wish. That you will always have any musical instrument you desire. That I will endeavor to sell your music. That the money goes to you.'

She swept a hand around the room. 'The weddings that took place here? Those couples had a regard for each other. We do not.'

His eyes pierced hers. 'You do not have a regard for me?'

She glanced away.

'I assure you…' his eyes bored into hers '…I have a regard for you, Phillipa.'

'Do not jest with me.' She pointed to her scar. 'Look at me.'

He pulled her hand away from her face. 'Your scar has never mattered to me. Listen to me. In your family you will always be dependent—'

This was no argument. She cut him off. 'You will make me dependent upon you.'

'No. Because I can give you independence. Money of your own.' He paused as if thinking of something for the first time. 'If you prefer, I can simply support you, but I fear that will cause both our families some distress and it will limit you in society.'

She almost laughed. Think of the gossip. The handsome Xavier Campion taking disfigured Phillipa Westleigh under his protection.

But the ridicule would be the same if he married her.

What was she thinking? 'I cannot do this to you, Xavier. Or to myself. You cannot want me for a wife.'

His gaze did not waver. 'I do want you for a wife.'

'Why?' It made no sense. A man like him wanting to marry her.

'You are being treated shabbily,' he said. 'I can fix it.'

She turned away.

'Think of it, Phillipa,' he pressed. 'You may play your music to your heart's delight. You will run your own household, decide on your own invitations. Your own activities. You will not be dependent upon your mother or brothers.'

She would only be answerable to him.

'Trust me.' It was as if he read her mind.

She stared into a future with her mother. She would be a spinster. As her mother aged she would be called upon to be her companion. When her mother was gone, she'd be shifted from one brother's home to the other.

If she married, though, she could live her own life. Was that not what her mother had always done? Her parents had paid little heed to each other's activities. Would marriage with Xavier be like that?

Could she endure it?

There must be something of self-interest in this proposition. 'What advantage would marrying me provide you?'

He glanced into her eyes. 'Would you believe me if I told you I would marry you because I love you?'

The words pierced her heart. 'Of course not.'

'I thought as much.' He smiled, but the sadness

did not leave his eyes. 'Marry me anyway and leave this place.'

It was as if he'd offered freedom from a dungeon. The question was, could she resist, when she knew it was guilt or obligation or honour or whatever that led him to make this offer?

She could not.

He offered her music and that was the one offer she could not resist.

'Very well, Xavier.' She would marry him.

He seized her hand. 'Good, Phillipa. Good.'

'But there is one thing.'

His brows rose. 'That is?'

'We must marry quietly. Only you and me.' She refused to be put on display, not even in front of family.

He raised her hand to his lips. 'It will be as you say.'

Xavier released a pent up breath. She'd said yes.

Music was the key.

She could not live without music.

He appearance this morning was even more alarming than the day of the wedding. She wore her hair pulled back into a simple cap that hid all her curls. Her lips were thin and her eyes pained, and she was so pale, the discolouration of her scar became even more prominent. He wanted to see her flushed with pleasure again. He wanted to see her joy at making music.

He pulled a paper from his coat pocket. 'I took the liberty of procuring a special licence. We can marry anywhere, any time. We want only witnesses and a clergyman.' He smiled. 'We could do it today, if you wish.'

'Today?' She looked alarmed.

'Tell me when.' He wanted to assure her the independence he'd promised her. She must decide.

Her chin rose in determination. 'Tomorrow, if you can manage it.'

He reached across the distance between them and touched her cheek. 'I am determined it should be exactly as you wish. I will send word if I am unable to make the arrangements.'

Her eyes searched his as if trying to determine whether she should believe him.

'Do not worry,' he told her. 'Leave it to me. I will call upon you at eleven o'clock.' He stood. 'I should take my leave. I have much to accomplish.'

She rose as well and walked with him to the drawing-room door.

He reached for the latch, but her hand stilled his. 'Are you certain of this, Xavier?'

He lifted her chin and leaned down to place his lips on hers. 'I am certain, Phillipa.'

The butler, who was attending the hall, handed Xavier his hat and gloves and walked to the door to open it for him.

Xavier turned to the man as he reached for the doorknob. 'If you have any affection towards Lady Phillipa, sir, perhaps you could refrain from mentioning my visit to Lady Westleigh.'

The butler's expression did not change, but he said, 'If her ladyship does not ask if Lady Phillipa received any callers, I see no reason I should mention it.'

Xavier smiled. 'Thank you. That is all I ask.'

He walked out to the street and turned towards Bond Street. There was much to be accomplished and only one day to accomplish it all.

Which he was determined to do.

Phillipa's heart pounded as she watched Xavier leave the house and hurry down the street. Could it really be true? Would she be able to leave this prison her mother had created for her and be free?

She walked out of the room and made her way to the stairs, feeling as if she were sleepwalking.

Mason stood in the hall. 'Is there anything you require, m'lady?'

She wanted to tell him not to tell her mother about Xavier's visit, but was he an ally or would he report to her mother?

No, she must pretend Xavier's visit was nothing of significance, nothing worthy of mentioning.

'If you would find Lacey and ask her to attend me, I would be grateful.' She had to risk asking for Lacey's help. Even more, she needed to tell someone what had happened. And what was going to happen.

'Very good, m'lady.' He bowed and she started up the stairs. 'One moment, m'lady,' he called to her.

She turned to him.

He looked up at her. 'Lady Westleigh never enquires if you have had callers.'

How odd for him to say. 'I rarely do have callers.'

'Precisely.' His voice did not change from its typically formal tone. 'Which is why Lady Westleigh never asks.' He paused. 'And I, therefore, have no reason to answer her.'

She suddenly understood. 'Thank you, Mason.'

He bowed.

On impulse she rushed down the stairs again and gave him a hug. 'Wish me happy,' she whispered in his ear. 'I am going to be married. Say nothing to my mother or anyone else.'

He broke into a smile, but just as quickly composed his features. 'If Lady Westleigh asks me if you are to be married, I shall be compelled to answer.'

She laughed. 'If she asks, do tell her!'

She ran up the stairs to her room. It looked remarkably unchanged. Her needlework lay on the chair by the window. Her music box sat on the table. Her brush and comb remained on the dressing table. She glanced in the mirror.

Even she did not look changed, even though everything she expected in her life would now be different. She turned a full circle, scanning every corner.

'I'll not see this room after tomorrow,' she said aloud. 'Of that I am immensely glad.'

A knock sounded at the door and Lacey entered the room. 'You wished to see me, m'lady? Is there something I may do for you?'

Lacey felt sorry for her, Phillipa knew, and also very guilt-ridden for telling her family about sneaking out at night.

Phillipa was about to give her a second chance. 'I have something to tell you, but you must promise to tell no one.'

Lacey wrung her hands. 'Oh, m'lady! I will swear on everything holy. I will say nothing. Not even if they torture me or threaten to sack me.'

'You won't be sacked, but you may be promoted.' Phillipa made the girl face her. 'Do you know that Mr Campion called today?'

Lacey nodded. 'One of the maids saw him walk to the door. She and I took a peek at him when he left. He is a sight to see, as you know.'

Even the maids were not immune to his good looks. 'Will you tell the maid to say nothing to anyone about seeing him?'

'Yes, m'lady. If you wish it.'

Phillipa hugged herself. 'You see, I have agreed to marry him.'

Lacey squealed. 'You do not say! Marry him? A man like him? Who would have thought?'

Even Lacey could not believe a perfect man like Xavier would marry an imperfect woman like herself.

'But you must tell no one.' Phillipa repeated. 'No one.'

'Yes, m'lady.' The girl giggled. 'No one. I promise. Not even the maids.'

'Especially not the maids.' She told Lacey of the plans for the next day. 'We must pack a portmanteau for me. I will write my mother a letter, which you may tell her about if she asks for me, but not before noon. I'll send word where to deliver the bag. I have not the faintest idea where it will be. We must sneak a portmanteau into this room without anyone knowing. Can you do it?'

'I can, m'lady.' She returned a calculating look. 'But what did you mean by a promotion?'

'If you wish it, you may come live with me. I'll need a lady's maid. Because you will be maid to the lady of the house, you must receive more pay for what you do.'

The girl's eyes widened. 'I would live with you and Mr Campion?'

'When we are settled.' Phillipa did not know where they would live. She did not care as long as it was not here.

And as long as it had a pianoforte.

Chapter Thirteen

Xavier searched out the jarvey who had driven them to and from the gaming house. He hired him for the day so that he would be directly at hand. None of the distances they would travel were too far to walk, but he would not have her walk this day.

At precisely eleven o'clock in the morning the hack pulled up to the Westleigh town house. Xavier had no more alighted than the door opened and Phillipa emerged.

Against the pale-grey brick she was a bloom of colour. Her dress was pale pink with a matching coat fastened only at her bosom so that its skirts billowed behind her as she walked towards him. Her face was hidden under her bonnet and her customary netting.

He strode towards her and took her hand in his. 'Look who drives us.'

She lifted the netting up to see the driver. 'It is you!'

He pulled his forelock. 'It is, indeed, miss. I am yours for the day. And what a day it is, eh?'

'I am happy to see you.' She sounded happy.

Xavier's heart swelled. 'Phillipa, you look lovely.'

She cringed at his words.

He bit his tongue. He did not wish anything to spoil her day.

'Come. Let us set off. Johnson knows all the stops.' He helped her into the coach as he had done so many times before.

'Where are we bound?' she asked.

He took her hand again. It trembled under his. 'Allow me to surprise you.'

The coach stopped on Piccadilly in front of a red-brick church.

Xavier said, 'This is our first stop.'

He helped her out. 'St James's,' he said.

'We are to be married in a church?' Her voice was breathless.

'We are indeed.' He'd made the right choice. 'We'll enter on the south side.'

They walked up to an elaborate Ionic doorway and went inside.

As soon as they entered, the church's organ exploded into Handel's music.

Phillipa gasped. *'The Arrival of the Queen of Sheba!'*

The organist had informed Xavier that the organ dated back to the late 1600s. The man suggested playing Handel, but Xavier had not known what pieces he'd select. As it was, the first piece was rather appropriate.

Phillipa laughed, but the sound was almost a sob. 'Oh, Xavier!'

She threw her arms around his neck and he held her close against him, surprised that the music pleased her that much. She wept on his shoulder and he could feel her whole body shaking. Curse her mother for depriving her of this—this food for her soul.

The feel of her in his arms affected him more than he'd ever have expected. He did not want to release her.

But she did pull away and they walked slowly towards the altar, the music wrapping itself around them like a warm cloak against harsh weather. In the centre of the church, she paused, her eyes closed and he waited, letting her have the moment to herself.

The first piece ended and the second began, much softer than the first.

'Water Music.' She smiled and she took his arm as they walked down the aisle, past the Corinthian columns, beneath the vaulted ceiling with its rich plasterwork, to the altar where the clergyman waited, prayer book in hand.

* * *

Phillipa let the music sink into her, filling all the empty spaces inside her. She had not expected this. She thought he'd bring her to the Masquerade Club and they would be married in the drawing room there. She'd start weeping again if she dwelled on how wonderful this was of Xavier.

Nothing could have been better.

As they neared the altar the clergyman stepped forwards to greet them. He was a young man, younger than Phillipa herself, she'd guess. Newly ordained, perhaps, and so very obliging to perform this ceremony on such short notice.

Standing nearby were MacEvoy and Belinda, one of the Masquerade Club's croupiers. MacEvoy winked at her and Belinda smiled. They knew her, she realised. Xavier must have told them.

'Are we ready?' the clergyman asked, glancing from one to the other.

'One moment.' Xavier took the netting on her hat and lifted it away from her face. 'I must see you,' he murmured.

Her impulse was to cover her face, not to hide her scar, but to preserve her identity, although that was silly, because soon the world would know that Adonis-like Xavier Campion had married the scarred Phillipa Westleigh.

Xavier indicated he was ready. Was she? Her heart pounded. It was not too late to change her mind. Save the handsome Adonis for a Venus worthy of him.

The music swelled.

No. She would not change her mind, selfish as it was. She needed music too much.

'Dearly Beloved, we are gathered here in the sight of God...' The words the clergyman spoke were the same they'd heard only a few days before, when Ned and Rhys married, both for love.

Not for a pianoforte.

She faced Xavier as he repeated his vows. 'I, Xavier, take thee, Phillipa, to my wedded wife...'

The sun shone through the stained-glass windows, casting his face in a riot of colour. His blue eyes were as clear and bright as the glass and they gazed upon her with abundant good will.

It was her turn to make the vows that would alter her existence. And his.

She made her voice strong. 'I, Phillipa, take thee, Xavier, to my wedded husband....'

When she finished her vows, the clergyman asked for the ring. Phillipa expected a thin gold band. Xavier, instead, placed a large ring festooned with diamonds upon the prayer book.

The clergyman handed the ring back to Xavier.

He spoke. 'With this ring I thee wed, with my body I thee worship, and with all my worldly goods I thee endow....'

He placed the ring on her finger. It sparkled in the light, like a musical composition with many notes. She stared at it. Why had he chosen this ring? This very special ring?

The clergyman recited the prayers with more meaning than had been evident in the other weddings. The words sound more personal, created just for them.

'...Those that God has joined together let no man put asunder...' And finally to the end. 'I pronounce that they be Man and Wife together.'

The music grew louder, more joyous. The allegro from the *Music for the Royal Fireworks*, composed over half a century ago, but still as beautiful and happy as one could wish.

Xavier captured her hands and squeezed them. 'We have done it, Phillipa.'

She pulled him down to whisper in his ear. 'Thank you, Xavier.'

MacEvoy and Belinda hurried up to them with congratulations. They all went back to the church office to sign the papers. In no time at all Xavier and Phillipa were back in the coach, headed to the next destination.

* * *

It was back to her mother's town house. Phillipa's spirits sank. Was he going to leave her there?

'I thought you might want to collect some of your things,' he said. 'We'll have to have it all sent to us eventually, but I did not have time to find us a place to live.'

'You have done much more than was necessary.' She swallowed, relieved. 'I have a portmanteau packed, but I do not want to go inside. I do not want to speak to anyone or to have them see me. Especially my mother.'

He moved to climb out of the coach. 'I am counting on your mother being out.' He jumped down and turned to her. 'I will go in. How do I ask for it?'

'Have Mason send for my maid. She will hand over the bag.'

He strode to the door, walking with a masculine power that seemed unique to him. He sounded the knocker and, as she had hoped, Mason opened the door.

The butler glanced to the coach and met her gaze. She smiled at him. His expression softened and he nodded. A very few minutes later Xavier reappeared with the portmanteau. As he carried it to the carriage, Lacey appeared at the window, waving.

Phillipa waved back.

Xavier climbed back in. 'Here it is.'

'My mother—?' Phillipa started to ask.

'Not at home.'

She leaned back against the leather upholstery. 'Good. I wrote her a letter. My maid will see that it is put into her hands.'

The hackney coach started off.

'Where to next?' she asked.

He grinned. 'Another surprise.'

The coach took them back to Piccadilly and stopped in front of the Pulteney Hotel, so fashionable that the Tsar of Russia himself once chose to stay there rather than at a royal palace.

'We are staying here?' she asked.

'We are.' He opened the door. 'One night, at least.'

They said good day to the hackney driver and entered the hotel, its hall as grand as the hotel's reputation. Soon they were escorted up to their set of rooms.

The servant opened the door and Phillipa entered first.

She gasped.

Prominently displayed in the room was a pianoforte, the prettiest she had ever seen. Its mahogany rectangular case was adorned with chevron-string inlay and hand-painted with pink roses above the keyboard.

She crossed the room to it, running her fingers down the keys.

'It is yours,' Xavier said.

She swung around to him. 'Truly?'

'Unless you want another.' His voice turned deep. 'I asked for the best one in the shop, but if there is another you would like—'

'There could never be one more beautiful.' She played a few keys. Its sound was wonderful, as well. 'You have been too good.'

Her throat twisted and she thought she would dissolve into a puddle of tears if she said more.

'Feel free to play.' He gestured for her to sit. 'Your music is there.'

'My music?' He'd thought of everything.

'And a book of country dances. Something frivolous I bought on impulse.' He pulled up a chair nearby. 'Play. Whatever you like.'

A maid appeared and Xavier handed her Phillipa's portmanteau. While the girl unpacked her clothing, Phillipa pulled off her gloves and sat at the pianoforte's bench. From memory, she played a few bars of *The Arrival of the Queen of Sheba*. 'Did you pick the music for the church?'

He shook his head. 'I left it to the organist. I know very little of music.'

'It doesn't matter.' The pianoforte had a lovely sound. 'You thought of music.'

She began to play the minuet from Haydn's *Surprise Symphony*, which she knew by heart. She was happy and this was happy music.

When she finished, he said, 'You make me feel like dancing.'

She started playing another piece. 'If I could play and dance at the same time, I would. I do not think I have ever been so happy.'

Xavier dismissed the maid and settled in a chair to enjoy hearing Phillipa play. He watched her face as her fingers flew over the keys. All the nights she played at the Masquerade Club, he had longed to see her face, to watch her expression as the music poured out of her.

He was not disappointed.

Her pallor disappeared and her face was flushed with pleasure. Her eyes shone with joy. She looked beautiful.

When he'd called upon her yesterday, she'd looked as if she were shrinking into herself. She'd looked as if she were dying. The music filled her, like nourishment. Ironically the music was also a feast for anyone lucky enough to be her audience. He felt content, just for listening to her.

He was satisfied with himself. It had been a new challenge for him to arrange a wedding with music and a set of rooms with a pianoforte in less than a day, but he'd done it.

He poured himself a congratulatory glass of brandy from a sideboard and sat back to simply take in the music.

He had the strong sense again that he was listening, not to music, but to her emotions. The emotions swirling inside her flowed into her fingers and emerged as music.

Even in the joyous pieces she chose to play there was an undertone of melancholy, as if she could not imagine being happy for very long, but that was another challenge he intended to meet.

This marriage would be a good one for her. And for him. He cared nothing for what others might say of it. He was determined to succeed as a good husband, one who made certain nothing hurt Phillipa again.

She looked up from the music and smiled at him.

Today was an excellent start.

Chapter Fourteen

Phillipa played all the music in her head, all her
sheets of music Xavier brought to the hotel for her.
He interrupted her once to tell her he must go out
briefly, but she lost track of time and did not know
how long he'd been gone. When he returned he sat
in one of the brocade-upholstered chairs, his long
legs stretched out in front of him. She resumed playing, soaking in the music like a flower parched from
lack of rain.

She lost herself in the music again until she felt the
touch of his hand on her shoulder. 'Our meal has arrived. You need to eat something.'

He'd ordered a lovely meal, dismissing the servant,
saying he would serve the meal himself. Turtle soup.
Salmon. Roast beef with side dishes of courgette and
potatoes. Peach tart waiting for dessert.

The scent of it roused Phillipa's appetite. 'I am suddenly famished.'

'I can imagine,' he responded. 'It has been hours since breakfast.'

She pressed her stomach. 'I did not eat very much breakfast.'

In fact, she'd not thought of food all day. She'd hardly thought of him either, or of being married, so lost was she in the music. It shamed her to realise it.

He uncovered the tureen of soup and served her. 'Have you enjoyed the pianoforte?'

She felt tears sting her eyes. 'I cannot tell you how wonderful it has been. I have missed the music so very much.'

His expression warmed. 'I am glad it made you happy.'

When had anyone been concerned with her happiness? Her father certainly never gave her a thought. Her brothers thought of her as much as brothers think of sisters. Her mother's attention had not been concerned with her happiness, but with a determination that she mix well in society. The only person she could recall who'd ever purposefully wanted to cheer her had been Xavier. When they'd been children, she'd worshipped him for it.

He poured her a fine claret.

She could not talk of the pianoforte or his kindness or she would weep in a manner he could not possibly understand.

'I wonder if my mother has yet discovered my absence,' she said instead.

Had her mother read the letter? Was she gloating in triumph or angry that her daughter had acted without her?

'I suspect your mother will approve,' Xavier said, piercing a morsel of salmon with his fork.

'She will approve of the marriage,' Phillipa responded. 'She will probably take full credit for it.'

He turned their conversation to her music. What she preferred to play. What she liked to write. It made it quite comfortable to converse with him.

When it was time for the last course, that lovely peach tart, Phillipa stood. 'You must allow me to serve.' She cut him a piece and placed it on his plate.

'Where did you go when you went out?' she asked him as she cut her own piece. 'If—if I may ask, that is.' Did she have the right to ask where he went, what he did?

'Of course you may ask.' He took a bite of the tart. 'I went to the *Morning Post*. An announcement of our marriage will be printed in two days' time.'

She froze, her fork in midair. 'Everyone will know.'

'The sooner the better, do you not think?' He looked concerned. 'Everyone must learn of it eventually.'

'I suppose.' She expected the notice would generate a great deal of gossip. *The Adonis married the scarred spinster. Can you imagine it? What was he thinking?*

He reached over and clasped her hand. 'I am happy to announce it, Phillipa. Let the whole world know.'

He was merely being kind again. Surely he would find the talk uncomfortable.

She slipped her hand away and cut him another piece of tart.

She changed the subject. 'Will you be at the Masquerade Club tonight?'

A quizzical look came over his face. 'Not tonight, Phillipa. MacEvoy will watch things there. I am not needed.'

She thought he would go about his routine. This wedding was not like Ned's and Rhys's. It was more like a favour he'd done her.

Tea arrived and the servants removed the dinner dishes.

Phillipa's eyes kept wandering to the pianoforte. It was much more comfortable to play her music than to think about him.

Her husband.

He placed his cup in its saucer. 'Teach me to play something.'

'You?'

'Certainly!' He took her hand and led her back to the pianoforte's bench. 'My sisters once insisted I learn to play. My lessons did not last long. I was much more interested in swordsmanship and shooting.'

'As a soldier ought to be,' she said.

He joined her on the bench and together they picked out the notes to some of the country dances he'd purchased for her. Fairly soon they managed a pretty terrible rendition of 'Miss Louisa Johnstone's Fancy' and 'The Fairie's Revels'.

Laughing too hard to finish, she covered her mouth with her hand.

He touched her ring. 'Does the ring please you?'

She held it up and watched the diamonds capture the light from the candles. 'It is the most beautiful ring I could ever imagine,' she answered truthfully, ashamed she'd not told him so before this.

A smile flashed across his face. 'I am glad.'

He stared at her, his eyes darkening. 'Have I made you happy today, Phillipa?'

Her heart beat faster. 'Yes.' Her voice trembled. 'Very happy.'

He leaned closer to her. And closer.

Very suddenly Phillipa forgot about music and pianofortes and rings. Nothing existed but Xavier, so very handsome and so very close. She felt his breath on her face, as soft as a butterfly's wing. His lips came nearer. They touched hers gently and she felt every part of her flare with sensation.

The kiss lasted only a moment, but when he moved away it felt like abandonment. He smiled again, but she was bereft. She needed that intimate connection with him. She needed to not be so alone any more.

He closed the distance between them again, wrapping his arms around her and again seeking her lips. This kiss demanded more of her. She pressed her lips against his and savoured the warm fullness of his mouth. His tongue touched hers, tasting of peaches and claret, a sensation that surprised her, especially because it made other parts of her ache in response.

She melted into his embrace, her hands flat against his back, feeling his muscled body even through his coat.

He broke away again. 'Shall I send for a maid to help you prepare for bed?'

Had she displeased him?

Something must have shown in her face because his brows knit. 'It is our wedding night, Phillipa. Do you not wish to share my bed?'

She blinked. 'I thought you were sending me away.'

He pulled her into an embrace. 'Phillipa, you are my wife. I would not send you away on our wedding night.'

Was he being kind again? She averted her face,

hiding her scar from his view. 'I—I never thought you would wish to bed me.'

His expression hardened. 'We are married, are we not?'

'But—but I thought you merely were marrying me out of pity.'

'Pity?' His eyes narrowed in pain.

Her heart sank. The last thing she wished was to upset him. 'I will share your bed if you wish it, Xavier.'

'I wish it. I wish for a marriage in every sense of the word.' His eyes pierced hers. 'In fact, I will not send for a ladies' maid. I will perform that function myself.'

He would undress her? Her eyes widened.

He cupped her chin. 'I will show you what a husband will do.'

Felicia, her best friend, had hinted at the pleasures of being married and Phillipa knew what occurred between a man and a woman in bed. Who could not know who grew up on a farm? Or attended school where older girls were only too willing to tell. She had just given up hope of experiencing it for herself.

He took her hand and led her to the bedchamber, a room so beautifully appointed she could understand why the Tsar of Russia chose this hotel over St James's Palace.

By the coals glowing in the fireplace she could see the maid had turned down the bed and laid out her nightdress. She watched the fire as he stood behind her and undid the laces of her gown, his fingers creating sensations so unexpected. So pleasant.

Her dress slid to the thick carpet beneath their feet. She stepped out of it and slipped off her shoes. He ran his hands down her bare arms, his palms warming her. His touch felt comforting. And thrilling. His lips touched her neck and sensation flashed through her. She'd never guessed that a man's kiss—Xavier's kiss—could be felt all over her body.

He untied her corset and loosened its laces so that it, too, joined her gown on the floor. All that covered her now was her thin muslin shift. He pulled the pins from her hair and combed through her curls with his fingers. To have him touch her hair was glorious. Who could imagine it to feel so different from a maid's ministrations?

Was this arousal? This feeling inside her? It surprised her and made her want more from him. He slipped his hands around her and cupped her breasts, stroking her until she thought she would go mad for yearning. He swept her into his arms and carried her to the bed. While she lay upon the feather bed, he rolled down her stockings, another sensation so intense she could not bear it. Nor bear for him to stop.

But he stepped away from the bed and removed his clothes, peeling off first his coat, then his waistcoat, then his shirt. His skin glowed from the firelight and she could not look away when he removed his pantaloons and stood before her like a Greek statue.

Adonis.

He climbed on to the bed. Closer, she could see scars on his abdomen.

She touched them. 'Xavier?'

He covered her hand with his. 'A few battle wounds.'

'You must have been gravely hurt!' He'd been stabbed. Sliced.

He took her hand away and kissed it. 'Your half-brother carried me off the battlefield.'

Rhys had saved him? She thanked God for her new brother.

Xavier took her face in his hands and kissed her again, a long, lingering kiss that made her forget about battlefields.

He lifted her shift and broke off the kiss long enough to pull it over her head. She lay naked next to him, a feeling so decadent she marvelled that it felt so right. Tentatively, she touched him again, this time feeling the contours of his muscles beneath her fingers.

He kissed her again and ran his hands down her naked body and back to her breasts. He traced around her nipple with his fingers and the glorious sensations returned. Who knew a man's fingers could create such sensations?

He lay her on her back. 'I will be gentle with you, I promise.'

Gentle? She was not certain she wished him to be gentle. She wanted all of this experience, not *pianissimo* but *forte*.

He touched her. Down there. And his fingers created new sensations, as *forte* as she could imagine, so intense she thought she could not bear it another moment. At the same time, she did not want him to stop.

She moaned with pleasure and need.

'It will bring you pleasure, Phillipa,' he reassured her.

He had already brought pleasure.

His fingers were clever, bringing her body to new heights of experience. Her muscles reacted on their own, rising up to give him more access, to keep him from ever stopping.

But he did stop and her body throbbed in disappointment. His body covered hers and she felt his male member touch her, press against her and then, as she trembled beneath him, slip inside her.

A quick stab of pain seized her and her muscles stiffened in response.

He froze, still inside her. 'Did I hurt you?'

She shook her head. 'No.' But she felt the dampness of her maidenhood flow from her.

A moment later, the pain receded and her need grew.

He moved inside her, slowly, rhythmically.

She must remember this rhythm, she thought. She must try to recreate it. In her mind she heard what it might sound like on the pianoforte. Low notes with a unique timbre and vibrato.

The tempo increased and the music he created inside her grew louder, more intense. Her need grew as well, so strongly that it frightened her.

Suddenly a sound from deep within his chest escaped him and he plunged into her and held her in place. She felt his seed spill inside her.

A child, she thought. They might create a child from this act.

The thought fled just as quickly. He pressed inside her once more and something exploded inside her. A crescendo of sensation. She cried out for the pleasure of it.

He collapsed on top of her and she felt his weight

for the first time. His skin was hot, damp, and his muscled body firm. He slid to her side and she took a breath. A strange languor came over her, as if her body had turned to melted candle wax.

'Did I hurt you?' he asked again.

She shook her head. She wanted to tell him how marvellous it felt, but words would not come. The music of it resounded in her mind, but even that faded and suddenly the idea that she was naked beside him made her shy. It had happened so fast, this lovemaking, this marriage, she'd not had time to think.

She'd certainly had no time to realise he'd want the physical side of marriage with her.

He rose on one elbow and stared down at her. 'Are you certain you are unharmed? I ought to have been more gentle. I am sorry for it.'

She found the bed sheet and covered her body with it. 'I am unharmed.'

He smiled and brushed her hair away from her face. 'The first time can be painful for a woman sometimes,' he explained. 'It will get better, I promise.'

It could be better than this? That defied logic.

He lay at her side, but continued to play with her hair, threading it through his fingers. He gazed at her face. 'You are beautiful, Phillipa.'

She tensed and turned her head away, hiding her

scarred cheek. She was not beautiful. This she knew. He could not possibly think so.

Her body turned numb and she turned away from him.

He cupped her cheek and made her look back at him. 'You must believe me. You are beautiful.'

She could not. He was merely being kind. He had been kind to marry her.

She thought of Lady Faville and all the other beautiful women he might have married and she was sorry he'd felt obligated to marry her. It could not have been more than pity for the shabby way her mother had treated her that led him to choose her over such worthy women.

'Phillipa?' He looked concerned.

She owed it to him to pretend everything was perfect, even though she knew it was not. He'd tried so hard to please her. He'd made such a sacrifice.

She reached over and kissed him, not a very good kiss, more like one given to an elderly uncle, but the best she could muster.

'Thank you for a perfect day.' She made herself smile. She made herself snuggle against him and pretend to fall asleep.

Although it took a very long time for sleep to come.

Chapter Fifteen

Xavier woke to sun streaming through the windows. And to an empty bed, an empty bedchamber. He rose and wrapped his banyan around him and walked into the sitting room. She was seated there, dressed in her nightdress, gazing out the window.

'Phillipa?'

She turned at the sound of his voice and smiled. 'Good morning.'

There was a reserve in her voice he could not like. He wanted her to feel comfortable with him, but perhaps the night before had upset her. He had not been gentle enough. His own need for her had surged too strong, too urgent. He had been able to bring her pleasure, of that he was certain, but they had a long way to go.

In any event, he must tread carefully with her and not expect too much of her. Theirs was not a typical marriage. It would take time for her to realise that he wanted them to get on well together, to forge a life together.

'Have you been up long?' he asked.

'Not too long,' she replied, which could have meant hours or minutes.

'And you have been sitting here the whole time?'

'Not all the time,' she said. 'I used the water closet. How marvellous for a hotel to have such a thing! I read about them, of course.'

He did not want to talk about the water closet. 'Did you sleep well?'

'Yes,' she replied.

This was still like talking with a stranger. Much too polite.

He sat in a chair across from her, but she seemed distant. 'Shall I order breakfast?'

She glanced down. 'May I be dressed first?'

'Of course.' He paused, uncertain how to anticipate what would make her most at ease. 'Shall I send for a maid?'

Her smile seemed stiff. 'Now? That would be fine.'

He sent for a maid and a valet and, after they were both dressed, he'd ordered breakfast. When they were eating it, she asked, 'What happens today?'

He wanted to please her. 'We need to find a place to live, but that is not likely to be accomplished today.

Would you like to stay here? Or we can stay at the Masquerade Club. Rhys no longer uses his rooms there. And he is away.' With his wife.

Having agreed to watch the Masquerade Club in Rhys's absence, Xavier could not take Phillipa on a bride trip of her own. Perhaps later she would fancy a trip to Paris or Italy. Or Vienna. Wherever great music might be found.

'I cannot see staying here if you will be needed at the gaming house,' she responded. 'It must be very expensive to stay here. You do not need to spend so much money on me.'

He wanted to spend money on her, but something in her tone told him to simply do as she said.

Later that morning Cummings opened the door to the gaming house and they entered. MacEvoy happened to be in the hall as well.

'I am glad you are both here.' Xavier said.

'Come closer.' MacEvoy gestured. 'Let us have a look at you.'

Phillipa stepped forwards and, with only brief hesitation, lifted the netting away from her face.

Xavier gestured to Cummings. 'Let me present you to my wife.'

Cummings bowed. 'Mrs Campion. Welcome back.' The corner of his mouth twitched.

'Welcome back? You remember me?' Phillipa asked.

'The *pianiste*,' Cummings said. Phillipa extended her hand. 'It is good to be back.'

Cummings rubbed his hand on his coat before accepting hers.

'Hope you slept well last night,' MacEvoy said with a wink.

'Yes.' Phillipa blushed. 'We slept well.'

Xavier said, 'We will be staying here until we find a house.'

Cummings took something from his pocket. 'This arrived. Delivered from Stephen's Hotel.'

'Thank you, Cummings.' It was from his parents. 'A pianoforte will arriving here today. You may have it put in the drawing room.'

He'd already closed his rooms at Stephen's Hotel and had his trunk delivered here. Perhaps today they could arrange for Phillipa's things, as well.

When they reached Rhys's private rooms, Phillipa asked, 'Is the letter from my mother?'

He shook his head. 'From my mother.'

He showed her the bedchamber and placed their bags there. 'Would you like to unpack?'

'In a moment.' She removed her hat and gloves and unbuttoned her coat.

He stepped over and embraced her from behind. 'Everything will turn out well, Phillipa. Do not fear.'

She stepped out of his embrace and he helped her remove her coat. 'I am trying to get used to it.' She looked around the room, turning away from the bed. 'Should you not open your letter?'

'I should.' He broke the seal and unfolded the paper. 'They are in town.' He glanced up at her. 'Would you be willing to call upon them with me?'

She turned away. 'Perhaps you had better see them yourself and tell them. You must tell them before they read it in the newspaper.'

'I agree, but come with me.' He wanted her to be used to them together. The more people who saw her as Mrs Xavier Campion, the better.

She faced away from him. 'This will not be happy news for them.'

He laughed. 'Do you jest? They will be over the moon about it! They have wanted to see me settled since the end of the war.'

'But to me?' Her voice was almost inaudible.

He made her look at him. 'Our families have always been friends. Why would they not want to see me married to you?' She tried to turn away, but he would not let her. 'I insist. You must come. We should call on them right away.'

She took a deep breath and released it. 'Very well. Help me with my coat again. Let us go now, before I lose courage.'

It was as Xavier predicted. His parents were surprised. Shocked. And Phillipa supposed they were also mystified as to why he had chosen her, of all women, but they had always been kind people.

Like their son.

Lord and Lady Piermont welcomed her with open arms, broke out a bottle of sherry to toast to their future and insisted that Xavier and Phillipa come to dinner. Worse, Lady Piermont also sent an immediate invitation to Phillipa's mother to also come to dinner and she sent her kitchen staff into a flurry of activity to produce a dinner worthy of celebrating a marriage.

Xavier and his father set off to look for lodgings for the newly married couple and Lady Piermont enlisted Phillipa's help in writing letters to all Xavier's siblings, informing them of the marriage. Fortunately none of Xavier's siblings was in town. Lord and Lady Piermont were only there on their way to the country house for the harvest and hunting season.

'You and Xavier must come to the country with us,' his mother said.

Her natural good cheer could not help but lift Phillipa's spirits. 'He must attend to the gaming house in my brothers' absence. He promised Rhys.' At her new mother-in-law's disappointed look, Phillipa added, 'Perhaps when Rhys returns.'

That made Lady Piermont smile.

Phillipa took the opportunity to write letters of her own, to her brothers, to Felicia, and even to her father, who was not likely to care much. They had not finished their task when a footman brought Lady Piermont her mother's response.

Phillipa was confident that her mother would refuse the invitation. She never went anywhere on short notice. She kept writing as her mother-in-law opened the note.

'Oh, excellent!' the lady cried. 'Your mother accepted.'

'She accepted?' She did not wish to face her mother.

'Yes, indeed,' Lady Piermont went on. 'She is going to bring a friend. General Henson. I do remember him from Brighton several years ago.'

Of course her mother would bring General Henson.

'Isn't that lovely?' Lady Piermont exclaimed.

Phillipa stifled a groan. 'She will expect me to dress. I should get a note to my maid to send over a dinner dress.'

Lady Piermont rose to her feet. 'Nonsense. You

are similar in size to me. I will wager I have a dress that will fit you.'

She led Phillipa up the stairs to her bedchamber. Phillipa longed to ask the woman if she and her husband shared a bed, if their marriage had been a love match, or had they made it one after the ceremony?

Lord Piermont was a handsome, silver-haired man with kind blue eyes as brilliant as his son's, but it was clear that most of Xavier's looks came from his mother. In her early sixties at least, her dark brown hair was only threaded with grey. Her lips were full like Xavier's and her face was oval, like his. Like her son's, her nose was straight and perfectly formed. She moved with grace, as did he, although in a masculine way.

She was tall, like Phillipa, and slender. Though her waist was thicker—she'd had eight children, after all—Phillipa thought a dress of hers might, indeed, fit her.

Lady Piermont summoned her maid and instructed her what gowns to bring. One was a lilac silk with embroidered flowers in matching thread on the bodice and puffed sleeves so unusually made they reminded Phillipa of lace, but it was just the fabric.

Lady Piermont smiled. 'I see by your eyes you like this one. Let us have you try it on.'

The maid helped her into the dress and both she and Lady Piermont pulled and tucked the fabric.

'It needs only a *leetle* bit of sewing.' The maid spoke in a French accent.

Phillipa gazed in a full-length mirror and thought it looked lovely—if you looked at the dress, that is, not at her. 'I do like it.'

'I have a *leetle* something to make you look *très belle, madame*.' The maid touched her scar. 'We paint this and it disappears. *Voila!*'

Phillipa covered the scar with her hand. Her mother had always suggested she paint her face to make her scar less visible, but she always resisted. If people wished to meet her, then they would have to take her precisely as she was.

But no one at this dinner had seen her any other way than scarred.

Or masked.

Late in the afternoon Xavier came to collect Phillipa so they could walk back to the gaming house and dress for dinner, only to find Phillipa had made other arrangements. Or his mother had done.

'We shall surprise you,' his mother said, sending him off.

He returned and found the surprise. Phillipa's

mother…and General Henson. Surely this would not please Phillipa.

'Lady Westleigh.' Xavier bowed. 'General.'

They were alone in the drawing room, which was fortunate. He did not mind speaking frankly.

Lady Westleigh greeted him warmly. 'Xavier, my boy! I am in raptures that you succeeded in convincing Phillipa to do the right thing. It was wrong of her to decline in the first place.'

Xavier glared at her. 'No. You were in the wrong to deprive her of her pianoforte. Wrong and cruel.'

'See here, Campion!' the general piped up.

Lady Westleigh motioned for him to keep quiet. 'It is all right, Alistair. Xavier and I may speak with frankness.' She turned back to Xavier. 'If you are blessed with children, you may then choose to criticise me. You will learn that sometimes a parent must be cruel for a child's own good.'

'She is a grown woman who knows her own mind,' he countered. 'You made it impossible for her to do as she wished.'

'I made her see what was best for her. To see what her life would be like if she remained a spinster, subject to the whims of her relations.' She spoke with conviction. 'She made the right choice. Although she made a terrible mistake to keep the wedding secret. It ought to have taken place amongst family and special guests. She ought to have had a wedding breakfast.'

'I am grateful she could choose for herself how to be married,' he countered. 'She did not want to pretend a celebration she did not feel.'

Lady Westleigh rolled her eyes in exasperation. 'She has been running from attention since—since you-know-when. How could she expect to get married if she hid herself away?' Her eyes narrowed. 'I did what needed to be done and now all is as it should be.'

Except that Phillipa had not wished to marry him and he would need to work hard to convince her not to regret it.

His father entered the room. Xavier presented the general to him.

'We've met.' His father shook the general's hand. 'In Brighton. Years ago, I am certain of it.'

'That is so, my lord,' the general responded. 'I'd not expected you to recall it. So long ago.'

The two men talked of mutual acquaintances until Xavier's mother came and more greetings took place. They were all talking at once when Phillipa walked in.

Xavier was first to notice her.

She wore a flowing gown in a light purple colour that make her skin look luminous. It seemed to flow around her, like a dress a fairy might dance in. Her hair, too, looked fanciful, curls floating around her face, moving when she moved.

Her gaze went directly to him. He crossed the room to her, leaned down to her ear and whispered, 'You look lovely, Phillipa.'

Her hand flew to her cheek and she lowered her eyes.

'There she is,' his father boomed. 'Our new daughter! And does she not look a treat!'

His mother came up to Xavier's side and took his arm. 'I told you we had a surprise for you.'

He blew out a breath. 'I thought the surprise was her mother.'

She laughed. 'I suppose that was a surprise as well, wasn't it?'

A footman poured glasses of claret and handed one to each of them. 'A toast to our new member of the family.' His father lifted his glass. 'May she and our son be happy and fruitful!'

Xavier tapped his glass against Phillipa's. 'Happy and fruitful,' he repeated in a low voice.

After the toast, Phillipa's mother walked up to her. 'Phillipa, dear.' She touched Phillipa's cheek. 'You have applied cosmetics. Well done.'

'Very well done,' added the general. 'You can hardly see the scar.'

Phillipa's face turned red.

Xavier stared at her again. He'd not noticed what was immediately obvious to her mother.

The dinner went well enough. Lady Westleigh enquired about all the details of the wedding, which Xavier was obliged to tell.

Except he said nothing about the music played during their nuptials, nor did he tell them about her new pianoforte.

Lady Westleigh asked to see Phillipa's ring and Phillipa, her expression frozen on her face, extended her hand.

'Oh my!' her mother exclaimed. 'That is quite a ring.'

Xavier felt a quiet triumph.

When Phillipa put her hand back at her side, Xavier clasped it. She squeezed his fingers in return, a small gesture, but enough to cheer him.

After dinner they were forced to accept a ride in Lady Westleigh's carriage.

'I do think you should not be living atop a gaming house, Phillipa,' her mother said. 'It will cause talk.'

'No one will know unless you tell them,' Phillipa countered.

Xavier admired her. For the whole evening, Phillipa had more than held her own with her mother. The only time Xavier had seen her mother rattle her had been with the comment about her scar.

The ride was a short one, thank God. And they were soon back at the Masquerade Club. Phillipa covered her face with the netting on her hat when they entered.

The place was already abuzz with activity. There was not much to do in London at this time of year, so those remaining there used the Masquerade Club as their entertainment.

Xavier and Phillipa hurried inside and climbed the stairs to the private rooms. Once inside the bedchamber, Xavier helped Phillipa off with her coat.

'Tomorrow I must send for my maid,' she said.

He grinned at her. 'I take it my services are unsatisfactory?'

She coloured. 'I hate to trouble you.'

Could he not even jest with her? 'It is my pleasure to help you. I can help you out of your dress before I go downstairs, if you wish it.'

She frowned. 'I thought I would go to the supper room and play.' She faltered. 'With your permission, that is.'

He put his hands on her shoulders and made her look at him. 'You do not need my permission. Play, if that is what you want to do. We have missed you in the supper room.'

She lifted her chin. 'But I do not want anyone to know who I am. Who I am to you. I want to wear a mask, the same as before.'

'I'll let Cummings, MacEvoy, Belinda and anyone they might have told to keep mum about who you are.' He stroked her neck with his thumbs. 'Who you are to me.'

Suddenly he wished for nothing else but to share her bed and try again to please her with lovemaking.

When a masked Phillipa entered the supper room carrying her music, she expected nothing more than to sit at the pianoforte and play.

The room was unchanged from when she'd last been there, even though her life had gone topsy-turvy. Some of her regulars sat at their regular tables, Mr Anson and Mr Everard among them.

Anson rose when she entered the room. 'Miss Songstress! You are back!'

Others also rose and soon she was encircled by a throng of gentlemen, all asking questions of where she'd been. Had she been ill? Had she been in Brighton? On the Continent? Was she back to stay?

She laughed, more gratified by her reception than she wanted to admit. 'I am well. I was not ill. I was away, but I am back.'

She asked them about their lives in the past weeks. She was a bit sad to see Mr Everard here still. It meant that Lady Faville was also still here and that Everard was still pining for a woman who did not see he existed.

Phillipa knew all too well what it was like to be invisible.

As the wife of Xavier Campion, she would no more be overlooked. She would merely be talked about.

'What would you like me to play?' she asked her admirers.

They all wanted her to sing, which she did not mind, but it was her skill on the pianoforte that was the more important to her.

She sat and played and, as before, knew the instant Xavier appeared in the doorway. With him was the ever-present Lady Faville. They still made the perfect couple. How much more suited to each other were they than Phillipa was to Xavier. Xavier, though, walked away from Lady Faville and stood alone to watch Phillipa play. He did not stay long, but he had never stayed long when his duties lay primarily in the gaming room.

During her break Lady Faville approached her. 'Miss Songstress! I have missed you so! It has not been at all the same here without you.' She laughed charmingly. 'You can see I am still here, still making a cake of myself over dear Xavier. He is more comfortable with me now, I think, so I am progressing, I suppose.' She took a breath. 'But you must tell me all about where you have been. I do hope it has been for a romance!'

The beauty did not give Phillipa much of a chance to respond. 'I have been away, that is all. Now I am back.'

Lady Faville laughed again. 'Oh, so secretive. Yes. It must have been for romance. I hope soon to have a romance of my own to keep secret!'

What would Lady Faville think if she knew the object of her desires had married? She would find out, perhaps that very morning if she read the *Morning Post*. Phillipa could almost feel sorry for her.

'Well, I suppose I ought to return to the gaming room. Xavier will be wondering where I am, no doubt.' Lady Faville gave Phillipa her most beaming smile. 'Please do say I will see you again tomorrow?'

'I think so,' Phillipa managed before the lady turned and swept out of the room, all masculine eyes following her every move.

By the time the last card players finished their game, dawn's light was appearing in the sky. Daphne and three gentlemen who were obviously vying for her favour finally stacked the cards and scooped up their counters. The croupiers running the tables had already left and the only other person in the room was a very weary Mr Everard seated at a table near the door.

And Xavier.

She laughed her musical laugh and glanced his way. He stood, arms crossed over his chest, impatient to go upstairs.

And join his wife in bed.

Maybe this would be the last he'd see of Daphne. He could hope anyway. He'd done nothing to encourage her, but still she attended the Masquerade Club several nights a week with the poor, faithful Mr Everard in tow. Xavier had made it clear her interest in him would never be returned, but still she persisted. Flirting with other men in hopes that he would become jealous. Always at his side at some point in the night lest he forget her.

The other men left the room while she handed her counters to Everard. 'Will you turn these in for me? And have Cummings fetch my cloak?'

Of course Everard would.

And, of course, Daphne would linger, giving herself an opportunity to speak to him.

She came too close. 'I won tonight, is that not marvellous?'

She more often lost. 'Very good, Daphne. You are

the last to leave. Please do not dally. I am eager to go to bed.'

Her voice turned low and breathy. 'Why, Xavier, is that an invitation?'

His face grew hot. 'You know it is not. You waste your time here, Daphne. I have made that clear from the beginning. You've compromised your reputation for nothing, coming to this gaming house.'

'What we once had together cannot be changed.' She touched the lapel of his coat.

He pushed her hand away. 'It was nothing then and it is nothing now. It never will be.'

He walked out of the room, but waited on the other side of the doorway to close the door after she finally walked out.

She approached him again, putting her arms around his neck. 'Change your mind, Xavier. Come home with me.'

Mr Everard was waiting with her cloak. His features twisted in agony.

Xavier seized Daphne's wrists and peeled her off, not gently. 'Stop this, Daphne!'

She looked for a moment as if she would cry, but she collected herself and, instead, smiled brightly. 'Eventually you will stop being angry at me. I will be waiting right here.'

With any luck, in a few hours she would read the

Morning Post. Seeing the marriage announcement would convince her.

Daphne allowed Everard to place her cloak on her shoulders and escort her to the door. Cummings opened it and they left.

'Are they the last to go?' he asked Cummings.

The man nodded.

'Thank God.' He crossed the hall to the stairs. 'Do you and MacEvoy need me any further?'

'No.' Cummings gestured to the stairs. 'Go to your wife.'

Xavier grinned and clapped him on the back. 'With pleasure!'

He climbed the stairs with renewed energy and quietly opened the door to the bedchamber.

She would be in bed. Asleep, of course, and he would try not to disturb her, but he greatly wanted the comfort of her lovely body sleeping next to him. Once inside the room, his senses heightened as he caught sight of her, exactly where he expected, curled up on her side, her hair in a loose plait that he longed to take apart and wind through his fingers.

He washed his face and hands and brushed his teeth, trying to be as quiet as possible. It was a novel experience to be thinking of another's sleep instead of his own. He quite liked it. He quickly shed his clothing and laid it on a chair. Eager for her warmth, he climbed into bed, moving close to her. To his delight, she nestled against him and even though her nightdress prevented him from the glorious contact with her skin, he was content. He put his arm around her and, too tired for words, fell instantly to sleep.

A voice roused him from slumber. 'No, Mama. Wait for me, Mama. Wait for me.'

Phillipa was talking in her sleep. She sounded exactly as he remembered her sounding on that fateful day in Brighton.

She thrashed about. 'Mama! Mama!'

Should he wake her?

She cried out again, 'No!' and sat straight up in bed, blinking.

The dream had jolted her awake.

He sat up, too. 'You were having a dream.'

She peered at him as if puzzled to see him there. 'You slept with me?'

'Yes.' He wanted to touch her, but hesitated. 'We are married, remember.'

She could not meet his gaze. 'I just thought—' She waved a hand. 'Never mind what I thought.'

He could not resist. He reached over and swept some loose curls from her face. 'What was the dream?'

She lifted her hands to her head. 'It was as though

I was there again.' She stared into his eyes. 'Xavier.' Her voice was little more than a whisper. 'I—I remembered something.'

Chapter Sixteen

Xavier moved behind her and held her against him. 'Tell me what you remembered,' he murmured.

Her muscles tensed as she began to speak. 'I remembered following my mother all the way to the beach. It was getting dark and I was scared, too scared to go back alone. She was on the beach, arguing with a man.' She turned her head towards him. 'It was General Henson, I am sure of it.' She turned back. 'They were so angry. I pulled on my mother's skirts, but she did not heed me.' She paused. 'She ran after the man and then I woke up.'

His muscles tensed. 'Can you remember anything now.'

She grew still, as if trying to bring the memory back.

She shook her head. 'Nothing.'

She moved out of his arms and scooted around to

face him. Her gaze flickered over his bare chest and, to her credit, she did not turn missish.

She looked directly at him. 'I thought you would sleep in a different room.'

He was puzzled. 'Why?'

She lowered her gaze. 'This is not a love match.'

That was a sabre thrust. 'Maybe not, but I do want a real marriage. Children. All of it. Not separate beds and married in name only.' He lifted her chin to look at him. 'We will do well together as man and wife. Tell me you are willing to try.'

She covered her cheeks with her hands.

He pulled them away. 'I want you to be happy.'

She averted her gaze. 'You have done nothing to make me unhappy.'

He moved until she was forced to look at him again. 'Does my sleeping with you make you unhappy?'

'No.' She recovered more of her courage and looked at him again. 'I merely did not expect you would want such—such intimacy with me.'

He released her hands and stroked her hair. 'You must shake off this idea that I would not want you as a husband wants a wife, because, I assure you, I do.'

He leaned forwards and touched his lips to hers, but she was not so warm and willing as she'd been for that first kiss. Still, he'd accept the challenge of winning her over. He knelt in front of her, placing her between his knees so he could hold her close. He kissed her again, this time lingering on her lips. His body flared into response, all too visibly.

She trembled beneath his kiss and strained against his embrace.

He released her and backed slowly away. 'We have a lifetime to sort this out.'

She gazed at him with wide eyes, as if she had not expected either the kiss or his retreat.

Perhaps, later on, he could ask her what had made her withdraw from him. She had passion—their first lovemaking surely revealed that. It was not unlike what came out in her music. All he needed was to make her want to express that passion with him.

He rose from the bed and opened his trunk for clean linen. 'What would you like to do today?' He glanced back at her and caught her staring at him.

Yes. They would sort out the lovemaking. He was confident of it.

She quickly averted her gaze and rose from the bed herself. 'I would say play music, but since you rescued me from my mother's prison, I have quite refilled the well. Performing at the gaming house tonight will be sufficient for me.' She poured some clean water into the basin and washed her face.

'There is some place I would like to take you.' He turned away purposely so she could remove her nightdress without him watching. There would be time for watching eventually.

'I will be at your disposal, then,' she said.

'First thing,' he said, pulling on his pantaloons, 'we send for your maid and your trunk. I had hoped it would be here by today.'

'I expect my mother delayed it.' He heard her moving behind him. 'So that we would have to call upon her in order for it to be sent.'

'Then we must call upon her first thing.' He donned his shirt and dared a glance.

She was in her shift and corset, but was struggling with its laces. He strode over to her.

She allowed him to tighten them. 'I suppose we have no choice.'

He tied a bow. 'Shall I call upon her alone with a coach and Cummings? We could take your trunk by force, if necessary.'

She laughed. 'Surely you do not mean it.'

She stepped into her dress and put her arms through its sleeves.

'I do mean it.' The gown had buttons down the back. 'I'll call upon your mother, fetch your maid and your trunk and you may amuse yourself here. Play the pianoforte.' He glanced around. There was clothing and such scattered everywhere. 'Or pick up this room.'

She swung around. There were mere inches between them. 'I would scrub the chamberpots rather than call upon my mother today.'

Hardly words to provoke passion.

Undaunted, he leaned down, closer, his eyes fixed on her lovely pink lips. 'Play music,' he murmured. 'Leave the pots to the maids. In fact, leave this room to the maids. Play music.'

He forced himself to move away lest he seize her in his arms and take the kiss he so very much desired. The ease between them had returned and he had no wish to risk losing it again.

Their comfort with each other lasted through breakfast and Xavier saw Phillipa comfortably seated at her new pianoforte, now in the drawing room, before setting out to call upon Lady Westleigh.

He walked to Davies Street, telling Cummings to meet him there in a short time with a hackney coach.

The September day was chilly and damp and he quickened his pace to keep warm. When he reached the Westleigh town house, he sounded the knocker.

The butler answered the door, his quizzical look something more than expected.

'Mr Campion to see Lady Westleigh,' he told the man.

'Right away, sir,' the butler responded. 'You may wait in the drawing room.'

He gestured for Xavier to follow him, but instead Xavier said, 'I can find my way.'

The man nodded and started to climb the stairs. He stopped and turned back to Xavier. 'Begging your pardon, Mr Campion, but how fares your wife?'

Xavier grinned. 'She is very well. I will tell her you asked about her. Last I saw her she was playing her new pianoforte.'

The corners of the butler's mouth turned up for a fleeting moment. 'How very good, sir.'

Moments later Lady Westleigh swept into the drawing room. General Henson was right behind her. 'What is it, Xavier? Is something wrong?'

'Good day, my lady. General.' He bowed. 'Nothing is wrong. I am here to pick up Phillipa's trunk and to bring her maid to her.'

'Where is Phillipa?' Lady Westleigh asked. 'I wanted to speak with her.'

'To beg her forgiveness?' he asked.

Her eyes flashed. 'No. To tell her you should live here. Or with your parents. Until we find you rooms of your own.'

'Lady Westleigh.' His voice was firm. 'Stop managing. Release the trunk and the maid and let us go about our lives.'

'Watch your tongue, sir!' the general broke in.

Lady Westleigh motioned for him to be quiet. 'You cannot leave Phillipa to her own devices, Xavier,' she told him. 'She will simply closet herself away. You must make her mix in society. Limit her music—'

'Never.' His voice deepened and he leaned closer to her. 'I will never limit anything she wishes to do. Certainly not her music.' He stepped back. 'Now, if you please, summon her maid. My coach will be here very soon.'

She walked to the door and stepped out of the room to speak to the butler. 'Find Lacey and bring her to me,' Xavier heard her say.

The general took that moment to talk to him. 'Campion, I will not have this insolence towards Lady Westleigh. She does not deserve it. The welfare of her daughter has been her greatest concern, I promise you.'

Xavier straightened. 'Removing Phillipa's pianoforte was a terrible cruelty. It will take time for either one of us to forgive her that.'

'She meant it to be instructive.'

It had almost taken the life out of Phillipa.

Xavier met the man's gaze. 'Keep Lady Westleigh entertained, General. Keep her busy. Do not let her interfere. No more involving herself in what Phillipa does or does not do.'

Lady Westleigh re-entered the room. 'I will always involve myself with my children.'

'Not with Phillipa,' Xavier said. 'Not unless asked.' He made certain she knew he was speaking in all seriousness. 'No more interference or I will break my vow to you and tell what I've sworn never to tell.'

About Phillipa's accident.

Lady Westleigh blanched. 'You would not dare!'

He did not back down. 'I suggest you do not test my resolve.'

A few minutes later the maid appeared, her gaze sliding towards Xavier. 'Yes, m'lady?'

'Apparently my daughter wishes you to be her lady's maid, but I must tell you that it means living above a gaming house which is not at all respectable. You do not have to go if you do not wish it. You may stay here.'

The woman was attempting to manage the maid's life as well as her daughter's. And his.

'I do not mind living atop a gaming house,' the maid said.

Lady Westleigh took a breath. 'Very well. Pack my daughter's things, and yours, as quickly as you can. Mr Campion will take you there right now.'

'All is packed, m'lady,' the maid said. 'Since yesterday.'

The hackney coach arrived and Cummings and a footman carried Phillipa's and the maid's trunks out to the coach. The maid said quick goodbyes to the other servants and, in no time, they were on their way.

In the coach the maid looked tiny seated with the two men.

'It is Lacey, is it not?' Xavier asked her.

'Mary Lacey, sir,' the girl replied.

He introduced her to Cummings, who nodded.

'Lady Phillipa will be very glad to see you,' he told the girl.

'Yes, sir.' She blushed.

Phillipa heard the carriage pull up in front of the gaming house. She left the pianoforte and walked to the window. Xavier returned. With Lacey.

She hurried down the stairs and opened the door for them.

'M'lady!' Lacey cried, skipping to her.

'I am so very glad you decided to come.' Phillipa clasped her hand. 'Come in. I will show you around.'

'I cannot believe I'll be living in a gaming house!' the girl cried.

'It is just temporary, but I'm sure you will find it very comfortable.'

She introduced Lacey to MacEvoy, who bowed and looked very pleased to meet her. Xavier introduced both Phillipa and Lacey to the kitchen servants and the maid-of-all-work. They left Lacy to the disorder in the bedchamber and went out again.

'I almost forgot.' Phillipa pulled a note from her pocket. 'This came from your father.'

He stopped to read it. 'He says there is a small town house very near here that we might be able to let. Shall we go see it?'

'I am willing,' she said. 'But where else were you going to take me?'

He placed the note in a pocket. 'Let me surprise you.'

The leasing agent was not far and, after a surprised glance at Phillipa's scar, declared himself delighted to show the Earl of Piermont's son the town house.

'Tenants are few and far between this time of year,' the man said as he led them to a second-rate town house on Dover Street, directly across Piccadilly from St James's Street.

'The walk would be only a little more than a street,' Xavier remarked.

The agent unlocked the door. 'I am certain the interior will please you.'

The hall was unremarkable, but there was a comfortable study and a dining room behind it. The first floor had a nicely decorated drawing room, with plenty of space for a pianoforte, and a bedchamber behind.

One bedchamber with dressing rooms on each side.

There was another bedroom on the second floor and a maids' room with three beds. They descended the stairs again and examined the kitchen area and more servants' rooms.

She could be living here with Xavier, Phillipa thought. She would be in charge of the house, the meals, the servants.

'We can assist you in finding excellent servants, as well,' the agent said. 'There are several good people from whom to choose.' He smiled. 'Do you wish to take the house?'

Xavier looked to Phillipa.

She was to make the decision? 'It—it seems satisfactory.'

Xavier turned to the man. 'We will take it.'

They returned to the agent's office, signed the papers and received the keys.

'Shall I send some servants for you to interview, ma'am?' the agent asked.

This was all too sudden.

Xavier answered for her. 'Let us contact you about that tomorrow.'

By the time they walked out of the agent's office Phillipa's head was spinning. She walked numbly at Xavier's side, not even heeding where they were headed.

Xavier finally spoke. 'Please tell me you wanted that house, Phillipa.'

She slowed her pace. 'I assure you, it is all I could want.' She took a breath. 'I am simply dumbfounded. Two days ago I was completely under my mother's thumb. Now I am a married woman with a house to manage.'

He threaded her arm through his. 'I share your amazement. These are good changes, Phillipa. You must believe me.'

She wanted to assuage his concerns, but could not. 'I am too shaken by the changes to declare them good or bad.'

He pulled her closer. 'They will be good.'

They walked towards Piccadilly.

'Where do we go now?' she asked.

'To the hack stand,' he replied. 'To Cheapside.'

'Cheapside?' What could be there?

They walked to Piccadilly and Bolton Street, where the hackney cabs waited for passengers. They were immediately hailed by a familiar voice. 'Mr Campion! Over here.'

It was their hackney coach driver. He stood with his horses while they drank from buckets of water. The waterman waited nearby.

When the jarvey saw Phillipa, he pulled on his forelock. 'G'day to you, ma'am. Will you be wanting a ride today?'

Xavier opened the door of the coach. 'Take us to King Street in Cheapside.'

The waterman picked up the buckets and the driver climbed up to his seat. Xavier helped Phillipa into the carriage. She'd no sooner settled in their seat than the horses set off.

'Why do we go to Cheapside?' she asked. 'Are we to do some shopping?'

'You will see,' he answered cryptically.

The coach wended its way through streets filled with wagons, horses and other carriages, until it pulled up to a shop with a newly painted sign, Jeffers Cabinetry.

Why bring her here? He could not have known they would lease a house. Besides, that house already had all the furniture one could wish.

Phillipa and Xavier alighted and Xavier paid the jarvey.

'I can wait for you at the stand, if you like.' The

jarvey gestured to a place down the street where several hacks waited.

'Good of you,' Xavier said. He rejoined Phillipa.

'We are visiting a furniture shop?' A furniture shop was his surprise?

'We are indeed.' He reached for the door handle, but paused. 'Phillipa, I must tell you. This shop is run by one of the men who attacked us.'

She shrank back. 'No! Then why bring me here? Are you going to see to the man's arrest?'

'Not at all.' He turned the handle and held the door for her to enter.

The shop displayed a variety of wooden cabinets, tables and chairs, all of simple, unembellished but pleasing design. She could hardly heed them, however, wary at encountering a man who had attacked them in the street and attempted to rob them.

A shop clerk—not the man she feared—greeted them. 'May I be of assistance, sir?'

Xavier answered, 'I am here to see Jeffers. Tell him Mr Campion wishes to see him.'

The clerk's eyes widened. 'Mr Campion!' He snapped to attention. 'I will find him right away, sir.'

The clerk's reaction seemed very odd.

It took no time at all for this Jeffers to emerge from a doorway covered by a thick curtain. It was the man Xavier cut with her knife. It must be the man, because a scar remained, still red from recent healing. But rather than gaunt and menacing, this man wore a pleasant, welcoming expression. His pleasure at seeing Xavier was genuine.

'So good of you to come.' He shook Xavier's hand.

'I brought someone with me.' Xavier stepped aside so Jeffers could see Phillipa.

The man blanched. Even through the netting on her bonnet, he recognised her.

'Ma'am. Ma'am,' he entreated. 'I beg you to forgive me. It was a foolish act to accost you. I am heartily ashamed of my part in it.'

She stiffened, the anger from that night resurfacing. 'Why did you do it, then?'

Xavier interrupted. 'Phillipa, first allow me to present Mr Jeffers to you. Mr Jeffers, this is Lady Phillipa, my wife.'

The man bowed respectfully.

Xavier gestured to the doorway behind the clerk's counter. 'Let us go in the back. I would like my wife to see it.'

In the back, three men worked on building furniture. One put the finishing touches on a cabinet. Another worked on a chair. The third, a table.

Jeffers led them to a corner where a set of completed chairs and table stood, far enough away from the workers that they would not be overheard. 'Let me pour us some tea.'

Phillipa did not want to share tea with this man!

But Xavier held a chair for her and she had no choice but to sit. Jeffers took a water kettle from the fireplace and poured water into a teapot.

After he poured the tea into cups, he sat as well. 'I will answer your question now, m'lady. There was no good excuse for attacking you. It was wrong of me.'

'He was starving,' Xavier explained.

Jeffers lowered his head. 'That I was, ma'am, but, even so, I should not have done what I did. Not to you, not to anybody.'

'No, you should not,' she said curtly, not so willing to forgive him as Xavier had apparently done.

Jeffers nodded. 'I agree, ma'am. I do not deserve this opportunity Mr Campion has given me. I do not know what would have become of me if he had not found me that day.'

'Opportunity?' She did not understand.

'Mr Campion provided the money for this shop. We are just getting started, but we will make a success of it.' He gestured to the men at work. 'It has been manna from heaven to these men and to me. We had no work, but now—' He glanced around the room again. 'Look at us.'

* * *

Xavier tried to gauge Phillipa's reaction. Would she disdain him for running a shop? For helping Jeffers? Her face was too shrouded by her hat's netting for him to tell.

'They are all former soldiers,' he explained to her. 'Let go from their regiments and reduced to begging on the streets. Or worse.' Like Jeffers, turning to crime. 'I had money to invest. I thought why not make good use of it?' He might as well tell her all. 'I also have a candle maker.'

'And I've a line on an ironmonger, if you fancy an ironmonger's shop,' Jeffers said.

Xavier glanced to him. 'Excellent idea.'

She gaped at them both.

He faced her again and continued. 'I had the idea from the Burlington Arcade. I was tired of seeing so many soldiers begging on the street. Why not put them to work.'

'You did this to give men work?' Her voice sounded stunned.

'Never you fear, my lady,' Jeffers broke in. 'We will be paying Mr Campion back and then some. He will have a share of our profits, from now to for ever.'

He was a shopkeeper. Better for her to know it now. It would have been better still if he had told her before marrying her, but he'd wanted nothing to keep her from saying yes.

He waited for her to speak now.

She turned to Mr Jeffers. 'Did you make all the furniture in the front in this short space of time?'

Jeffers looked proud. 'We did our best. Cannot make money without goods to sell.'

'It is a remarkable feat,' she said.

Jeffers beamed. 'It is furniture for ordinary folk. That is who we expect to buy our cabinets.'

She stood. 'I spied a cabinet in the shop that interested me.'

She'd given no indication.

Jeffers popped out of his seat and led her back to the front of the shop. She pointed to a small commode, lacking the usual elaborate decoration.

'I quite like this piece,' she said. 'What is its price?'

'My lady.' Jeffers was near fawning. 'It is yours. We shall deliver it to you today.' He turned to Xavier. 'We found a soldier with a horse and cart to make our deliveries.'

'Deliver it to my residence.' He gave Jeffers the direction to the gaming house.

After the arrangements were made, they were back on the street, walking towards the coach stand.

Once back in the hack, Xavier could wait no longer.

'You needed to learn about the shops. About Jeffers.' He paused. 'It is not the sort of business a gentleman engages in, but soldiers needed jobs and I could create them. I'm not stopping with one or two. I'm determined to have several shops and to have them all succeed. They will make money, never fear.'

She turned to him and lifted her netting. 'I do not know anyone who would do what you did.'

'It begs for society's censure. I realise that.' He could point out that her family had invested in a gaming house. Were shops any worse? 'But no one knows, except you. And my solicitor. But not my parents. Not even Rhys.'

'Why did you tell me?' she asked.

'I could not withhold from you that I was in business with a man who had tried to rob us. Or that I'd turned shopkeeper.'

Her gaze turned even more intent. 'It is good you told me. I detest it when I am *protected* from the truth, as you well know. I would be unhappy indeed if you kept secrets from me like my family did.'

Except he was keeping one secret—what he knew about her accident, and was honour-bound not to tell.

Chapter Seventeen

They fell silent in the carriage. Phillipa pulled down her netting, but only so she could look at her husband without him knowing.

What sort of man would do what he'd done? Members of the *ton* looked down their noses at any man who ran a shop. *He smells of trade*, they would say.

But Xavier invested in shops for only one reason—to give unemployed soldiers decent jobs. He'd even saved Jeffers from a life of crime or a hangman's noose.

'Xavier.' Her voice came out low and husky.

He turned to her.

'I am glad you brought me to Cheapside.'

His features relaxed for a moment then tensed again. 'The shops will be successful, you will see.'

'I have no doubt,' she responded. 'Jeffers and the other men will work hard for you.'

He took her hand and brought it to his lips.

'There is just one thing,' she went on.

'What is it?' he asked.

She smiled. 'I believe my mother will have apoplexy if she discovers this!'

He laughed. 'My parents as well.'

She shook her head. 'You are wrong there. You could not displease your parents no matter what you did.'

The netting on her hat did not protect her from the intensity of his gaze. She felt as if he was searching to see if she really approved of his shops.

She did approve. In fact, her chest swelled with pride for him.

'Phillipa,' he whispered, lifting the netting away from her face and kissing her lips, a long, lingering, tongue-to-tongue kiss that made her body ache, a sweet ache that begged for more from him.

Before their first night together she would not have known what the yearning inside her meant. Now she knew she wanted him inside her, creating that sweet music with her.

He pulled her on to his lap and she felt his arousal. Did he want her?

He was under no obligation to make love to her at this moment.

She kissed him back to show him she intended to

please him the way a wife should—in bed, or in the cab of a hackney.

The excitement inside her surged and she plunged her fingers into his hair.

He groaned and cupped her breast, his hand driving her need to greater heights. She felt giddy and light-headed and lost to awareness of anything but him.

'I have an idea.' He broke away from her and opened the window to the jarvey. 'Take us to Dover Street.'

The coach turned right off of Piccadilly on to Dover Street and stopped.

'Here, sir?' the jarvey called through the window.

'Here will do,' Xavier replied.

He opened the door and helped Phillipa out.

'What is your idea?' Phillipa asked.

He raised a finger for her to wait and paid the jarvey.

'Thank you, Mr Campion,' the man responded enthusiastically.

He turned back to Phillipa and pulled something from his pocket.

The key to the house he'd leased.

She still did not understand. 'We are visiting the house again?'

He smiled. 'We are indeed.'

He unlocked the door and they entered the house.

As soon as he closed the door behind them and locked it again, he scooped her up in his arms.

'What are you doing?' she cried.

He gave her a quick kiss. 'Carrying you to our bed.'

Xavier's spirits soared as he carried her up the stairs to the bedchamber.

To the bed.

He turned the covers down and lay her on the bed linens, but she immediately sat up, untying the ribbons of her hat and pulling it off her head. She put her arms around him and kissed him with an energy that merely aroused him more.

When he had time to take a breath, he asked, 'How do you feel about making love to me in the daylight, in the afternoon? There is no one here to know. No one but you and me.'

She lowered her lashes. 'I am willing to try.'

He grinned. 'You never disappoint me, Phillipa.'

She glanced up at him as if surprised.

He was determined to convince her that he desired her. At the moment his desire was so strong he wanted to ravish her. He kissed her lips, her nose, her once-wounded cheek. 'May I love you, Phillipa?'

She nodded and returned his kisses, gently touching her lips to his mouth, his nose, his cheek, so innocently passionate it made even his heart ache for her.

He peeled off his coat and reached around her to untie her laces. As she wriggled out of her dress, he removed his waistcoat and untied his neckcloth. She spun around on the bed so that he could reach the strings of her corset. He untied the undergarment, loosened its laces and pulled it over her head. He threw off his shirt and undid the buttons of his pantaloons. Just in her shift, she watched him, her face flushed.

It was bold of her to watch him so brazenly. He felt a surge of pride in her because of it. He enjoyed her heated gaze as he stripped himself of his pantaloons and drawers and stood before her naked. And aroused.

Her eyes did not leave him as she lifted her shift and revealed herself to him. The afternoon light from the window made her skin glow. Her breasts were high and firm and her nipples a dark rose against skin, so smooth it begged for touching. She was lean, but not delicate, her waist narrow, but not tiny, her hips just full enough. He let his gaze wander over her, savouring her like one might savour a fine wine. His eyes lowered to the dark patch of hair between her legs.

He climbed up on the bed and took her in his arms, lifting her on top of him, luxuriating in the feel of those breasts, that skin.

His body urged him to lift her on to his erection and take her quickly, but he forced himself to a slower pace. He did not want to cheat her of her climax. She'd learned of that pleasure in their first lovemaking and he would not deprive her of it now. His pleasure alone was not enough. This time he was determined to show her what pleasure they could create together. He rolled her to his side and stroked her arms, her neck, and let his hand slip down to her breasts.

His palm scraped her nipple and she moaned with pleasure.

This was what he'd longed for between them all those nights when they'd been alone. He'd never truly compromised her, but it was not for want of desiring to. Now she was his wife. He could look forward to night after night like this. Making love. Sharing passion.

He slowly rubbed the tip of her nipple with palm of his hand until she trembled against him. Was there any sensation to compare? This intimate touch. This skin against bare skin.

His hand moved down her body until he fingered her most feminine place. Her legs parted for him and he circled his fingers, feeling her grow wet for him.

As before he slipped his fingers inside her, immediately relishing the sensation of warmth that greeted him. She writhed beneath him, covering his hand with hers as if she feared he would move his away.

No chance of that. He stroked her most sensitive spot, feeling her sensation build, greater and greater. He would show her. He could give her pleasure this way first and still bring her to climax with him inside her. He stroked with his fingers until her glorious spasm erupted.

'Xavier!' Her voice was half-question, half-demand.

He could wait no longer. He needed to be inside her.

'There is more, Phillipa,' he rasped.

'Show me,' she cried.

He rose above her, his erection rock-hard and demanding release, but he banked the urge, instead forcing himself to ease into her slowly. Her body was still unused to this and he wanted to spare her any pain or soreness.

Her hands flattened against his rear, pressing him against her, and her hips rose to meet him.

This was what it meant to be joined with her in marriage. Nothing would put them asunder, he would see to that. Nothing would stop them from making this a marriage even stronger than his parents'. He and Phillipa were meant for each other and had been since they were mere children.

A moment later those thoughts fled, all thought fled. His body moved faster, urgently plunging into her.

She kept pace with him, making it a physical kind of music with him that turned louder, stronger, and stronger still.

He felt her climax, a convulsion around him that drove him over the edge. His seed burst from him, long and gratifying.

He collapsed on top of her and moved to her side before his weight crushed her. He held her against him, never wanting to release her.

'Xavier,' she murmured.

'This is what it will be like for us,' he whispered to her before closing the distance between his lips and hers.

A little later they played the music again. Low and slow, but building to a frenzy of pleasure. He could have gone on to a third performance, but this was enough for one afternoon's interlude.

They had the rest of their married lives to complete the act.

Phillipa lay sated in his arms, her lids and limbs heavy, but her happiness danced upon the ceiling. Was it possible that this was what married life would be like? Could their nights be like this? Their afternoons?

He had desired her in this way. They'd created pleasure together. It was a good place to start making a real marriage.

He grinned at her. 'We have had quite a day, Mrs Campion.'

She sighed. 'Quite a few days.'

Her female parts still throbbed with pleasure. She wondered if they'd created a baby this afternoon. How wonderful that would be! She'd never dreamed she'd have babies of her own, but, because of Xavier, she could dream of it now.

She pressed her hand against her abdomen.

With Xavier anything seemed possible.

They sat propped up against the pillows. 'This is an adequate bedchamber, do you not think?'

A thrill rushed through her. This was *her* bedchamber. They would share their nights together here. 'I think it is a lovely room.'

'We should move in here as soon as possible,' he said.

They talked about hiring servants, how many they would need, agreeing on as few as possible to start.

'I'll contact the agent tomorrow,' he said. 'We can set up the interviews for the next day and perhaps be in this house in three days' time.'

She laughed. 'Will my head never stop spinning?'

He hugged her. 'First thing we move in is your pianoforte.'

Events might still resemble a whirlwind, but one thing was certain. She felt easy with him again. She could say whatever she wished to him and he would always be open with her.

'I have no need of living extravagantly,' she said, confident he would understand. 'In fact, I prefer to live quietly.'

He frowned. 'Do not hide yourself away entirely, Phillipa.'

She dreaded the thought of attending a ball or musicale with him. She could almost hear the talk. *He is so handsome, why did he marry her?*

He hugged her. 'And we must do something for your music. We must see about publishing some of your songs.'

'Do you think they are good enough?' She knew he would tell her the truth.

'To me they seem as good as the other songs you perform,' he replied. 'Some are better.'

She felt a rush of pride and delight.

Perhaps he had been correct. Even though he'd been honour-bound to marry her, perhaps they could be happy together. She loved him and perhaps in his way he loved her, too.

She snuggled against his bare chest and marvelled

at the feel of the rough hairs peppering his skin and of the hard muscles beneath.

She had always loved him.

The marred and imperfect Phillipa Westleigh was in love with Xavier Campion, the perfect man.

Chapter Eighteen

It was near the dinner hour when they returned to the Masquerade Club. To Xavier it seemed as if they'd been gone for weeks.

So much had changed between them.

Cummings and MacEvoy did not mark their absence as anything extraordinary, though. Even Phillipa's lady's maid had kept herself busy organising the bedchamber and sorting out their clothes. She'd already put to use the commode that had been delivered from Jeffers's shop.

Perhaps their absence had only been remarkable to the two of them.

Xavier felt altered. Not only was he becalmed as only sexual satiety could accomplish, but he felt hopeful and content. He'd made Phillipa happy today.

He wanted to make her happy every day.

* * *

By the time he and Phillipa had changed out of their clothes into their evening attire, dinner was ready and was shared in the comfortable camaraderie they'd engaged in since making love. After dinner they sat in the drawing room. He sipped some brandy and listened to her play her pianoforte, the one that would soon be moved to their own house.

It astonished him how comfortable the time was spent in this manner, as if they had always shared a life together.

When the time came, he left her to attend to the gaming house. Patrons had begun to trickle in, even as the croupiers were still setting up. Because the announcement of his marriage to Phillipa had appeared in the *Morning Post* that morning, he made certain the rest of the gaming-house staff knew of it.

As Phillipa had requested, he did not tell them his wife was the masked lady who played the pianoforte and sang in the supper room. It was a fortunate thing they were soon to be in their own lodgings, because the staff would soon figure out that secret.

He made his rounds, talking with each of the croupiers and receiving their good wishes. He liked that Rhys paid them well and treated them better.

He did not mind running the gaming house now in Rhys's absence. Not now that Phillipa was back. When Rhys returned, though, Xavier wanted to pull back. He'd relish spending his nights with his wife and he wanted to take her to the opera and to concerts. He even wanted to dance with her again at a ball.

'Campion!' Anson, one of the patrons, approached him. 'You devil. I read your announcement in the paper.'

Xavier braced himself. Many of the patrons would have read the *Morning Post*.

'Bit of an epidemic here, is it not?' Anson went on. 'First Rhysdale, now you.'

'We are both lucky men,' Xavier responded.

Anson laughed. 'Except Rhysdale's off on a bride trip and you are stuck here.'

Xavier smiled. 'There is that.'

Anson leaned towards him conspiratorially. 'I wonder how Lady Faville will take this news.'

It was too much to expect that others had not noticed Daphne's single-minded obsession with him.

'I must say,' the man continued, 'I always thought she would be the one to get you in the parson's mousetrap. I am certain she always thought so, too.'

'I always made it clear to her that would never happen.' That sounded harsh, but it was the truth.

Another patron came up to them. 'Campion! Leg-shackled, are you? The Earl of Westleigh's daughter? What a coincidence, eh? The man who cheated his own son here.'

'We have known each other for many years,' Xavier explained.

The man gestured to his own face. 'Isn't she the disfigured one? Scarred on the face? Can't imagine a man like you with her.'

Xavier's eyes flashed. 'Why not?'

The man stuttered, 'D-d-don't know why. Just didn't.' He made a hasty exit.

Anson spoke. 'Damned idiot.'

'Indeed.' Xavier had nearly put his fist in the man's face.

'Expect you will hear that sort of thing more than once tonight.' Anson sounded genuinely sympathetic. He poked Xavier with his elbow. 'Take care. Here is Lady Faville.'

Daphne paused in the doorway only long enough to find Xavier in the room. She marched on him like a column of Napoleon's soldiers.

'Xavier, I would speak with you alone, please.' She sounded near tears.

'I am working, Daphne.' He did not wish to speak with her at all.

'I said alone, *please.*' She glared at Anson.

Anson, thank God, showed no inclination to move away.

Xavier also did not budge. 'Say what you have to say here.'

She sent another scathing look towards Anson before riveting her gaze on Xavier. 'Tell me that foolish wedding announcement in the *Morning Post* was a hoax.'

'I placed it myself,' he told her. 'I am married to Lady Phillipa Westleigh.'

'It cannot be!' Her voice rose. 'She is an ugly old thing! A recluse.'

Xavier glared down at her. 'Daphne, you are speaking of my wife.'

She waved her hand as if to shoo away his words. 'You cannot mean to defend her! Did she trap you? Did you need money? You should have told me. I have money! I have lots of money!'

'I need money,' Lord Anson said.

She tossed Anson another withering glance and turned back to Xavier. 'I cannot bear this. I cannot. You led me to believe—'

He held up a hand. 'I led you to believe nothing. I have been honest with you from the first night you appeared here. You simply chose not to listen to me.'

'You were not serious,' she countered. 'We were in love.'

'We were not in love, Daphne!' he snapped.

She went on as if he had not spoken. 'You should

have told me you were about to be married! I would have helped you.'

'You are speaking nonsense now.'

She fell against his chest. 'I am desolate.'

He seized her wrists. 'Enough, Daphne. Stop making a fool of yourself. Calm yourself or I'll be forced to have Cummings remove you.'

She immediately stilled. He released her and walked away.

After Xavier left, Phillipa sat at the pianoforte and tried to recreate the rhythm of their lovemaking. She played the lower keys, starting slow, then increasing the tempo. It wasn't quite right, but it replayed it in her head, as well as her time with Xavier replayed in her head.

When she looked up at the clock on the mantel it was almost her usual time to appear in the supper room. She hurried to get ready, tying the ribbons of her mask last thing. Before she descended the stairs, she watched from the second floor to be certain no one would see her coming from the private rooms. The hallway below her was empty so she hurried down the stairs, stopping a moment to compose herself before entering the supper room.

Upon seeing her, several of the gentlemen stood. 'Miss Songstress, you are here again!'

Several of them walked over to her, greeting her warmly and making requests of specific musical pieces she had played before.

Two of the pieces were her own works, which made her smile.

'Please sit, gentlemen,' she said. 'Give me time to prepare.'

'Did you read in the *Morning Post* that Campion is married?' one of the gentlemen asked.

'I knew of it,' she said quietly.

She sat on the bench and put her music in order, but bits of conversation from the tables reached her ears—*Campion married...Lord Westleigh's girl... scarred.*

Lady Faville flounced up to her. 'Miss Songstress, I am in such need of a friend!' She sounded greatly distressed. 'Do you know what has happened?'

'What?' Phillipa just wanted to play her music and wait for Xavier.

'He is married!' Lady Faville's voice cracked. 'Xavier is married. What am I to do?'

'I do not know.' At least the woman did not know it was Miss Songstress who had married him.

'He is married to Lady Phillipa Westleigh and I am certain he is made unhappy over it.'

Phillipa tensed. 'Why are you certain he is unhappy?'

The lady blinked. 'Of course, you would not know. Lady Phillipa is a monster.'

Phillipa felt her face flush. 'A monster?'

Lady Faville nodded vigorously, her artful blond curls bobbing prettily. 'I should say she looks a monster. She has a horrible scar that distorts her face.'

Phillipa's hand rose. She stopped herself before touching her face. 'Have you seen her?' She did not recall ever having met Lady Faville before the Masquerade Club.

'Once. I saw her in a shop. I asked who was the deformed creature looking through the music sheets.' Lady Faville lowered herself to the bench right next to Phillipa. 'How could he have chosen to marry her? He must have been forced.'

Had he been forced? Forced by honour. By her mother? Had he preferred Lady Faville? The optimism Phillipa felt moments ago crashed to the floor and shattered.

She turned back to her music. 'My lady, I am sorry for your disappointment, but I must play the music now.'

Lady Faville squeezed her hand affectionately. 'I will leave you, then, but I know you will find out the reason he married, will you not? I am depending upon you.'

The lady rose and walked off before Phillipa could refuse.

Phillipa's hands shook as she placed her fingers on the keys. Instead of the rousing tune she'd planned to play to open her performance, she began to play Beethoven's *Moonlight Sonata*. Though she'd intended it to calm her nerves, the underlying emotion in the piece merely unsettled her more.

She transitioned to a gavotte by Hook.

Lady Faville eventually left the supper room. She'd taken Mr Everard with her, so Phillipa could only think the lady had left the gaming house as well. That was some relief.

She'd left her words behind her.

It seemed the supper room remained abuzz with news of Xavier's marriage. She overheard it over and over. He could have had any woman. Why marry her, scarred as she was? Such a marriage was destined to be notorious, they said. It would be forever talked about.

She played through her usual time for a break, because she needed the music to ease her spirit and also because she had no wish to hear more about the marriage of handsome, eligible Xavier Campion to the scarred spinster daughter of a dissolute earl.

By the end, her music calmed her and the applause gratified her and she'd reassured herself that her marriage would not be forever talked about. It might remain notorious, but people would tire of it and go on to gossip about other things. At least, wearing a mask, she'd not been required to endure the inevitable stares. People who'd forever tried not to look at her would now wish to examine her to see why Xavier could possibly pick her for a wife.

She curtsied to the patrons and stacked her music to take upstairs with her. As she walked through the supper room, several gentlemen stopped her to compliment her on her play. In those first days of performing in the supper room she'd enjoyed such attention. This night she merely wished to make her escape and return to the bedchamber above. Lacey would assist her in dressing for bed and afterwards Phillipa would wait for Xavier.

She finally reached the hallway, but needed to wait for it to clear.

When she finally thought she might make it to the upper floor unseen, she heard hurried footsteps on the stairs below. Lady Faville appeared, rushing up to her.

The lady was all smiles. 'There you are! I knew I would find you still here.' She laughed. 'Xavier is still here and he escorts you home, does he not?'

'Not always,' Phillipa said stiffly.

If Lady Faville noticed that Xavier did not leave

the gaming house, she might have a clue that Phillipa had not left either.

'I have to leave,' Lady Faville said. 'I wanted to find you. I wanted to tell you that I arranged for Xavier to meet me tomorrow! Is that not grand?' She danced with excitement. 'I must give up the notion of marriage, of course, but marriages are not love, are they? Love can never be extinguished.' She made a dramatic transition from giddiness to tragic solemnity. 'If the only way we can be together is as lovers, then so be it.' She hugged Phillipa. 'Goodnight, then, my dear Miss Songstress. Tomorrow night I will tell you all about my tryst with Xavier!'

Lady Faville released Phillipa so quickly she pushed against her and Phillipa, standing right at the top of the stairs, almost lost her balance. She grabbed for the railing to keep from falling. Lady Faville did not even notice. In a flurry of skirts, she hurried down the stairs and out of sight.

Shaken again, Phillipa's vision grew dark and she smelled the briny scent of the sea. The scene changed and she was no longer at the top of the gaming-house stairs. She was running up the stone stairs of the sea wall.

Until someone turned and pushed her and her hand found nothing to grip.

Chapter Nineteen

When the gaming room thinned to only a few patrons, Xavier asked Cummings and MacEvoy to take care of things and to tend to the closing up.

'Eager to get to bed, then,' grinned MacEvoy.

'Very eager,' admitted Xavier.

In his good humour, he did not even care that MacEvoy's comment was a bit too familiar. He wanted to bound up the stairs, but took them at a sedate pace, which probably did not fool the clerk.

He opened the bedchamber door quietly. There was still a lamp burning, but Phillipa was in bed and did not move, even with the sound of the door closing.

He paused to look at her, sleeping on her side, curled up like a girl. She lay on the scarred side of her face and it gave him an idea of how she might have appeared had she never been injured.

She was beautiful to him, even with her scar, and

she looked so innocent and peaceful, he did not have the heart to wake her.

He hurried to ready himself for bed, trying to be as quiet as he could be. Like the night before, he must content himself with sleeping next to her and waking in the morning with her at his side.

He extinguished the lamp and climbed into bed. In the dim light from the fireplace, he watched her sleep and remembered how it felt to make love to her.

He brushed a curl from her face and her eyes opened.

'You are here.' Her voice was husky from sleep.

He pulled her into his arms and kissed her. Sleep made her pliable in his arms, but also gave her an expression of melancholy. He knew what that felt like, too tired to smile. He promised not to tax her, he would be content to merely hold her, but he wanted the warmth of her skin against his.

She stirred in his arms, urging him on top of her.

She wanted him? He was delighted to indulge her.

She opened to him and he eased inside her, joining himself to her again. He moved slowly, unhurried now, relishing the feel of being inside her. He felt the moment she became aroused by him, how it changed her, woke her to move with him.

This sense of melancholy lingered, although it made making love to her even more poignant. Whatever its cause, even mere sleepiness, he wished to free her of it with his body. Perhaps through his love-making he could erase all the pain inside her. From her scars. From her abominable family. From every-one and everything that had ever hurt her.

He was willing to try. More than willing to try.

He'd had his share of bedding women. Not as many as some might suspect, but he'd had some very erotic moments with some of them, starting with the days of his youth. Those women had taken what they wanted from him.

Phillipa was the first woman he'd wanted to give everything to. He wanted to convince her she was worthy of the love he felt toward her.

The sensation intensified and their pace quickened. This time, he did not lead her, but rather took his cues from her, responding to her every move.

With my body I thee worship. Was that not part of his wedding vow?

That was what he aspired to in this moment. He worshipped her with his body and hoped, in the end, she would feel adored.

But with the next thrust, her next rising against him, arousal took over and pushed him past the time of stopping or slowing. He rushed past the time of thinking. His need took over. It drove him into her, again and again, faster and faster, until the tortuous peak was reached and he convulsed inside her.

When he pressed against her in that final release of his seed, she cried out and he felt her reach her peak a moment after his.

As they both crashed down from that heaven, he held her tightly. He never wanted to let her go.

He loved her. He'd loved her when she was a child, but then it was as a brother loves a sister, a friend loves a friend, but from that evening before he'd been called back to war when he'd danced with her at a ball, he'd loved her as a man loves a woman.

Some day he would tell her this. Some day when she would believe him.

She mumbled something he could not understand.

'What did you say?' He wanted to add *my love*, but feared she would not yet believe even that endearment.

She answered him, only a little more clearly. 'Lady Faville.'

Daphne? Why the devil would she ask about Daphne? 'What about her?'

'Will see you tomorrow.'

He made a disparaging sound. 'Undoubtedly.' Would he ever convince Daphne to give up her fixation on him? She was a poison he and Phillipa did not need.

'Forget about Lady Faville,' he told her.

'Can't forget.' She sounded as if she were drifting to sleep. She mumbled something else. He caught one word only when she repeated it.

'Pushed,' she said. 'Pushed.'

When Phillipa woke the next morning, Xavier was leaning down to give her a kiss. He was fully dressed.

'I have to help MacEvoy,' he told her. 'Some problem with the figures. We need to work it out with the bank. Do not fear, I'll stop by the agent's on my way back and arrange for the servant interviews.'

'You are going to the bank?' Her mind was not yet clear. 'Only the bank?'

'One or two other errands, as well,' he said cryptically. 'I'll be back in a couple of hours, if all goes well. If not, it might be later.'

He kissed her a second time and was gone.

She lay back down in the bed. She remembered that he made love to her. It had been like a dream, all soft edges like sad music played pianissimo. She remembered asking him about Lady Faville. Had he answered her? She could not remember.

Was meeting Lady Faville one of Xavier's errands?

Phillipa suddenly could not tolerate another moment in bed, a bed still filled with the scent of him. She rose and summoned Lacey to help her dress.

While Lacey chatted with her, Phillipa's mind whirled. Was he meeting Lady Faville?

He was honest with her, even when no one else would be, but would he tell her if he were arranging a romantic tryst? What man would?

No. She could not believe it of him. She could not believe he would make love to her at night and plan to see another woman in the day. That was the sort of thing her father would do to her mother. Xavier was honest and honourable, not at all like her father.

As Lacey finished arranging her hair, her doubts still nagged at her, but something else waited inside her like unplayed notes.

When she was finished dressing and walked out of the room to the top of the stairs, she remembered. She gripped the railing.

She remembered being pushed. She remembered being pushed away by Lady Faville. She remembered being pushed away on a sea wall in Brighton.

She hurried down the stairs. Could she still catch Xavier? She had to tell him. She remembered. After all this time, she remembered what had happened at Brighton.

Cummings was attending the hall.

'Is Xavier still here?' she asked.

'No,' Cummings answered. 'Went out.'

'How long ago?' Maybe she could catch up to him.

'Quarter-hour.'

That was too long of a head start. 'Did he say where he was going?'

'Bank.'

That was consistent. She could try to catch up to him at the bank—

No, that was ridiculous. She did not have to chase him all over London. She could just as easily tell him when he returned.

She glanced at the stairway and the memory again flashed through her mind.

In fact, there was something she could do first, before telling him.

'Cummings, I must go out, too. If Mr Campion returns before I do, tell him I am calling on my mother. I will not be long.'

Phillipa walked alone to her mother's house, remembering the nights that she and Xavier had walked the same route in darkness. So much had happened since then.

She passed Brunton Mews, where they'd been attacked. This time she smiled, thinking how Xavier had made something good out of the horrible experience, the experience that also jarred loose Phillipa's memories. And now she knew more of what had happened.

Today, she hoped, she could put it all to rest.

She reached the familiar door on Davies Street and sounded the knocker.

Mason answered. 'My lady!' His unguarded pleasure at seeing her quickly changed to concern. 'Is anything amiss?'

She stepped inside. 'Nothing at all,' she told him, pounding those niggling doubts. 'I wish to see my mother. Is she at home?'

'She is in her sitting room,' he told her. 'With the general.'

'Of course.' She smiled. 'No need to announce me. I'll just go on up.'

She climbed the stairs and rapped on her mother's sitting room door.

'Come in.' Her mother's voice.

She entered. 'Hello, Mama.'

Her mother's face brightened and she rose. 'Phillipa!' Her eyes narrowed in suspicion. 'What are you doing here?'

'I wished to speak with you.'

The general had been seated near her mother. He stood.

'Good day, General,' she said. 'I am glad to see you here.'

Both he and her mother looked surprised at her words.

He glanced from her to her mother. 'Shall I leave you alone, my dear?'

'No, stay,' Phillipa said to him.

He was part of the memory.

Her mother sat again. 'I will not hear you complain of your marriage. What is done is done.'

'It is not about my marriage.' She sat.

'What is it then? A social call?' Her mother's tone turned sarcastic.

'No.' She took off her hat. 'I want to talk with you about this.' She touched her scar.

Her mother dipped her head and looked concerned. 'What do you mean?'

'I mean about how it happened.'

'You know how it happened.' Her mother spoke by rote. 'You went to the beach alone and you fell from the steps of the sea wall.'

'That is what you told me all these years, Mama. But it is not what happened.'

Her mother and the general exchanged worried glances.

Phillipa went on. 'I followed *you* to the seaside that evening, Mama.' She turned to General Henson. 'You were there, too. You were quarrelling with each other. The general strode away and, Mama, you ran after him.' She paused. 'I ran after you.'

Her mother gripped one hand with the other.

Phillipa trembled. 'I ran up the steps, trying to catch you, but you turned and shoved me.'

A gasp escaped her mother's lips. 'I will throttle him,' she muttered.

'You pushed me away, Mama,' Phillipa repeated. 'And I lost my balance and fell down the stairs. How could you keep such a thing secret from me?' Her mother opened her mouth to speak, but Phillipa stopped her. 'And do not dare tell me it was for my own protection.'

'Of course it was to protect you,' her mother snapped.

'She did not mean for you to be hurt,' the general added. 'It was an accident.'

'You were little and you did not remember,' her mother cried. 'Why would I tell you such a thing?'

'You could have told me when I got older,' Phillipa countered. 'You could have told me when I asked a few weeks ago. I wanted the truth, Mama.'

'It was more complicated than that,' her mother insisted.

'Were you afraid the story would become gossip? Were you afraid your friends would know you pushed your daughter down the steps?' Phillipa went on. 'Perhaps you were not protecting me, but protecting yourself.'

'She was protecting me,' the general broke in.

'She did not want her husband to find out she was with me.'

Phillipa's mother stood and waved her hands in front of her as if to make them both stop. 'It was neither of those things! You were such a beautiful child and I had disfigured you for life! Did you think I would want you to know it? To hate me for ever? I was your mother. Goodness knows you had no father to speak of. You needed me. I could not have you thinking I could hurt you like that.'

Phillipa was struck at the intensity of her mother's emotions.

The general shot to his feet and put his arm around her. He coaxed her mother back to sitting.

She dabbed at her eyes with a handkerchief. 'It was best you went on thinking you fell, that it was just something that happened to you. I tried very hard not to let you think it would mar your chances in life, but you just had to look in your mirror to know it.' She shuddered. 'You were never going to find your rightful place in life. All because of what I'd done. You would never forgive me.'

Phillipa lowered her voice. 'Mama, I could always forgive what was an accident. What I cannot forgive is how you have kept the truth from me. About this. About our financial problems. About what my father did. About the gaming house. And Rhysdale! I had a brother. You all knew I had a brother and you did not tell me.'

Her mother pursed her lips. 'You had enough burdens. You did not have to know of all the other horrible things.'

'She did it to make life easier for you,' the general said.

'I did not need to have life made easier for me,' Phillipa insisted. 'I have always been strong. As strong as my brothers. I did not need to be treated differently.'

'But you were different,' her mother said. 'You were damaged. And it was my fault! I made it up to you as best I could.'

'My face was damaged, Mama, not me.' Phillipa stood. 'And if making it up to me meant keeping secrets from me and manipulating my life, it has to stop. Do you hear me?'

Her mother glared defiantly.

Phillipa took a breath. It was too much to expect a simple apology from her mother, a simple acknowledgement that her mother had wronged her. It must be enough that the truth was out. Finally.

She picked up her hat and curtsied to her mother. 'That is all I came to say. I will take my leave.'

The general walked ahead of her to reach the door first.

When he opened it and Phillipa put one foot on the threshold, her mother's critical tone returned. 'Tell that husband of yours I wish to see him. I will have words with him.'

Phillipa turned. 'You wish to talk to Xavier? About what?'

Her mother blinked rapidly. 'About this.'

'What about this?' There was more her mother was not telling her.

Her mother gave her a haughty look. 'I wish to tell your husband he is a dishonourable wretch. He had the gall to reveal what he promised to keep secret.'

'Keep secret?' She was confused. 'What did he promise to keep secret?'

'Bad business,' added the general. 'Not at all the thing to break a solemn vow.'

'What solemn vow?' Her voice rose.

'Come now.' Her mother huffed. 'Did he not tell you that he swore he would never tell what he saw that day? I suppose he didn't include that piece of it.' She jabbed the air with her finger. 'Why he renewed that promise just yesterday! That goes to show how much he can be trusted. What does he do? Say one thing, then hurry up to do the other?'

'What he saw?' she repeated, still unable to believe the words. 'He saw what happened?'

'Sneaking around in the dark,' muttered the general. 'Spying on people. Had no business doing that either.'

Xavier had been there that day?

'Well, do not believe a word he says. That is my advice to you.' Her mother picked up her needlework, apparently considering the conversation closed. She glanced to the general. 'It is a rare man you can trust.'

Phillipa strode back to her mother. 'If ever you tell me the truth, I beg you do so now. Was Xavier there that day? Did he see my accident?'

Her mother looked annoyed. 'Do not act the fool, Phillipa. You know he was there. How else could you know what happened? You were blessed with no memory of it. God knows why he was not at home. A boy his age should have been, instead of spying on people in the dark. He was old enough to know about vowing to keep something secret, though.'

Phillipa trembled inside, but she forced herself to speak. 'He did not break his vow to you,' she said, because that was the truth. 'I remembered what happened.'

Phillipa walked out of the room without another word. If her mother or the general said more to her, she could not even hear it. She numbly made her way to the stairs and paused, holding on to the railing for support.

Xavier had been there the day of her accident.

He had seen what happened to her and, with all her struggles and fears about the memories bombarding her, he had said nothing to her. Because of some promise he made as a boy? Surely that did not count over what she had suffered? She'd thought herself insane because of the visions.

Mason was not in the hall. Or if he was, she did not see him. She let herself out, her mother's words ringing in her ears. *Do not believe a word he says.*

Chapter Twenty

Xavier hurried the last few steps to the gaming house. MacEvoy had gone on ahead while he stopped at the agent's office to arrange for the servant interviews. From there he'd made a quick trip to Cheapside to check on the candle shop. The candle maker told him a space had come available that would work for the ironmonger, so Xavier told the man to arrange for him to meet the landlord and ironmonger at the space. Perhaps that shop would be started soon as well.

Three shops. It was a good beginning, but there was always more he could do.

Xavier was finally free the rest of the day, such as it was. He was eager to get home to his wife and tell her what he'd accomplished.

Perhaps they might visit their new house again for an hour or two of lovemaking? He grinned and raised his face to the September sun before knocking on the town house door.

Cummings opened it for him.

'Thank you, Cummings,' he said in good spirits. 'How do you fare today?'

Cummings merely shrugged, but he also pointed to the hall table. 'A note came.'

Xavier picked it up and unfolded it.

The signature jumped out at him—*Yours, always, Daphne.*

He certainly had no interest in whatever she had written. He folded the note and climbed the stairs to the drawing room where he assumed he'd find Phillipa.

She was not there.

He looked in the bedchamber. The curtains were drawn and no lamps were lit. Where was she? He was about to leave the room when he spied Phillipa deep in the recesses of a wingback chair.

'Phillipa.' He dropped the note on a nearby table and walked over to her. Leaning down to kiss her on her forehead, he allowed his lips to linger a moment. 'Why are you sitting in the dark?'

'I was waiting for you.' Her voice was low and without tone.

'I hope not long.' He stepped over to the windows. 'Do you mind if I open the curtains?'

'No,' was all she said.

He tied back the curtains and the room flooded with light. He turned back to her.

She looked pale, so pale her scar shone more prominently.

'Are you unwell?' He crouched to her level and took her hands in his.

Her hands were cold.

She pulled them away and met his eyes. 'I called upon my mother today.'

He braced himself to hear of another cruelty her mother had inflicted upon her.

Her gaze drifted away and back. 'I remembered something. I remembered what happened in Brighton. How I fell. My mother pushed me down the steps.'

Yes. He could see it all again. Little Phillipa running after her mother who wanted only to catch up to the general. Xavier knew he should stop her from running up the slippery steps, but he stayed where he was while her small legs worked hard to climb after her mother. Phillipa grabbed at her mother's skirts. Her mother whirled around and pushed her away.

He felt the horror again of seeing little Phillipa fall down the stone steps and land hard on the rocky beach below. He was the first to reach her. He saw the blood pooling under her cheek.

Phillipa spoke and he jolted back to the present. 'You were there, Xavier. My mother said you were there. She accused you of telling me what happened.'

He nodded. 'I was there.' He had no need to hide it now.

She leaned forwards. 'Why did you not tell me?' Her voice shook with anger. 'Why did you not tell me when you knew the memories were returning?'

His excuse seemed weak. 'I had sworn not to.'

'You were a boy. Why was a boy's promise more important than me? I thought I was going insane. Remember?' She choked. 'You knew how it shook me. The memories. The not knowing.'

'I wanted to tell you.' But honour was honour. A promise was a promise, no matter what age it was made. 'I gave my word not to.'

'I despise being *protected* from the truth,' she said hotly. 'You, more than anyone else, knew that.'

He stood. 'I told you as much as I could, Phillipa.'

'I thought about this,' she went on. 'You've kept other secrets. Like about meeting Jeffers and helping him.'

'I told you,' he protested.

'Not when it happened. Only after we married.' She rose from the chair.

'Did it make a difference to you?' His temper was flaring. He was honest with her. When he could be.

Not when he'd given his word. 'Yesterday you did not mind me owning shops.'

'I do not mind it,' she shot back. 'I mind that you did not tell me when you first encountered him again.'

'I thought it would upset you,' he admitted.

'You wished to protect me.' She crossed her arms over her chest.

'No,' he answered. 'Yes. Yes. I wished to protect you from thinking of that night. At least until I knew what use he would make of the opportunity.'

'What else are you keeping from me?' she challenged.

'Nothing.' At least he could think of nothing. Only the events of the morning, which he'd not had a chance to mention. And some things that happened in war about which no soldier spoke.

'Nothing?' She lifted her chin. 'What about Lady Faville?'

'Lady Faville?' He forced an even tone. 'She is not important enough to speak of. If you wish to know my connection to her in the past, I will tell you, but I assure you, it is of no consequence to me now.'

'Are you not going to call upon her today?' Her voice wobbled.

He spoke through gritted teeth. 'She is the last person I would call upon.'

'You planned a meeting with her today. She told me.'

Leave it to Daphne to cause trouble. 'I planned nothing with her.'

Phillipa looked more wounded than angry. 'Do not tell me she means nothing to you. I've seen her with you so often here at the gaming house. She is always on your arm—'

'Not by my choice.'

She took in a shuddering breath. 'She believes you were trapped into marriage with me. She believes you still love her as you once loved her.'

He looked her directly in the eye. 'I never loved her.'

She turned away.

He seized her and made her look at him again. 'Phillipa, I care nothing for her.'

She glanced to the note on the table. 'I was in the hall when the messenger arrived. I took that note from him. I read it and gave it to Cummings to give to you.'

He felt the blood drain from his face. 'Good God, what did it say, Phillipa? I did not read it.'

'She says she will see you today as planned.'

He released her and ran a hand through his hair. 'This is madness. Why would you believe her and not me?'

She avoided looking at him. 'Because what she says makes sense. It makes sense that you would fall in love with her. You must admit that you would have never married me if it had not been for my mother's manipulations.'

'I will not admit that, Phillipa.' She'd refused to be convinced.

She pointed to the mirror. 'Look at yourself. You are so handsome, and she is so beautiful...' She lifted her hand to her face and covered her scar. 'I am not.'

His stomach suddenly felt as if filled with lead shot.

He turned away from her and walked to the window to compose himself. He heard her sink back into the chair.

He remained at the window as he spoke. 'You are like her. Like Daphne. Appearances are all that matter to you. I am not like that.' He turned to her. 'Your scar has never meant a thing to me. I do not think of it when I think of you. How it has hurt you matters to me. How it has affected the treatment you receive from your mother and other people matters to me. I do want to protect you from unhappiness; I admit that and I do not apologise for it. If I give my word to keep a secret, I will keep that secret. I admit that, as well. I keep my word. And I try to do what is right.' His chest ached as he spoke. 'If you cannot see that about me and can only look at my face, I do not know how to go on.'

She glanced up at him and quickly turned away.

He left the room.

Phillipa remained in her the chair, his last words stinging in her ears. When she heard him open the door she swivelled around and watched him leave her.

Anxiety clutched at her throat.

She rose from the chair and paced the room.

What was she to believe?

So much evidence on one side. Only his word on the other.

She lowered herself on to her chair at the dressing table and peered into the mirror. Her reflection was so well lit by the light from the window, she could see every tiny line on her face, every eyelash, every inch of her scar.

Had he been correct?

For all her self-moaning and protestations about how people only saw her scar, was that all she saw of herself, as well?

She touched her scar and leaned closer to the mirror to examine it.

She'd prided herself on accepting her scar and the limitations it placed on her life. Had she really done so? Or was it the first thing she thought of when she thought of herself? It certainly was the first thing she thought of when anyone looked at her.

Did she not think of her scar no matter what she experienced?

So what if the most handsome man in the ballroom had been coerced into dancing with her? Was that only about her scar? Other young ladies in their first Season were set up with dance partners. She was the one who attributed it to her scar. And, even if that dance had been only about her scar, she was the one who used it as an excuse to leave. How might that ball have been different for her if she'd stayed and merely enjoyed herself?

She rose from the dressing table and walked over to a table near the window where she'd left some music. She picked up one sheet and played the notes in her head.

Surely her music was unrelated to her scar.

She threw the sheet down again and sank her head in her hands.

Her music had everything to do with her scar. It was her distraction from it. Her way to hide.

Her excuse to hide.

The truth was she defined where she could go, what she could do, who she could speak to, by the presence of her scar.

By her appearance, just as Xavier had accused.

He'd said the same of Lady Faville.

If Phillipa's scar was always foremost in her mind, perhaps Lady Faville's beauty was all she thought of herself? It was all anyone ever noticed about her. All Phillipa noticed about her.

Phillipa was suddenly sad for the woman. In her way Lady Faville had tried very hard to make her a friend. What if Phillipa had embraced that friendship? Perhaps she could have done the lady some good. Steered her away from Xavier and towards someone who could love her.

Assuming Xavier did not love her.

Phillipa walked to the bed and leaned against the bedpost, holding on to it as if it were the mast of a boat being tossed by stormy waves. She glanced at the bed, in contrast to her emotions so tidy, showing no signs of their lovemaking.

She stared at it, not a wrinkle on its cover. Its appearance certainly deceived.

She closed her eyes and remembered the tangled bed linens, the feel of his hands upon her skin, the firmness of his muscled body, the thrill of him entering her and making them one.

Could men lie during lovemaking? Could Xavier have pretended such tenderness towards her? Could he falsify the glow in his eyes as he gazed at her naked body? Would he have held her all night if all he'd wanted was a release?

She pushed herself away from the bed and returned to the mirror.

Could she convince herself that he had made love to her because of her scar? That he saw only her scar when he gazed upon her?

She could not.

She gasped, covering her hand with her mouth.

Do not believe a word he says, her mother said, but her mother was wrong about him.

Phillipa was wrong about him.

She loved that he'd refused to allow her to walk the streets of Mayfair alone at night, even though she protested. She loved that he arranged for her to continue at the gaming house after the attack, because he knew it meant a great deal to her. She loved his loyalty to Rhys—Xavier had managed the Masquerade Club nearly as long as Rhys. She loved Xavier's forgiveness of Jeffers, his kindness in helping him and other soldiers. She loved that he cared about her happiness.

She even loved his sense of honour, although it truly hurt that he'd not told her of Brighton.

And, yes, she did love his smile, his blue eyes, his glorious body, but they appeared pretty far down her list.

'I must tell him,' she cried aloud. 'I must tell him before it is too late! Even if he never forgives me, I must tell him he is wrong.'

She loved him for far more than his appearance.

She hurried out the door, determined to find him.

Chapter Twenty-One

Xavier needed a walk out of doors. To clear his head. Quiet his emotions. Help him forget what just happened.

Help him decide what to do.

What could he do? He was married to her.

He loved her.

Which was why it was so cursed painful that he'd misjudged her.

No matter that their wedding day had been a delight. No matter that they'd made love in the afternoon. No matter that he'd done everything he could think of to see to her happiness. Her regard for him was as shallow as any woman's.

He descended the stairs and reached the hall where Cummings was in attendance.

'Did she find you?' Cummings asked.

'Who?' One of the servants? A croupier? He had

no wish to deal with anyone. Just let him be alone for awhile.

'That Lady Faville.' Cummings spoke with disapproval, using more expression than was his habit.

'Lady Faville?' What the devil was *she* doing here? First the note, now the visit.

'Said she knew where to find you.' Cummings shrugged. 'Went upstairs.'

Not to the private floor. He would have seen her. Good God. He needed to find her before she encountered Phillipa.

He took the stairs two at a time and checked the gaming room first, but it was empty. The supper room was next.

He opened the door and immediately saw that a lamp was burning on one of the tables. She was there, standing decoratively near the room's fireplace.

'Xavier!' she cried. 'I knew you would come!'

She ran to him and flung herself into his arms, smashing her lips against his.

He twisted around trying to extricate himself.

And saw Phillipa standing in the doorway.

'Xavier.' Her voice was barely audible.

He peeled Daphne off him. 'Wait, Phillipa. This is not as it seems.'

'It is as it appears to be,' cried Daphne in a triumphant voice. 'We were kissing.'

'Be quiet, Daphne,' Xavier snapped.

She seized his arm again. 'Is this your *wife*, Xavier?' She spoke the word *wife* as if it tasted rancid. 'Will you present her to me?'

'No,' He pried her hand from his sleeve. 'Leave.'

'Of course she must leave,' Daphne said, twisting his meaning. 'But it would be polite to formally introduce us first.'

'We have already met.' Phillipa stepped into the room and Xavier could not read her expression.

'We have not met.' Daphne gestured towards Phillipa's scar. 'I assure you I would have remembered.'

That was cruel. Xavier started to step in.

But Phillipa spoke first and, to his surprise, her tone was kind. 'I assure you we have met.' She covered her face with her hands as if they were a mask. 'You called me your friend.'

Daphne's eyes widened. 'Miss Songstress? But—but you pretended to be someone else.'

'I did not pretend to be someone else. I told you all along that I wished to protect my identity.' She smiled sympathetically. 'I am afraid that included not letting you know my connection to Xavier.'

'It was uncivil of you.' Daphne turned to him. 'Xavier, would you ask her to leave? I must see you alone.'

'She is my wife.' Xavier liked saying it. 'I will not ask her to leave.'

'You think you are being kind to her, Xavier,' Daphne insisted. 'But she should know the truth about how we feel about each other, about how you felt forced to marry her.' She swallowed as if experiencing intense emotion. 'About how we *love* each other.'

Phillipa looked past Daphne, directly into his eyes. 'Xavier?' Her voice was low and surprisingly calm. 'If you want her, I will not stand in your way.'

He returned her gaze. 'Phillipa, she's talking nonsense.'

'Do not say so!' Daphne's voice rose an octave. 'You love me, Xavier. You have loved me for years. Since our first meeting.'

Was the woman mad? 'Daphne.' He tried to speak gently to her, as Phillipa had done. 'There are many men who come here who, I suspect, are in love with you. But not me.'

She looked confused. 'You want me—'

'I do not want you, Daphne. Please believe me.' He turned to Phillipa and feared she would not believe him either. 'Phillipa, I love you. Forgive me. I spoke to you in anger before.'

Phillipa held his gaze. 'There is nothing to forgive. You were correct. At least in part.'

His muscles relaxed. 'I want you, Phillipa. Only you.'

* * *

Phillipa stared at him, the words *I want you* echoing in her ears. She did not need to hear anything else.

He went on, though. 'I did not ask Daphne to come here. I have nothing to hide regarding her. You must believe me in this.' He turned back to Lady Faville. 'Leave us now, Daphne. Please.'

Lady Faville's lip trembled. Phillipa now felt nothing but pity for her.

'You cannot prefer her over me,' Lady Faville cried. 'She is grotesque! And you and I will look perfect together.'

Her words still wounded.

Xavier's eyes flashed. 'I will not have my wife insulted. This ends now, Daphne. Do not come back. I will find someone to escort you home, if you wish, but you must go.'

Lady Faville looked afflicted.

Xavier softened his tone. 'It would be best if you do not come back, as well.'

Lady Faville dug in her heels. 'I will not leave. Not until I have spoken to you alone.'

'Then we will leave.' Xavier put his hand on Phillipa's back and leaned close to her ear. 'We need to end this with her.'

She nodded, more eager to be alone with him than Lady Faville could possibly be.

They walked towards the door.

'No!' Lady Faville stamped her foot. It sounded as if she pushed over a piece of furniture. 'I will not let you leave me!'

Glass shattered behind them. They whirled around to the sight of flames.

She'd thrown the lighted lamp. Its oil and fire scattered. A curtain caught fire. Xavier ran to it and pulled it down.

Lady Faville screamed and backed away in a panic. The hem of her skirt was on fire and she was shaking it, making it worse.

'Stop her!' Xavier cried, attempting frantically to smother the flaming curtain.

Phillipa grabbed her and struggled with her, knocking her to the floor and beating out the flames. Lady Faville screamed throughout. When Phillipa released her, she scrambled to her feet and ran out the door.

'Get help!' Xavier cried.

The fire had spread to another curtain. And another. Phillipa ran to one of them and pulled it down. He battled with the other.

'Get out!' Xavier cried. 'Don't stay here.'

'No!' There was too much fire for one person to fight.

'Phillipa, go!' he cried again.

'No!' She grabbed a tablecloth and tried to beat out the small flames with it. The cloth itself caught fire and she slapped out the flame with her hands. The smoke stung her eyes and burned her throat. She was very aware that her own skirts could go up in flames, but the idea of leaving Xavier alone with the fire, risking him being engulfed in flames, was too terrible to endure.

'Phillipa, run,' his voice rasped. 'Grab your music and run. We might lose the house.'

Her music? What good was her music if she lost him?

There was a bucket of sand by the fireplace. She carried it to the fire and scooped handfuls of it on to one flame after another.

The carpet caught fire.

'Help me!' Xavier cried. He pushed the furniture away.

She ran to him and together they rolled up the carpet, smothering the flames inside it.

A voice came from the doorway. 'What? Fire!' It was Cummings, who immediately jumped in to help.

'Leave now, Phillipa,' Xavier ordered. 'Get more help.'

This time she obeyed. She ran down the stairs, shouting for MacEvoy, who appeared from the servants' floor below.

'I smell smoke,' he said.

She seized the front of his coat and pulled him to the stairs. 'The supper room. Fire.'

He ran upstairs and she went down to the kitchen, startling the cook and kitchen maids. 'There is a fire in the supper room.'

'A fire!' One of the girls screamed.

'Can you go get help?' She glanced around. 'Where is Lacey?'

Lacey entered the kitchen. 'I am here, my lady.'

Cook put down the pot she'd held. 'We must leave the house.' She turned to the maids. 'You both run ahead and find some men to help.'

Lacey wrapped her arm around Phillipa and led her outside.

When they reached the street, Phillipa began to cough.

The maids found more help and they watched more men run inside.

'Where is Mr Campion?' Lacey asked, keeping her arm around Phillipa.

Phillipa looked up to the windows on the first floor, picturing him with flames around him.

'He's in the fire,' she answered.

* * *

An hour later they sat at a table in the kitchen while Cook slathered their hands with a salve she promised would heal their burns in no time. Xavier's burns were much worse than Phillipa's and Cook wound them in bandages.

He winced when Cook touched a sore area.

Phillipa felt the pain in her own stomach. 'Your poor hands.'

He shrugged. 'Better a few burns than losing the house to fire. How could I face Rhys and your brothers if I let the place burn? Or, worse, what if the fire spread to other houses?'

'It was not worth risking your life.' She saw him again surrounded by flames, relived her fear.

He smiled. 'Actually, it was worth the risk. As long as this is all it cost.' He glanced to his hands.

Cook tied the last bandage. 'There you go, sir. All set. Keep the bandages clean and dry and I'll change them tomorrow.'

'Thank you, Cook. I feel better already.' He stood. 'But we should leave you to your work now.'

Xavier closed the Masquerade Club. The supper room was the only room damaged and that damage was primarily to the carpet and curtains, but the gaming room smelled strongly of smoke, and also the private rooms and the maids' rooms to a lesser extent.

Every window in the house was open and dishes of charcoal and vinegar were placed everywhere. Still, it would take days to restore it to normal.

Phillipa and Xavier climbed the stairs to the supper room where the maids, Cummings and MacEvoy were scrubbing the floor, ceiling and walls. The carpet, the curtains and all the linen were gone. Phillipa glanced at the pianoforte, which, thankfully, seemed undamaged.

'How are you all faring?' Xavier asked them.

'Making good progress,' replied MacEvoy in a good humour. He turned to the others. 'Are we not?'

Cummings grunted, but the maids voiced their agreement.

The poor maids, Phillipa thought. This was an arduous task, but she was pleased to see the lovely paint and plasterwork emerging again.

They continued up to the private rooms and immediately felt the chill from the open windows. In the bedchamber, Lacey wore a shawl and laid out clothes on every possible surface so they could benefit from the fresh air.

She curtsied when she saw them. 'How are your hands?'

Phillipa raised hers. 'Stinging a little, but Cook's salve has done wonders.'

'And you, sir?' the girl asked Xavier.

He showed her his bandaged ones. 'Cook says they will heal quickly if I do what she says.'

'Then you must do as she says,' Phillipa told him.

They changed into clean clothes. When done, Xavier turned to Phillipa. 'We do not need to stay here. We have a house to go to. Cook can pack us a dinner and Lacey can pack a change of clothes—'

A few minutes later they were ready to leave with a picnic basket and a portmanteau. As they opened the door, Mr Everard stood on the outside, ready to sound the knocker.

'Oh!' He startled, then bowed. 'Mr Campion. My lady. I wonder if I might have a word with you.'

'You have seen Daphne?' Xavier asked, standing aside to allow him entry. 'Was she injured in any way?'

'Nothing to signify,' Everard responded. 'But, as you can imagine, she is rather distraught.'

'She ought to be. The whole street could have burned,' Xavier said.

'She is, perhaps, not yet thinking of anyone but herself.' Mr Everard looked apologetic. 'I came to inspect the damages, however, and to inform you that she will pay full restitution.'

Xavier nodded. 'Arrange it with MacEvoy. He is in the supper room. Please include generous restitution to him, Cummings and all our servants. They bear the brunt of the cleaning up.'

Mr Everard inclined his head towards Xavier's hands. 'You are injured.'

Xavier shrugged. 'I will heal.'

'Well.' Everard cleared his throat. 'I will not keep you. I cannot tell you how sorry I am for—for all this.'

Xavier acknowledged his apology and Mr Everard started up the stairs.

'Everard!' Xavier stopped him.

Everard paused on the stairway.

Xavier said, 'Make certain she does not come here again. Or approach me in any way. Or Lady Phillipa.'

'I will, sir.' Everard continued up the stairs.

'One more thing,' Xavier called to him.

He paused again.

'She should go away.'

Everard's brows rose.

Xavier spoke firmly. 'I am serious. She should go to the Continent.'

Everard nodded. 'I will make the suggestion.'

Xavier and Phillipa continued out the door.

She stopped him, 'Why did you say Lady Faville should go to the Continent?'

'For the same reason your brothers sent your father away.' He took her hand, but winced in pain. 'Daphne has opened herself to scandal. But everyone will forget if she is away.'

She threaded her arm through his. 'I suppose the scandal will reach us, as well. People are already talking about us.'

He gave her an understanding hug. 'It will be worse for her, though. She will be alone.'

They reached Piccadilly and finally Dover Street and stood in front of the door to what would be home. He put down the portmanteau and tried to reach in his pocket for the key. His bandages made it difficult.

'I will get it for you.' Phillipa set down the basket of food.

Her fingers stung, but she reached in his coat pocket, an act that seemed very wife-like. It made her smile. With the key in hand, she unlocked the door.

Her hand was on the latch when she turned back to Xavier. She threw her arms around him and hugged him, never wanting to let him go. She'd almost lost him. To the fire. To her own folly.

'We are home, Xavier,' she cried.

It had been just as she'd dreamed as a child. Xavier had indeed whisked her away—in a hackney coach, not on horseback, and to a town house on Dover Street, not a castle—though he was and would always be her prince.

She imagined a crescendo of music, louder and faster, from the lower keys to the higher.

He returned her embrace. 'When I am with you, I am home.'

It was the perfect final note.

Epilogue

London, May, 1820

Phillipa would not say there was a crush of people in the drawing room, but there were enough that she had to crane her neck for a glimpse of her husband. He stood at the opposite end of the room, speaking to her half-brother, Rhys, father of John Rhysdale the junior, the reason for this celebration. They were probably talking business. Of Rhys's steam engines and Xavier's shops. He owned five now and she could not be more proud of it.

Watching Xavier was a thousand times more pleasurable than listening to the chatter of her sister-in-law, who'd parked herself at Phillipa's side and made no signs of ever moving away.

Or of going silent.

'It was a lovely christening, was it not?' Adele said for the thousandth time. 'Did we not make fine godparents? I am so glad you held the baby, because I am certain I was so nervous I would have dropped him....'

Xavier had indeed made a fine godfather, so handsome in his new coat, as much of an Adonis now as he had been in his regimentals all those years ago at Lady Devine's ball. He'd assured Phillipa that she looked her finest, but the old insecurities poked at her throughout the ceremony. She'd taken to using a bit of cosmetics to minimise her scar, but she'd wager a night's take at the Masquerade Club that someone in the church had commented on how unbelievable it was for Xavier Campion to marry Phillipa Westleigh—the Adonis and the scarred spinster.

Such comments had never entirely stopped.

Adele sighed. 'I do hope dear Ned and I conceive soon. It seems unfair that Celia has had the first baby in the family, although one cannot quite credit this baby as a Westleigh, seeing as they'd had to marry and my baby will be heir to the family title...'

Empty-headed Adele had no idea how insulting she could be.

Phillipa pressed her hand to her abdomen. Her sister-in-law would likely soon learn of another baby in the family, but for now it was a delicious secret, hers and Xavier's.

She glanced over at Celia, Rhys's wife, holding

little John, so tiny in her arms. How would it feel to hold Xavier's baby? To know that a living creature could result from their act of love?

A woman's laughter broke into Adele's monologue. It was Phillipa's mother, arm in arm with General Henson, conversing with the clergyman who had performed the christening. Her mother was happy now and for that Phillipa was glad.

Xavier caught her eye, smiled, and started across the room to her. Phillipa's cheeks flushed, just as they had all those years ago when he'd crossed a ballroom floor to dance with her.

He winked and turned towards Adele. 'Forgive me, Lady Neddington, I must steal my wife from you.'

Adele opened her mouth to respond, but Xavier already had taken Phillipa's arm and led her away.

'You have rescued me once again,' Phillipa said. 'Where are you taking me?'

'Not far.'

It was a thrill to have his hand firmly on her arm, to be close enough to inhale the scent of him, now so familiar to her. Ladies' heads still turned as he passed and she supposed one or more of them would repeat the familiar refrain—*how could a man like that marry her?*

He loves me, ladies, she pretended to reply. *That is why.*

Two rooms had been opened into one long one to accommodate the guests. He led her to the far end where a violinist and cellist were setting up their instruments next to the pianoforte.

'Musicians!' Phillipa cried. 'I did not know Celia and Rhys hired musicians.'

'I thought this might interest you.' Xavier smiled.

'Surely they are not to have dancing as well?' That would be odd at a christening.

'Unfortunately, no dancing,' he replied.

'Unfortunately?'

He put his arm around her. 'I enjoy dancing with you.'

Their opportunities to dance together had been rare. Only one ball in the autumn and none yet this spring.

'Now that mourning for King George III has been lifted, we may dance again.' She lifted a shoulder. 'If we receive any invitations, that is.'

'We will receive invitations.' He squeezed her tighter. 'Do you remember dancing with me at Lady Devine's ball? It was right before I was to return to the regiment in Holland.'

'I remember.' That ball, that dance, had changed everything for her.

The musicians began tuning their instruments, the

discordant sounds a fitting accompaniment to memories of that night.

Xavier went on. 'I do not think I ever enjoyed a dance more than that one we shared.'

She gaped at him. 'You enjoyed it?'

He looked surprised. 'Of course I enjoyed it! I'd been away so long, and home on leave so briefly, everyone seemed like strangers to me. Some of the young ladies, I certainly had never met. Then I saw you, my dear friend. I was so happy to see you, dancing with you was...' He paused. 'It was very special.'

She made him look directly into her face. 'No. My mother made you ask me to dance.'

His brow furrowed. 'Your mother? I do not recall seeing your mother until afterwards when she told me you'd gone home ill. I could not call upon you to enquire about your health, because I had to leave for Holland the next day.'

'My mother did not set it up for you to ask me to dance?' She couldn't believe it.

'Indeed not.'

Her knees suddenly felt so weak she might have sunk to the floor if he had not been holding her. All this time she'd thought—

How her life might have altered had she known at the time that he'd chosen her.

He inclined his head towards the *pianiste* and two other musicians. 'They are ready to start playing.'

Phillipa's head was already swimming. It took several bars of music for her to notice the familiar tune. 'They are playing my sonata!'

He grinned. 'As I requested.'

Before Christmas he'd sold several of her music pieces to a publisher. She'd seen them for sale at a music shop, but never performed. In fact, she'd never heard this arrangement anywhere but in her own head.

She glanced around the room, but Rhys's guests seemed to take the music in stride. 'I feel like shouting aloud that they are playing my sonata.'

'Shall I?' He made as if he would do so.

'No.' She pulled him back. 'Just listen.'

The pianoforte dominated, then the violin, then the cello. The composition had been inspired by the sounds of the gaming room at the Masquerade Club and Xavier had once remarked upon the version she'd written just for the pianoforte. It seemed fitting that this sonata should be played at this celebration of Rhys's and Celia's child. The Masquerade Club had played such an important role in their romance.

As it had in Xavier and Phillipa's romance.

She leaned her head against Xavier's shoulder as

the music filled her ears and happiness filled her heart.

'You make beautiful music, my dear wife,' Xavier murmured to her.

* * * * *

Discover more romance at

www.millsandboon.co.uk

- ❤ WIN great prizes in our exclusive competitions

- ❤ BUY new titles before they hit the shops

- ❤ BROWSE new books and REVIEW your favourites

- ❤ SAVE on new books with the Mills & Boon® Bookclub™

- ❤ DISCOVER new authors

PLUS, to chat about your favourite reads, get the latest news and find special offers:

- f Find us on facebook.com/millsandboon
- 🐦 Follow us on twitter.com/millsandboonuk
- ❤ Sign up to our newsletter at millsandboon.co.uk